W9-BNH-054

Of Manners and Murder

Of Manners and Murder

A Dear
Miss Hermione
Mystery

Anastasia Hastings

MINOTAUR BOOKS
NEW YORK

This is a work of fiction. All of the characters, organizations, and events portrayed in this novel are either products of the author's imagination or are used fictitiously.

First published in the United States by Minotaur Books,
an imprint of St. Martin's Publishing Group

Printed in the United States of America. For information, address St. Martin's Publishing Group, 120 Broadway, New York, NY 10271.

Design by Meryl Sussman Levavi

ISBN 9781250848567

For David

Of Manners and Murder

My dear Miss Hermione,

I must open my heart to you and share a secret I cannot tell another soul. In my years of attending school at Miss Simpson's Academy for Young Ladies, I thought I'd learned all I needed in order to be a proper wife.

Now, I am not certain. You see, Miss Hermione, I have recently married and I know I should be the happiest woman on earth. I am, indeed, the happiest woman on earth! My husband's love radiates through all he does for me. We are compatible and congenial. And yet, lately . . . oh, Miss Hermione, I feel so bunglesome. Just thinking about my dearest husband makes me forget myself and lately, my head has been so much in the clouds, I have had a number of foolish accidents. I dread it will happen again and that in itself has made me so overanxious and apprehensive, I am sure my darling will see me as artless and not worthy of his love. Please help me, Miss Hermione.

A Desperate but Hopeful Wife

Dear Desperate but Hopeful,

You poor lamb! I blame no one at all for the predicament in which you find yourself as much as I blame the outmoded—and dare I say it, preposterous—expectations of Society.

We hold Love in high esteem and think of it as otherworldly and miraculous. Thus blinded, we expect all who are drawn to Love to be swept away, quite removed from their ordinary lives. Stuff and nonsense!

Certainly, Love has brought you to the happy state in which you find yourself, but now, Desperate but Hopeful, you must do your part.

The less you worry about how you might impress others with impossible perfection, the more confidence you'll feel and the fewer accidents you'll have. Realize your true worth and make your way in the world, not simply as an adjunct to your husband but as his equal. Certainly, you should wish to please him, just as he should do the same for you. But you are only human. Cast aside your worries and your uneasiness. Your husband has found the woman of his dreams. Now she needs to plant herself firmly in reality, ease herself into the new role of wife, and start living.

You may be Hopeful about these matters, my dear, but when it comes to such things, neither you—nor any woman—should ever feel Desperate.

Miss Hermione

Chapter 1

Violet

London
June 29, 1885

It should be known from the beginning, I am no flibbertigibbet. Nor am I inclined to the sorts of vapors which often envelop my half sister Sephora and cause her to swoon—usually when there is an attractive young man in the vicinity to offer assistance.

No, I, Violet Manville, am levelheaded. Commonsensical. Well ordered of both habit and mind.

Perhaps that is why I felt especially vulnerable that particular morning standing in my aunt Adelia's library, the inner sanctum I had never before been allowed to enter, scanning the labels written on the drawers of the filing cabinets in front of me.

Unfaithful Husbands
Comportment
Disrespectful Children
Mothers-in-Law

My heart beat double time. My jaw went slack. An instinct of self-preservation kicked in and I stepped back, putting distance between myself, those oak cabinets, and all I had just learned they meant.

It hardly helped. An invisible hand tightened around my throat and I gasped for air like a doomed sailor submerged in an icy sea. At that moment, every bit of wit abandoned me. But then, there was little room for it considering I was filled with trepidation.

"But, Aunt Adelia . . ." Drawn as a moth to flame yet fully aware of what happens to the unfortunate insect when it gets too close, I looked again to the cabinets. Their labels were written in a flamboyant, flowing hand that belied what I suspected was the serious nature of the contents of each drawer.

Manners
Morals
Mourning

"Aunt Adelia . . ." I gulped, a sound that betrayed my apprehension. "You must surely be mistaken. You cannot possibly think I could—"

"Of course you can." My aunt bustled from desk to bookcase, from bookcase to armoire, from armoire to the desk again, retrieving a gold cigarette case, casting aside a pair of kid gloves and unwanted papers that fluttered to the floor like so many fallen flower petals.

She stopped her marauding long enough to offer a smile, but I wasn't fooled by it for a second. Smile or no smile, I knew better than to imagine she'd ever change her mind. Adelia was a rock. A fixed force in a universe where the sun had been supplanted by Adelia Henrietta Georgina Tylney Manville and the planets revolved around her and her alone. As if to prove it, she lifted her chin. "I am never wrong, dear Violet. You should know that by now."

"I do. But—"

"I decided. A year ago. Soon after you and Sephora came here to live with me. I suspected you were the right woman for the task all along, all those years we corresponded when you traveled with your father. I'd hoped to have time to gradually ease you into this new role I have prepared for you, but . . ." She rounded the desk to stand in front of me. Aunt Adelia is something of a nonpareil, matchless when it comes to her impeccable clothing. Unlike me, for I preferred understated styles in colors that were just as inconspicuous, Adela adored bright hues and hats adorned with feathers. That day, she was dressed in a traveling suit the color of plums. Her hat was on the desk, and she reached for it and perched it on her head at the precise angle to make the most of her chestnut hair, her slim nose, her wide eyes. "Hamish is an unpredictable sort. It is part of his charm. He did not propose this journey to me until last night and so you see, until then, I did not know I was leaving. And before you ask, no, I do not know when we might return. That is why I need you to be a dear and handle this for me. Do not be cross. There is no way I could have told you sooner. He's waiting for me now outside in a hansom, the train leaves Charing Cross in just another hour, and I have every confidence in you." She gave me a peck on the cheek. "You'll do very well."

Just a short time before, I had been sitting quietly at the table reading the morning's newspaper while enjoying a cup of tea and a slice of perfectly crisped toast provided by

Adelia's incomparable housekeeper, Bunty, nothing more on my mind than a visit to the British Museum that afternoon. Now, here I stood, my world turned upside down by my charming, outspoken, incorrigible aunt and all she had planned for me. Can I be blamed for raising my voice and stomping my foot?

If nothing else, my fit of pique got my aunt's attention. Already moving to the door at her usual cyclone's pace, she whirled to face me.

I inched back my shoulders. I am not as tall as Adelia. I am not nearly as broad. As she is nearing forty, I am her junior by sixteen years. I had been raised better than to disrespect my elders, and I reminded myself of that fact while I struggled to make her listen to reason.

"Miss Hermione is the most celebrated agony aunt in all the Empire," I said, my voice, too high-pitched, bouncing over the words. "She is talked about everywhere. Her wisdom to those who write to her for advice is admired and extolled. Her column in *A Woman's Place* magazine is fabled."

"Well, of course it is. Really, Violet, you don't need to preach what I already know." She turned again to the door, but I was not done.

"Her true identity has been a mystery all these years and now . . ." When I stepped forward, Adelia dropped her hand from the doorknob, but kept her back to me. "You cannot reveal to me that you are Miss Hermione at the same time you tell me you are leaving for the Continent for an undetermined amount of time and you want me to take over the writing of your column."

Slowly, she pivoted to face me, her eyes wide, her lips pursed. The picture of innocence. "Why not?"

"Because I don't know what I'm doing."

"Bosh!" Her laughter had the clear, sweet ring of the clink of champagne glasses. "You'll be far more successful than I've ever been. You have a great deal of common sense and I have absolutely none."

As if it would somehow emphasize what I'd just learned about the aunt I'd always thought had little more to her than a cadre of interesting friends, a paramour now and then, and the sometimes-inconvenient habit of laughing at the wrong things at the wrong time, I swept an arm toward those filing cabinets. "Yet for years you've been dispensing advice to all and sundry about things like mothers-in-law and unfaithful husbands."

"Yes! It is quite the funniest thing, isn't it? It started as a lark and simply grew." Another laugh and she set her hand again on the brass doorknob. "Now, dear Violet, Miss Hermione will give you her final piece of advice. A lady is wise to let a man wait for her so that he tingles with anticipation at the thought of her coming and rejoices when she finally arrives. However . . ." She grinned. "She cannot possibly expect the railway, too, to wait." She threw open the door and glided into the hallway where Bunty stood at the ready, Adelia's traveling cloak over one arm and the carpetbag my aunt would carry to the station sitting nearby.

"Bunty will assist you," Adelia told me, then leaned forward and lowered her voice. "Bunty knows the secret, as do a few select others. Remember, you cannot tell anyone. Especially Sephora. You know she never misses reading Miss Hermione's columns. She even clips them and keeps them in an album. No, no. If she knew Miss Hermione's true identity, she would be far too excited to keep the news to herself, and Miss Hermione's mysterious persona is part of her allure."

I thought back to the labels on the cabinets.

Disrespectful Children?
Mothers-in-Law?
Husbands Faithful or Unfaithful?

"But I know nothing of the subjects you wish me to consult about," I creaked.

"Bunty will help." She did now, holding out Adelia's cloak so she could slip it on. "Bunty is always here for you. And you may write to me whenever you wish. Bunty will know what to do with your letters."

"But—"

It was just as well the sound of the post arriving interrupted whatever objection I might have offered. My protests fell on deaf ears.

Bunty left to retrieve the letters and when she came back, she handed my aunt the bundle. Adelia riffled through them. "These will be your first," she told me. "And you'll see how simple it all is. Some silly girl asking what to do when the boy at the stables smiles at her. A woman not sure of the proper way to welcome her son's wife to the family."

"But . . ." Thinking, I tipped my head and looked from the letters to my aunt and back to the letters in her hand. "If no one knows who Miss Hermione is, how is the secret kept if the letters arrive here?"

Adelia threw back her head and laughed. "Didn't I tell you, Bunty? Didn't I tell you the girl is intelligent enough to handle whatever Miss Hermione's readers can put in front of her? You mustn't worry, Violet. It is all very simple. The letters go first to the magazine office, where my editor there forwards them to a certain Mr. Harrison at the Pig and Ox public house."

"And this Mr. Harrison, he sends the letters on to you?"

Clearly, I'd suggested a plan not nearly convoluted enough. Adelia frowned.

"Harrison has them messengered to Mrs. Doris Sykes, the dressmaker," she told me. "And Doris's helper, Dolly, who is conveniently not very intelligent and has no idea what the packet she sends contains, takes them to the post. And from there . . . Voilà!" She waved the morning's letters at me. "As I said, it is all very simple and quite efficient. And I promise, the inquiries will be easy enough for you to handle. You have plenty of wit, and you can call on a good deal of charm, too. A few practical bits of advice and . . . oh!"

Adelia's hands stilled. Her brows lowered. Her bottom lip caught in her upper teeth, she studied a letter she pulled from the packet. "I recognize the hand," she said, though if she was talking to me or to Bunty, I could not be sure. "It is from a woman Miss Hermione heard from a month or so ago. I do hope there is nothing more to the letter than to thank me for the advice I offered. She was uneasy in her role as a new bride, you see, and I do believe I told her she needed to be kinder to herself, to ease into the role love had brought her to. But . . ." She put the letter in my hands. "Be a dear and get to this one first," she said. "Just in case."

In case of what, I never had the chance to ask. The front door flew open and Hamish MacGill, a man who reminded me of a red-haired bear, strode into the house.

His voice boomed against the walls and fairly made the orange flowers on the indigo wallpaper dance. "Are ye comin', woman?"

Adelia gave me a sly smile and a wink. "What was it I said about making them tingle with anticipation?" She grabbed the carpetbag from the floor and swept down the hallway. "No doubt Sephora is upstairs fussing with her hair, but I've already said my goodbyes to her. And you, Violet . . ." At the door, she turned just long enough to reach for my hand and give it a squeeze. "I am sure you will do me proud."

Side by side, Bunty and I watched them leave. Adelia was as delightful as she was maddening, as interesting as she was mercurial, and when the hansom disappeared around the nearest corner, I realized I would miss her. Especially in light of the task she'd given me.

"Tea?" Bunty asked when the hansom was out of sight.

"Yes." I stepped back into the house, the reality of my new responsibilities settling on my shoulders and stiffening them with resolve. "If you would, please, you may bring it into the library."

ↂ

It was my desk—at least for the foreseeable future—so really, I shouldn't have stepped into the library and approached it as if it were one of the terrifying tigers I'd seen while traveling in India with my dear, late papa.

"Ridiculous," I grumbled, giving my head a shake and propelling myself forward. "I can certainly write a letter. How difficult can the job of Miss Hermione be?" Like so many millions throughout the country and indeed, the Empire, I had over the years read Miss Hermione's column. Unlike so many millions—my half sister included—I no sooner finished reading Miss Hermione's advice than I completely put it out of my mind. How silly was it not to listen to one's own common sense when it came to life's conundrums and to instead ask the advice of a stranger?

Thinking about it, I couldn't help but chuckle. It was certainly the perfect job for Adelia! She loved nothing better than to let everyone know her opinion—even when they didn't ask for it. I was a much more private person and not so inclined to force my viewpoint on others. At least not unless they were sorely in need of it. For now, my only task would be to read over Adelia's latest work, to understand her system and how she chose to organize things and . . .

A closer look at the desk and my resolve disappeared. There were papers scattered across the desk and piled on the nearby chair, a Kashmir shawl in shades of blue and green flung over the inkwell, a canvas lawn tennis case bound in black leather tossed atop an array of pens. Opera glasses. A bar of carbolic soap. The delicate porcelain cup I had once sent to Adelia when Papa was posted with the Foreign Office in Hong Kong.

Try as I might to tell myself it could all be cleaned up and handled, arranged and managed, I could not pull my gaze away from the jumble, not even when the library door snapped open.

"What am I going to do, Bunty?"

I heard the rustle of her skirts behind me. "You're going to do the only thing there is to do when it feels as if you're being thrashed about in a storm. You're going to sit down and have a cup of tea."

She was right. Tea was the only sensible way to start on a project as overwhelming as this. I swept around the desk and to the settee near where Bunty poured. "You'll have a cup with me?" I asked her.

She poured a second cup and sat in the chair nearest mine, and for a few, quiet minutes, we considered our circumstances.

My tea finished, my courage bolstered, I looked her way. She was a small, round woman with a head of silvery hair and thin lips, and she had been in Adelia's service for years. Bunty was reliable, dependable, intelligent, and—as I had seen her talk terms and haggle about prices with the merchants who came to the kitchen door—I knew she could be canny, too. Just the ally Miss Hermione needed.

"Will you help me, Bunty?"

"All I can."

"You can tell me where to begin."

"Miss Adelia has already told you as much," she said quite simply. But then, Bunty was a practical woman, and not one to beat about the bush.

"She did. Of course!" The letter Adelia had singled out was on the settee beside me, and because I knew I'd never find a letter opener on the desk even if I searched, I carefully slid a finger under the envelope flap. "There is a note," I told Bunty. "And . . ." I peered into the envelope. "Newspaper clippings." I started with the letter.

"'My dear Miss Hermione,'" I read, "'It is I. again.' I. again," I tipped the paper to give Bunty a better look at the words written in a strong, even hand. "Odd, isn't it? A full stop after the *I*?"

Bunty leaned nearer and squinted. "Or an ink smudge."

"Yes, surely." I got back to reading the letter. "'I have tried my best to follow the kind advice you provided in your column, dear Miss Hermione. I have done all I can, as you so wisely counseled, to relax and remind myself a new wife has many responsibilities. I have tried, Miss Hermione. Truly, I have tried.'"

"Look. Here." Again, I tipped the page and this time, pointed so Bunty did not fail to see what I did. "The ink is lighter here, the letters dashed off. It is as if the writer has grown more frantic." I kept on reading. "'I am sorry to report, the Matter is far from settled. In fact, the situation has grown grave.'"

"What matter do you suppose she's talking about?" I asked Bunty.

She'd just poured another cup of tea, just taken a sip, and she swallowed before she shook her head and said, "I suppose she's referring to whatever it is she wrote about the first time."

"And how would we find out exactly what that might be? Aunt Adelia mentioned the woman was uneasy in her new role as wife, but I would like to know exactly what her letter to Miss Hermione said."

When Bunty glanced toward the filing cabinets, my hopes rose. There might be a simple answer to my inquiry, an easy way to look back over old correspondence. That is, until Bunty's lips pinched.

"Miss Adelia, she was never what you might call organized," she confided. "Has her own way of doing things. Her own way of keeping track of letters and replies. Her filing system was never up to snuff, if you catch my meaning. Still, I could sometimes make some sense of it. But since Mr. MacGill has been in her life . . ." Bunty sighed. "I'm afraid Miss Adelia has been thinking even less clearly than usual. Her head is full of the man, as is her heart." The small smile which played around Bunty's lips told me that while she would have liked to, she did not hold this against my aunt. Nor did I, except for the fact it apparently meant her cryptic filing methods were more slipshod than ever.

I'd already risen from my seat to go to the cabinets and start a reconnoiter when another thought occurred and my spirits rose.

"Bunty, I am a dullard!" I swept out of the library. "When you want to know what readers ask Miss Hermione, you ask one of the readers."

At the bottom of the stairs, I called up to my sister, Sephora. She poked her head over the bannister, her golden hair atumble, her cheeks smeared with almond cream. "What are you going on about, Violet? I'm busy getting ready to go around to Margaret Thuringer's. We are going to take a stroll and watch the boats on the Serpentine and then go to the shops for the afternoon. I'm determined to find just the right hat to go with my new blue tea gown."

"I won't delay you. I need you only for a minute," I assured her. "You, and the clippings you keep of Miss Hermione's column."

A few minutes later, still in her dressing gown, slippers on her feet and the cream wiped from her face, Sephora joined me where I waited in the parlor, seated at a table covered with the red and yellow paisley shawl Adelia had once thrown over it because, she claimed, the room needed cheering up. Like our aunt, Sephora certainly knew how to make an entrance.

Her precious album of Miss Hermione clippings clutched close to her heart, she paused in the doorway so as to allow a stream of sunshine from the nearest window to gild her hair and highlight the natural blush of her cheeks. While I took after our father and Aunt Adelia in looks and coloring, Sephora was a twin of her late mother, the woman Papa married after my own mother succumbed to fever in Bombay. Sephora was small and delicate, with pale skin and eyes that, at least according to Sephora, more than one smitten young man had compared to sapphires.

It was not only our looks which set us apart. I was the daughter of Clara Umberly Manville, an intelligent, practical woman my papa, Edward Manville, met while serving the Crown in China. Clara's parents were missionaries, and my mother's life reflected theirs. She had a good and generous heart, a kind demeanor, and a love for all people. She was as poor as a church mouse, but that meant nothing to Papa. He fell in love and proposed within weeks of meeting Clara. He once told me it was the only spontaneous thing he'd ever done. And he didn't regret it for one moment.

He was heartbroken when Mother died, but he had me—a headstrong twelve-year-old—to contend with, and he knew he could not fulfill his parental duties on his own. When he caught Elizabeth Broadsley's eye (for Papa was a handsome man!), he hoped she would provide the maternal love and guidance I needed. I had always thought them poorly matched. Papa was adventurous, intelligent, curious. Elizabeth's family owned a prosperous tea plantation, and she was used to a life of privilege. In the years before she, too, succumbed to tropical fever, she grew increasingly bored with the life of a civil servant and so poured all her energies into her lively, beautiful only child, Sephora. She indulged my half sister's every whim, and she trained her to behave decorously and to not worry her pretty head over anything more momentous than the latest fashions. Though I never heard her admit it, I was sure she didn't want Sephora to make the same mistake she'd made when she married. A nearly penniless civil servant? That was hardly the match Elizabeth wanted for Sephora. She taught her to set her sights high and to use her charm and beauty to get noticed.

And I? I do believe Elizabeth saw me as unredeemable. I was too opinionated, too wild in her eyes, and so I was largely ignored when it came to her lessons on how to behave like a lady. I was just as happy for it. After all, it was only right

Sephora should get all the attention. Eventually Elizabeth's family fortune went to Elizabeth, and her fortune would be Sephora's once she reached the age of eighteen. With Elizabeth and Sephora so wrapped up in each other, I had time to explore, to read, and to learn the cultures of the places we lived.

Sephora had money to her name, and I had very little.

We were far enough apart in age that we had nearly nothing to do with each other. Even once Elizabeth was dead, while Papa still lived, Sephora and I did no more than go through the motions of a relationship. After he, too, was gone, we had no need to pretend. We had no mutual interests. We had nothing to discuss. We never shared secrets because I was sure Sephora's were too trivial to care about and she, I am certain, believed I couldn't possibly have anything to confide. Sephora had a coterie of friends whose company she preferred to mine. She did far too much shopping and read far too many novels written by the likes of Hardy and Austen and the Brontë sisters, and her sole aspiration in life was to fall in love and marry well. Though, in fact, her reading matter should have taught her that the idea of living happily ever after was a tenuous dream at best.

As for my own dreams, in spite of the handicap of being a woman, I had longed to become a scholar and study the ancient civilizations of the Eastern countries I knew so well. As I had spent the last years acting as Papa's hostess and Sephora's companion, though, it was not meant to be.

And now, here I was instead, consigned to answering letters from lovesick swains and shy young misses, and this woman who said, "It is I. again" and begged for Miss Hermione's help.

"What is it you're looking for?"

Sephora's question drew me from my thoughts and I waited to respond until she sat down in the chair opposite mine. Even as I watched, her expression transformed from merely curious to jubilant. "Are you looking for fashion advice? Oh, Violet, I am so happy! Our mourning for Papa is over, and yet you still wear dreary colors and plain styles that don't at all flatter you. Not with your dark hair and eyes. You need to add some color to your wardrobe if you ever hope to attract a husband."

I did not bother to reply. It was a conversation we'd had before: I, reminding Sephora I was more interested in serious study than in a husband. Sephora, who was sixteen and simply didn't know any better, trying to reason her way through to why any woman would wish to remain unmarried and thus, in charge of her own destiny.

"I am looking for a letter." I tapped a finger against the leather-bound album she'd set on the table. "A letter Miss Hermione answered in her column perhaps six weeks or a month ago."

She opened the album and flipped through its pages of carefully cut clippings. "What is the letter about?"

I thought back to all Adelia had said. "I believe it was from a young bride saying she was uneasy in her new role."

"Young bride. Uneasy." Sephora mumbled the words while she scanned through the letters. She turned a few more pages. "Yes, here it is." She showed me the letter. "This might be the one you're looking for."

"What does it say?"

She cleared her throat and read the letter aloud, and when she reached the end, she looked up and said, "It is signed, 'A desperate but hopeful wife.'"

I considered all Sephora had just read. This must surely be

the Matter the writer spoke of in her latest letter. "And Miss Hermione, what does she say in reply?" I asked my sister.

Again, Sephora scanned the clipping in front of her. "That the woman must realize her life has changed and she must ease into the role of wife." She flipped the album shut. "I would certainly not need such advice," she assured me. "It seems such an easy thing, don't you think, going from miss to missus?"

This, I could not say. I thanked Sephora and told her she'd better move quickly or the best of the boating would be done for the day, and I went back to the library and closed the door behind me. I was just in time to see Bunty turn away from the filing cabinets.

"I found it," she said, waving a letter at me. "Only the good Lord knows how, as it was not filed where I thought it might be. But I found the original letter."

"Sephora had the clipping," I informed her, but nonetheless, looked over the letter. Yes, just as Adelia had said, the handwriting was the same, and it was not signed. Not surprising. I imagined most of the correspondence to Miss Hermione arrived anonymously. What was surprising . . .

I took a closer look and then, because I wanted to be sure, took the letter to the window. "There is no name, of course," I told Bunty. "But where a signature would be, the young wife has drawn a picture of a plant."

Bunty retrieved the letter, which had arrived just awhile earlier. "This one, too," she said.

"And that explains it!" I held the letters side by side. "When she said, 'It is I. again,' the writer was giving us a clue. About her name. It must surely be Ivy."

Together, Bunty and I sat on the settee. She, holding the first letter and me, looking again at the second, we got back to the business at hand.

I kept reading from where I'd left off. "'I am sorry to report, the Matter is far from settled. In fact, the situation has grown grave. Please believe me, Miss Hermione, I do not reveal this information lightly. But I must tell you what is in my heart. I must urge you to help me. I cannot be so bold or so wicked as to reveal their names in writing, but I do believe there are a number of candidates for what I suspect. Dear Miss Hermione, I do believe someone is trying to kill me.'"

Chapter 2

"Surely this is the stuff of fiction." I could not tear my gaze away from the letter in my hands, not even when Bunty clicked her tongue before she went on. "This Ivy, she cannot possibly think—"

"And yet you saw it yourself, Bunty." As much as I wished to, there was no denying the truth. "Her handwriting is more and more agitated as she goes along. She is certainly upset. Fiction or not, Ivy believes she's in danger."

Bunty scowled. "Then it's a pity she does not know who might want to do her bodily harm."

"On the contrary . . ." I looked over the letter again. "She says she cannot be so wicked as to reveal the names in writing. That tells me she knows exactly who she suspects. Perhaps the clippings in the envelope will tell us more."

I set the letter aside so I could reach into the envelope and draw out the newspaper clippings, then quickly scanned them. "They are all from the same edition of a single newspaper," I told Bunty. "The *Mercury,* from a village in Essex called Willingdale. And look!" I stared at the clipping on top of the little pile, and my blood ran so cold, it took a minute for me to collect myself and read over the paragraph of type below a drawing of people enjoying tea beneath a striped tent. "There has recently been a fete in Willingdale," I said, my voice suddenly breathy, "and this is a picture of one of the events. Bunty, look, Ivy has circled the face of one of those in attendance."

As I have mentioned, Bunty is shrewd. Just as I did the moment I set eyes on it, she knew what the circle meant. That would explain why her face paled, why she clutched her hands on her lap so the bones showed beneath her skin. "She refused to put the names in writing, but she's telling you, isn't she? She saying who's trying to kill her." She ran her tongue over her lips. "That man is one of the people she suspects. Who is he?"

The picture showed a youngish man with a long nose, a sweeping forehead, and ears too large for his slim face. "According to what is written here, he is Simon Plumley, the vicar of St. Christopher's Church."

"A vicar trying to murder someone?" As if she'd been slapped, Bunty flinched, and just as quick as that, the concern which had momentarily robbed her of breath and softened her cynicism disappeared in a strangled gasp of outrage. "That not only seems unlikely, it is preposterous."

"And yet Ivy believes it is true." Thinking, I tipped my head. "I wonder what brought her to the conclusion. He looks a pleasant enough fellow. What could the reverend have done to make Ivy think he's a threat to her? And Bunty, do you suppose he's the husband she mentioned in her first letter?"

Bunty wrinkled her nose. "No way of telling. Unless she's said more there in those other pages."

Hoping to be enlightened, I looked at the next clipping, a drawing of a group of men watching a game of cricket. There were no answers to be found there, not when it came to Reverend Plumley. In fact, the second clipping only introduced more questions. The face of a man with a drooping mustache was circled.

"Here, apparently, is a second possibility. Richard Islington, the local physician."

Bunty thought this over. "A physician, at least, might have reason to want a person dead. They know secrets, don't they, doctors? Things folks don't tell others. If he knows Ivy is wicked, if she's done something terribly wrong and will never be punished for it by the law, he might seek his own justice."

In spite of the serious nature of our conversation, I laughed. "Now who's talking fiction?" I set this clipping down on the settee with the first I'd examined. "No, no. We cannot possibly know what this man's motive might be or what he's done to make Ivy suspect him. Not unless Ivy tells us."

"And does she?" Bunty wanted to know. "Is there more?"

There was, though it had nothing to do with motive or means. In fact, it only introduced more possibilities and so, even more questions.

"A woman named Edith Cowles." I showed Bunty the picture of a woman in a trim gown with long fitted sleeves and a bustle behind which made her look rather like a whale breaching the surface of the ocean. "Two women. Yes, I could see how that might cause friction, how some slight or a word or a rumor might make Ivy suspicious. But as I said, we cannot assign motivation when we know nothing about circumstances." I moved to the last item in the envelope. This drawing showed a woman in a fashionable postilion hat with a narrow brim and a high crown like a flowerpot. The hat was trimmed all over with ribbons and lace, all a match to the ornamentation on the woman's elaborate dress.

"Lady Betina Thorn," I read.

Bunty pursed her lips and color flooded her cheeks. "A vicar, a doctor, what looks to be a respectable lady and now, a member of the gentry? We can make up reasons and excuses all we like, but the truth of it is, this is clearly nonsense! Why would the likes of any of them be wanting this Ivy girl dead?"

I knew there was no more writing on it, but I turned over Ivy's letter once again, and looked through the clippings, searching for any clue. "She doesn't say why," I said. "But I think it's very likely this is what she was talking about in her first letter to Adelia . . . er, Miss Hermione. She mentioned being clumsy, having accidents. But, Bunty, think about it. What if those accidents were no accidents at all?"

"You mean one of these people here . . . ?" Bunty gave the clippings a dubious look. "You think she is afraid one of them is causing those accidents?"

"We cannot know. Not for certain."

As if to show me just how preposterous she thought the idea, Bunty stood and smoothed the skirt of her black gown and the white apron she wore over it. "If this woman is making accusations and seeing danger all around her, she sounds a bit unsteady to me. I hope you'll do the wise thing and ignore her letter."

"Is that what Adelia would do?"

Instead of answering, Bunty gathered our cups and took the tea tray to the door. "You cannot even think to publish such a letter. Not when it is so scandalous, so repugnant in all it implies."

"Agreed. But Miss Hermione might still answer Ivy. Privately."

"I do not believe that's wise." Bunty's gaze skimmed to the desk and she muttered, "Which is exactly why Miss Adelia would probably do exactly that. But really, Miss Violet, if you insist on such a course of action, perhaps you could ignore Ivy's ravings and simply offer some discreet advice."

I liked the idea and was encouraged at the thought of doing something practical, helpful. After all, dear Papa had never been one to doubt my intelligence, my skill, or my ability to take care of myself. Even though I was a female. Yes, I had been protected within the confines of the Foreign Office compounds where, no matter where we were in the world, we lived an English life. But Papa prepared me for those times I ventured out to mingle with the public. I knew how to shoot a pistol. And as I had proved one eventful evening at the market when the youngest son of a petty rajah mistook me for one of his concubines who had run off with her lover, I was reasonably adept at throwing a punch and landing a well-placed kick. (Contrary to popular gossip at the time, he was later able to father children. Six of them to date, so I had been told.)

I would be forever grateful to Papa for instilling such useful knowledge in me and now, I was pleased I could pass it on.

"I might offer advice on how Ivy can protect herself," I proposed, standing and pulling back my shoulders. "And suggest ways she might look more deeply into this matter so she might determine which of these people are causing the accidents that have befallen her."

I wondered if Bunty had ever dared offer Adelia the sort of sour expression she shot my way. "I was thinking more of how you might tell her she needs to get a little fresh air, to take a few invigorating strolls. You know, to clear her head of these mad ideas."

I reminded myself I was in England now, not in the back

of beyond with Papa, where we needed to be careful of where we stepped for fear of annoying poisonous snakes and be mindful of what we said so we did not insult the people, many of whom were already resentful of Crown rule. I lived in the center of civilization, where surely the things Ivy suggested did not commonly happen. And yet, worry and despair colored each word of Ivy's letter. And I had been entrusted with dealing with it.

My mind raced, and a plan formed, but I knew this was not the time to reveal it to Bunty. If I did, she would do all she could to discourage me. I might not know what to do with the rest of Miss Hermione's letters, but I saw my way clearly with Ivy's. I wanted to help her.

"Perhaps you are right," I told Bunty. "Perhaps Ivy's mind is playing tricks on her." I moved a stack of papers from the chair so I could sit at the desk.

Just as I'd hoped, my words convinced Bunty I'd seen the error in my thinking. She smiled, placated. "I will remind you that you need do nothing immediately. The way the letters are sent, then forwarded here from the magazine office, I would say Ivy posted her letter only two or three days ago. She won't be expecting an answer anytime soon. You'll have time to think on it and decide the best way to handle the problem."

Bunty closed the library door behind her and I was alone with the thoughts that caromed through my head.

Bunty could very well be right. The plot against Ivy might be nothing more than a figment of her imagination. But what if it wasn't? What if Ivy was in real danger? If that was the case, I simply could not sit here, safe and comfortable behind the Miss Hermione persona, with my head in the sand. Ivy needed to know she wasn't alone. She needed to be prepared for any eventuality that might befall her. And it seemed to me that the only one who could provide assistance was the very person she'd implored for help.

Miss Hermione.

June 30

The village of Willingdale was forty miles north and east of London, its proximity and the dependability and efficiency of the railway making it the ideal setting for the grand country homes legendary in that part of the island. Many of London's Society set spent their weekends in the countryside of Essex and I'd read that their rural residences were even more elaborate than their city dwellings and thus well suited to their status. For a good deal of the trip, I looked out the window of my first-class train compartment, hoping to catch a glimpse of one of the stately mansions.

I should have known better. Country estates are nestled in acres of land, not near railway lines, and rather than grand houses, I watched a watercolor version of the countryside fly by in shades of gray just beyond the fog that settled close to the ground and whooshed and swirled as the train sped along its way.

It was a damp, chilly morning and I was glad I'd searched through my trunks for the black cloak I'd worn on the voyage back from the Far East after Papa's passing. Sea travel can be cold, no matter the time of year, and a journey by train is always beset with problems, not the least of which is the residue of dust and dirt which settles on a traveler's shoulders. A dark-colored coat was ideal, especially as I could take it off and look more presentable when I introduced myself to Ivy.

I had waited until the morning after I received her letter to make the journey, and because I neither wanted nor needed what I was sure would be endless questions from Sephora about where I was going and why she couldn't accompany me, I left early. This strategy also meant I was able to avoid explaining myself to Bunty. It was good to feel adventure course again through my bloodstream as it so often had when Papa and I explored far-off places. The fact that I might be able to help Ivy, too, only served to boost the anticipation that buzzed through me. The train whistle shrieked, indicating our near-arrival in Willingdale, and not for the first time, I reviewed how I planned to broach this very tricky subject with the woman I'd come to meet. I could not tell Ivy I was Miss Hermione, so I'd constructed a fiction of my own: I was the mysterious writer's private secretary, she had passed Ivy's letter on to me and asked if I would kindly check on her. Miss Hermione was caring and concerned, and I was instructed to act as Ivy's advocate, to advise her about what she should do and how she might protect herself. I was quite pleased with my little story, and greatly looking forward to seeing if it—and I—was clever enough to convince Ivy with it.

The station in Willingdale was much as I expected, a solid stone building with a platform outside it where, just as I also anticipated, I was able to find a cart and driver for hire.

He was a man with rheumy eyes and a puff of white hair around a face like a rumpled blanket, and he chomped on the end of an unlit pipe when I told him where I wanted to go.

"I'm afraid I do not know her married name," I said. "But her Christian name is Ivy and I know she lives here in Willingdale, and if you could take me to her, I'd be grateful."

"Yeah, yeah." Since I had no intention of staying in the village longer than it took to converse with Ivy, I'd brought no luggage, so there was nothing to load. The driver offered me a hand up so I might sit on the wooden seat beside him. "I know Ivy well enough. Everyone around these parts do. Especially these days. I can take you to her."

I was grateful, and I settled in for what turned out to be a short ride. Outside St. Christopher's, a gray stone church with a square Norman bell tower, the driver stopped and I couldn't help but think back to Ivy's letter, to her singling out of Simon Plumley, the vicar there, as one of her suspects.

"Is Ivy the vicar's wife?" I asked the driver.

The sound that gurgled from him might have been a laugh. He jumped from his perch to assist me to the ground, then poked his chin toward the churchyard. "Over to the side" was all he said before he climbed back into the cart. "I daresay you'll find Ivy and the rest of them easy enough."

I took him at his word and made my way through the graveyard, the way he'd indicated. The church was to my left and all around me, gravestones rimed with lichens and time poked from the ankle-high grass like dragon's teeth. Eddies of fog drifted over the tops of my boots and snuck under the hem of my cloak and I shivered.

When I rounded the corner of the church, I found a clutch of people dressed in black, their backs to me. Simon Plumley faced me. No longer just the sketch of a vicar in a newspaper, he stood, flesh and blood, at the head end of a casket, his prayer book open in his hands.

I'm sure I can be excused for freezing in my place. I had not meant to interrupt a service, and I hoped to find a way to extricate myself from the scene before anyone noticed an intruder threatening the solemnity of the occasion. And yet, I could not tear my gaze away from the vicar with his long solemn face, the mourners with their heads bowed, the mahogany casket already in the ground, its color like dried blood in the lusterless light.

When the vicar spoke, his voice was clogged with tears. "We ask Your mercy on us and on all who have gone before us into the light of Your presence, and we commit to You, O Lord, and to the grave from which she will rise again on the last day, the body of Your daughter, Ivy Clague Armstrong."

Chapter 3

I did not mean to emit a tiny gurgle of surprise and yet I can hardly be faulted. It was enough of a sound to make those gathered around the grave turn to see who had disturbed this, the most sacred of moments.

The collective gaze of the assembled bored into me, their expressions a mixture of outrage, surprise, and curiosity. In that moment, I will admit to considering the coward's way out, to turning and running, to fleeing to the train station and back to London so I might put as much distance as I could between my embarrassment and the sobering realization that Ivy was dead.

I did not budge, though, and I would like to say it was because I was strong and determined, but I think, rather, I was paralyzed by horror and the ideas that exploded in my brain. Ivy thought someone wanted her dead. And now here she was, brought to the churchyard on this cold, sunless morning, waiting for body and memory to be covered over by the earth.

It was impossible to work my way through the possibilities and consider what this unforeseen turn of events meant—not there, not then. My breaths suspended, my insides icy, I did my best to look calmly back at the mourners, realizing as I did so that Ivy's suspects were among them.

I stood directly across from Reverend Plumley, only the length of the casket between us. His eyes were rimmed with red; his long, slim nose was the same color and raw as well. At my unexpected arrival, his prayer had dissolved and he lost his place in the reading and took the opportunity to pluck a handkerchief from his pocket and dab it to his nose. He did not look the sinister type, I decided, at the same time I reminded myself any person might be a threat. If they had motive enough.

Dr. Islington was to my right, easily recognized by his bristling mustache. He was enveloped in a black coat, his hands encased in leather gloves, his top hat held respectfully at his chest. He was a thick man with wide shoulders and a way of standing, his chin lifted, his feet set apart, that told me he would make a stalwart ally. Or a formidable enemy.

Edith Cowles was beside him and quickly identifiable, too, thanks to the large bustle she wore, just as she did in the drawing in the *Mercury*. Styles had changed, and currently, bustles were smaller and supposedly more delicate and feminine, yet Edith, though she was older than me by only ten years or so, kept with the older, cumbersome undergarment. I'll admit I judged her for it, though I liked to think I had good reason. Years in the tropics had taught me to dress more for comfort than fashion, and I was a believer in the Aesthetic movement and so, not a wearer of petticoats or bustles. Not for the first time, I was witness to the inconvenience of so-called fashion: because of Edith's bustle's magnificence (not to mention its sheer size), the row of people behind her had to keep a good distance, lest they be poked by the stiff shelf of her behind.

Edith's hands were clasped at her waist, and her gaze raked me with little more than passing curiosity. I, though, studied her with interest. Here was another of the villagers Ivy suspected wanted her dead, yet watching her there at the graveside, I couldn't help but think a woman with Edith's thin lips and weak chin would never have the nerve. That is, until I saw her glance toward the casket, something like steel in her eyes. A woman who was confident and stubborn enough to wear a fashion so clearly out of date might do anything. If she was moved by great emotion.

Lady Betina Thorn was nearest me, just to my left. As she had been in the picture in the *Mercury,* she was fashionably dressed, her clothing sturdy enough to keep out the chill and ornamented with just enough jet to be tasteful—and still make her stand out in the crowd. She was a woman of some sixty years, full of face and wide in the hips, and after the initial surprise of finding someone unexpectedly so close, she did not spare me another moment's notice, but turned back to the service. Like the reverend, she seemed harmless enough, encased in black and somber-eyed, yet the casket there at our feet told a different story.

There were others present, too, whose faces were not familiar to me and whose interest in me and my breach of manners ended the moment the vicar turned back to the service. There was only one person who had paid me no mind at all: the man who stood at the reverend's side. He was dark haired, his expression as stony as the grave markers all around us, his face as colorless as the fog-shrouded landscape. The pain in his eyes was palpable. What had Ivy said? That she and her new husband were compatible and congenial? That his love for her radiated through all he did? This was surely that man. Even my intrusion could not bring him to tear his gaze away from the casket of his beloved wife, there in the hole just inches from his feet. I did not even know his name and yet my heart broke on his behalf.

After but a dozen uncomfortable seconds, Reverend Plumley's prayer drew the attention of the crowd away from me and allowed me to collect myself.

Edith Cowles concentrated on the casket and the widower.

Lady Betina kept her back fully turned.

Reverend Plumley, his voice choked, began the next prayer.

Only Dr. Islington did not look away. His eyes, small and gray, studied me as if I was an odd species of butterfly, ensnared and pinned to a board. His mustache lifted when his top lip curled.

Uneasy, I shifted from foot to foot, but the ground there in the churchyard was damp and my right boot sunk further into it. Rather than take the chance of slipping and thus causing even more commotion, I forced myself to keep my place and bowed my head just as the rest of the assemblage did, repeating the words of a familiar prayer.

It was impossible to feel any genuine grief, for I did not know the woman in the casket except through her correspondence, and yet my eyes filled with tears just as my heart squeezed with regret. Should I have come to Willingdale sooner? What had happened to Ivy? Was there anything I could have done to stop it? And was one of the mourners who stood close by a murderer?

Again, I chanced a look at the crowd, evaluating and considering, and coming to only one conclusion: whatever had happened to Ivy, she had put her trust in Miss Hermione. She had asked for help. I was not able to provide it for her while she was living. The least I could do now was offer her some peace in death. As Reverend Plumley said the last of the prayers for Ivy's soul, I knew I was obliged to find answers.

For Ivy's sake.

The idea presented itself and settled deep just as Reverend Plumley said the last "Amen."

The word was echoed by voices muffled by emotion and the damp, and then Ivy's husband threw a handful of soil onto the casket. The sound of it hitting the mahogany reverberated through the churchyard like the crack of an Enfield rifle.

Edith Cowles flinched and turned away. Reverend Plumley hung his head. The jet beads on her clothing catching what little light there was, Lady Betina walked to a grave not thirty feet off, where she stood with her head bowed. After the rest of the crowd dispersed, Dr. Islington plunked his hat atop his head and put a hand on Ivy's husband's shoulder to lead the unfortunate widower from the grave.

"You're a stranger here." I tore my gaze away from the doctor and his charge to find Edith standing not three feet away, appraising everything from my boots to the cut of my coat. I had no doubt she noticed my lack of a bustle, too. "You knew Ivy?"

I stepped back, not eager to tell a lie so close to the deceased, but determined to follow through with the course I'd set. "We were old friends. In fact, I have just come from London to visit. When I arrived, it was the first I'd heard what happened."

Edith's dark brows rose a fraction of an inch over eyes that were as brown as chestnuts. "Friends? Really? Ivy spent all her life here in Willingdale. I should think we were acquainted with her friends. All of them."

"Miss Simpson's Academy for Young Ladies." Sending up

a quick thanks for my excellent memory, I offered as much of a smile as was proper considering the circumstances. "Ivy and I were at school together. I've recently had a letter from her and—"

"Have you? Had a letter?" Edith cocked her head and caused the black feathers on her Gainsborough with its rounded crown and turned-up brim to twitch. "You must tell me all about it. You'll be joining us? At the funeral luncheon?"

Instinctively, I backed away. I could not face the mourners in so private a setting. I needed more time to prepare, more information on Ivy herself. "I really don't think that would be proper. I haven't been invited."

"I'm inviting you." Edith stepped to my side and wound an arm through mine. "After all, you are an old friend. And you were on your way to visit Ivy." She cast a look over the gravestones scattered around us. "Where is your luggage?"

"Left at the station. To be delivered later." I managed to speak the words with all sincerity. "I think it best if I simply claim it and return to London by the next train."

"There are trains all day. And into the evening. That settles the matter. You must come to luncheon, if for no other reason than to offer Gerald your condolences."

"Ivy's husband? He won't mind?"

Edith's expression softened. "Gerald is the kindest of men so no, of course, he won't be bothered in the least. In fact, I think it's certain he'll be grateful you're here. I know he'll appreciate hearing your reminiscences about Ivy's school days."

I could only imagine he would, and as I untangled myself from Edith's grip to zigzag my way through the maze of gravestones, I wondered how many such stories I could cobble together that might actually sound genuine.

Edith and I proceeded to the road where the horse cart driver had left me. There was no carriage waiting, and as if reading my thoughts, she remarked, "Willingdale is not so large a place. We can walk to Gerald's for the luncheon. Unless you object?"

"Not at all." Outside the confines of the graveyard with its sad reminders of the brevity of life and the lasting sting of grief, I felt better able to breathe, to think, and I was grateful for the opportunity to spend some time clearing my head. We started down a street lined with sturdy brick Georgian buildings that housed the town hall and small shops that sold everything from poultry to flowers. There were timber-framed cottages interspersed, each with a square of garden out front.

Edith noticed how I studied the place. "We must seem terribly unpolished here in Willingdale," she commented. "What with you coming from London."

We were just making our way past a garden chockablock with roses of every color and I stopped to admire them and gather my thoughts as I told her, "Not at all. This is the kind of scenery Londoners only dream of. It's lovely."

"Is it?" Edith laughed. "It must all seem terribly rustic. I would think a woman such as you from a city such as London . . ."

"I spent many years away from London," I told her. "I traveled with my father in India and China and—"

"Oh!" She clapped a hand to her heart and her eyes flew open. Her complexion, best described as sallow, got paler still. "How terribly brave of you. Traveling in such savage lands!"

"I can assure you, they are more wondrous than savage. There is so much to admire in different cultures. The history and the artwork are astonishing!" The memories flooded me and filled me with longing. "The people are lovely."

"Really?" Edith's nose twitched. "And what about the food?"

"We ate mostly the same foods that we eat here. Except on the days we were lucky enough to venture out with the native populations. Then there was no end of glorious spices and teas we are not familiar with here, and so many other culinary delights. Curry and chicken tikka masala and—"

"All that, and yet you seem not uncivilized."

I imagined Edith meant this as a compliment, and because we had just left a funeral, I did not go so far as to correct her. Instead, I steered the conversation in another direction.

"I haven't seen Ivy in a long while," I said, my voice as innocent—or so I hoped—as the expression on my face. "Tell me about her."

"About her? But you must surely know about her since you are friends."

"Well, yes, but about her marriage then. As a new wife, she's been busy and we haven't had much communication. With this visit, we were counting on pleasant days and long conversations. You said her husband's name was Gerald. How long have they been married?"

"Six months last Thursday." Edith's words had the ring of authority. She was a woman who knew her facts and prided herself on keeping them straight.

"They were happy?"

She slid me a look. "Did Ivy say she was happy?"

"Well, yes." It was the truth so I did not feel the least bit guilty relaying it. By then, we were nearing the wide village green with its neatly trimmed lawn and I pictured it as I'd seen it in the drawings from the *Mercury,* with striped tents, crowds of merrymakers, and perhaps, a murderer in attendance.

I shook off the chill that skittered up my spine and focused on the pub nearby, the George and Dragon, with a sign outside showing a man in armor about to plunge a sword into a hapless serpent with green scales and sharp fangs. "Ivy did say she and Gerald were very happy. In fact, she told me—"

Edith didn't give me a chance to finish. A girl with mousy hair and ruddy cheeks stepped out of the pub and started our way, and Edith didn't waste a moment. She grabbed my arm and tugged me across the street. It wasn't until we got there that she realized she'd maltreated me.

She dropped her hand, backed away, and mumbled, "I am so sorry. I did not mean to catch you off guard. I just thought perhaps that we—"

"Should avoid the girl who walked out of the pub?"

The way she laughed told me I was right. "Betty? I hardly noticed her. And why would I be anxious to avoid Betty? No, no, that wasn't what I was thinking at all. I thought, perhaps, it wasn't so sunny on this side of the lane, though now that I consider it, you are probably used to sun. That is, due to the time you lived in tropical climates."

"It isn't sunny at all." I shouldn't have had to remind her, not with the way the wind whipped our dresses and the damp settled on our shoulders.

"Did I say sunny?" Another laugh, this even more unsure than the first. "What I meant is, the wind is far less ferocious here than it is near the green. I thought you'd be more comfortable."

Since there was no use disputing this or continuing to challenge her, I thanked her instead, and got back to the conversation I was quite anxious to have. "Tell me," I said, "what happened to Ivy?"

"You mean . . ." Edith chewed her lower lip.

"I mean, of course, she was a young woman and as far as I know, in good health. She was certainly in love and so, in good spirits. How did she die?"

She did not reply. Instead, her pace quick and determined, Edith led me further along the road and at a place where a small lane intersected the one we were on, we turned.

A few minutes later, we found ourselves at a stone bridge. To our right was a river with steep banks and water that raced its course around protruding boulders and fallen trees. Below us was a mill dam, perhaps five or six feet high, built to control the waters of the river. To our left was the millpond, a reservoir for the water used to power the grain mill at the opposite end of the bridge, a square, sturdy building that looked to have stood there for centuries.

"It happened here," Edith told me. "Just three days ago."

I ventured further onto the bridge for a better look, glancing down to where the water poured over the dam. Just beyond, it rolled and roiled into the pond.

"This is where Ivy died?"

"Fell." Edith lifted her chin in a way that told me though the information was both solemn and terrible, she felt obliged to convey it. While I'd ventured forward, she'd kept her place where land met bridge and now, she stepped closer.

I leaned against the waist-high wall. I am taller than most women, yet the wall was sturdy and seemed high enough, safe for anyone who might be passing.

"Ivy fell? Here?"

Edith nodded.

"It seems odd, don't you think? It would take some doing to trip and fall over this wall. It is a high enough barrier."

She clicked her tongue. "If you knew Ivy, you know there was no knowing what she might have been thinking. She may have been racing home. Or skipping. I've seen her skip, you know. So unladylike. Or perhaps . . ." As if even the thought was too much to bear, Edith wrapped her arms close around herself. "She might have been atop her bicycle and taken a spill. She rode one around the village. A bicycle. As if that is any way for a woman to travel."

Since I, too, enjoyed the exhilaration and efficiency of bicycle travel (and wore a split-skirt gown when I did) I did not agree with Edith's assessment. In fact, the very thought made me wonder, "Was Ivy's bicycle found? For surely if she was thrown from it, it would have been abandoned here, damaged."

"In the water, I imagine," Edith said. "And just as well. Bicycles are a menace to the general population."

Instead of considering it, I again judged the height of the parapet, the possibility of a person tumbling over it. "So, you believe it was an accident?" I asked Edith.

She blew out a breath of disbelief. "Of course it was an accident. What else might it have been? A terrible accident."

If it wasn't for the grim warning contained in Ivy's letters to Miss Hermione, I would have liked to believe her.

And for the fact that, though the light was poor and her face was shadowed by her hat, I swore I saw Edith smile.

Chapter 4

The redbrick Armstrong house was large and welcoming. Its location at the far end of the Willingdale green placed it at the center of village life while at the same time the wall surrounding the property assured its privacy. I quickly surmised that Gerald Armstrong was a man of business, and prosperous in his calling. Here, Ivy's life must surely have been comfortable. The walk to the front door was lined on either side with red rambling roses and there was a small garden up front where at this time of year purple lavender, pink hollyhocks, and blue delphinium grew in exuberant abundance. In sunny weather it was no doubt stunning, but because of the fog playing hide-and-seek around petals and stems, the glorious colors were muted so even the flowers seemed to be in mourning.

Edith and I fell into step behind a long line of black-clad neighbors who streamed into the house and we found ourselves in a wide entryway with a stairway directly ahead of us and rooms filled with people to our left along the hallway. A man whose expression was not as funereal as it was simply nonexistent took our cloaks and I again found myself in an awkward position. I had not anticipated attending a funeral, and the gown I wore was deep green with ochre trimmings.

A gold velvet chatelaine bag hung from my waist. In comparison with the sea of black around me, I looked a circus performer, or a music hall doxy, and I vowed my first order of business would be to offer my apologies to the widower.

That would have to wait. When Edith and I walked into the parlor, Gerald was deep in conversation with Dr. Islington and I did not dare interrupt. I would have time enough later to offer my condolences.

The parlor was a large, pleasant room with French windows that looked over the back of the house and another garden even more beautiful than the one out front. Most of the furniture had been moved to accommodate guests, but what had been left was tasteful and well made. There was a brocade couch with an elaborate walnut carved back across from the windows. Lady Betina Thorn sat there talking to a man with a shock of white hair. Armchairs were scattered here and there and a mahogany tall-case clock, its finials studded with brass, watched over us all.

"Tea?" Edith suggested, and when I told her I would get some in a bit, she went off to fetch her own from the table set against the far wall where there were piles of funeral biscuits wrapped in paper and sealed with black wax, meant to be taken home at the end of the luncheon. There also sat platters of ham and bread, cheeses, apples, and nuts. I moved to the side of the room to give the other guests easy access to the food and watched Edith fill a plate and chat with the people around her.

Here there was a piano and I imagined Ivy playing in the evening, and the pure, sweet sound of the music flowing through the house. There were two photographs there and, hoping to not be thought too curious, I took the time to study first one, then the other.

The first was that of a young woman standing beside a showy arrangement of flowers. Ivy. It could be no one else.

Ivy's hair was light and, in a style popular for the last few years, it was curled and piled atop her head. She had a wide nose and a round face, and she was short and substantial, with broad hips, small hands, and tiny feet. Ivy's expression was serious, her lips pressed so close together it made me think she was not comfortable posing for the camera.

Before turning to the second photograph, I looked from Ivy's portrait to the widower across the room.

Gerald's hair was raven dark and slick with macassar oil, his looks comparable to those classical statues I had once seen when Papa and I briefly visited Rome. He had a high, broad forehead, wide eyes, and a strong jaw.

Even at this, the most difficult of moments, his dark eyes sparked with energy. As he talked to Dr. Islington, he flashed what was almost a smile before the expression was again smothered beneath the weight of his heartache.

To me, the second photograph was far more interesting, and I turned from the widower to study it. In the photograph, Ivy and Gerald sat side by side, and the carnation in his lapel wasn't the only thing that signaled to me that it was taken on their wedding day. Ivy's discomfort was nowhere in evidence here. In fact, she had a smile on her face and it sparkled like the opal-and-diamond brooch pinned to her gown. Gerald's grin went ear to ear. Contentment radiated from the couple, infectious and complete.

"Just six months ago."

The voice startled me, and I spun to find Simon Plumley standing close behind me, looking where I was looking. His shoulders heaved. "So much can happen in so little time."

"Indeed." I nodded at him, giving only a small smile as

befitted the circumstances. "I am Violet Manville, a friend of Ivy's. I hadn't heard of her death until I arrived here in Willingdale to visit. Edith Cowles told me about the accident."

"Accident? Is that what she said?" Simon's gaze slid to mine, but stayed there but for a moment before he looked again toward Ivy's photograph.

"You don't believe it's true? That it wasn't an accident?"

Wherever his thoughts had traveled, I'd interrupted them, and Simon flinched. "I think . . ." He reached toward the photograph and touched a finger briefly to its silver frame. "She had secrets. Ivy always had secrets. She never wanted to reveal them for fear . . ." The reverend gave me a careful look. "You were a friend, you say?"

"Ivy and I were at school together."

"Then you know. About Ivy's mother?"

I weighed the wisdom of saying too much and learning nothing against saying too little and proving once and for all I had no business there. I toed the line carefully and as I did, I watched the reverend for some warning I was headed in the wrong direction. "Ivy was reluctant to talk about it."

"Understandable."

"She was such a private person."

"True, true," he clucked.

"And yet what she did share with me was very . . ." I hoped for some sign of encouragement, some gesture or bob of the head that would tell me if it was troubling or cheerful news I was supposed to have heard about Ivy's mother. When he gave me no help at all, I forged ahead. "She was circumspect, of course."

"Ivy was a kind soul."

"And I'm sure you did all you could to help her, reverend. She was very lucky to have you for a friend."

"Is that what she said?" He was thin and rangy and he reminded me of a scarecrow, all arms and legs and a black suit with trousers that were a tad short and a jacket that was a bit baggy. When he shrugged, it was in a way that was both modest and self-satisfied. "There is some small happiness in knowing she considered me a friend. The truth is, though, there was little I could do other than offer Ivy a shoulder to cry on. Not literally, of course." The reverend's cheeks colored. "She worried so about her mother, poor Clementine, but Clementine's woes were beyond the help of medicine. Which is, of course, why Albert, Ivy's father, was obliged to do what he did. Out of love. All out of love. But as I'm sure Ivy told you, such pain, such agony, it is impossible to deal with, heartbreaking to watch."

As if this were a pronouncement of great insight, I nodded. "Ah, illness!"

"Ivy hated that she was not allowed to spend more time with Clementine. Reading to her, perhaps. Praying with her. Or simply sitting to offer companionship and comfort. I do hope you have not had to deal with anything like it yourself, Miss Manville, but if you have, you know how terrible it can be. There is no hope. There is no cure for madness."

The word struck me like a blow to the midsection, but I dared not show it was a surprise. "It is one of the secrets Ivy kept."

"Obviously not from you." The look Simon gave me was benevolent, and I would have taken it as such if not for that letter from Ivy. For the picture of Simon, his face circled.

"I'm happy she had a female friend to confide in," he said, as sincere as I thought a murderer would never be. "Just as I am happy you were coming here to visit. Clementine has been gone quite some time now, but still, the sorrow of her life and her unhappy ending colored Ivy's every day. Talking about it might have relieved Ivy's burden. Instead, all Ivy did was put her worries on paper."

"Did she? Write about them? I mean, other than by corresponding with me?" I could not believe Ivy had confessed to confiding in Miss Hermione so I hoped there was more to this comment from Simon. "You're saying . . ."

"She kept a diary. Yes. She was always writing in her diary. If I could find it, then I would know."

"Know . . . ?"

His bottom lip pinched and Reverend Plumley once again turned his attention to the photograph. Not the one of Ivy and Gerald on their wedding day, I noted, but the first. Ivy and the flowers. A young woman alone. Uncertain.

His breath caught. His bottom lip trembled. Before he could say another word, Reverend Plumley spun on his heels and rushed out to the garden. He paused there, his back to the house, away from prying eyes, and his shoulders heaved.

"The man takes too much to heart."

This time, the voice that interrupted my thoughts came from my left, and I turned to find Dr. Islington with a plate of ham in one hand, watching Simon just as I was.

"When I was a lad, vicars attended to church business and church business alone, just as they should," he grumbled. "They didn't get involved in peoples' lives and their goings-on and their backstairs gossip."

"Is that why the reverend is upset?" I asked him. "Because of backstairs gossip?"

"Bah!" Islington dismissed the notion with a brusque wave of his free hand. "No telling what the young fool is worried about." He gave me a bow as curt as the motion he'd used to consign the vicar to a conversation for another time. "Richard Islington. You are new to the village."

I had told the lie so repeatedly that now it fell easily from my lips. "I am a school friend of Ivy's. As I had not seen her in quite some time, I came to visit. But I arrived today and found—"

"Yes, yes." He cut me off before there was any chance for awkward emotion. "Ugly business."

"And especially sad considering how short a time Ivy was married and how much marriage agreed with her."

Islington grumbled a sound I could not identify as either agreement or dissension. "You say you haven't seen her in some time. How would you—"

"We've corresponded." It was, for the most part, true.

"Frequently?" he asked.

"Yes," I lied.

"Recently?"

This question did not require prevarication. "Very recently. Ivy told me she was settling in. Getting used to married life." I glanced around the room with its lovely view, its appealing furnishings. "And to the house, too, I would think. It is quite lovely."

"The house, you say?" Islington looked down over his mustache at me and in my imagination, I saw him with a circle around his face, just as it was in the *Mercury*. As if he suddenly smelled something nasty, he wrinkled his nose. "It is the Clague home. Built by Ivy's father when he first married Clementine. Ivy lived here all her life."

I could not panic at the slip of my tongue, not if I hoped to keep up the façade of my friendship with Ivy and thus, keep asking questions. With no other choice, I called on a technique I'd seen Sephora use time and again to great advantage. When in doubt about what to say to a man, pretend confusion. Calling up a blush always worked for Sephora, too, but I'm afraid though my talents are many, that is not one of them.

"Oh dear, I'm afraid I have misspoken." Had we been anywhere else at any other time, I would have added a giggle here as Sephora always did to disarming effect. I would also have taken the time to consider that Ivy's family must surely have had a considerable income. Now she was dead, I assumed Gerald would inherit. "I did not mean to imply I thought Ivy was getting used to the house itself as much as I meant she was getting used to being the mistress of the house now that there was a husband in residence."

Islington sniffed. "Indeed. And what did you say your name was?"

"Manville. Violet Manville."

"Well, Miss Manville, if you'll excuse me—"

"I would like to ask you . . ." When he backed up a step, I moved forward. "As you know, I arrived here in Willingdale at a most inconvenient time and I have yet to hear all the details of what happened to dear Ivy. I am loath to ask her husband, of course, and yet I'm eager for an understanding of the event."

His mustache bristled. "Are you sure?"

"Should I not be?"

"Well, you will, no doubt, hear it from a dozen other people and I'm certain they won't have the facts straight so you might as well hear the truth from me. I am sorry to tell you, Miss Manville, for it is surely distressing, but Ivy took her own life."

"No!" I did not have to pretend shock. Edith had told me

Ivy's death was an accident. "I didn't know. I hadn't heard. Why would she—"

"You needn't be coy, Miss Manville." His look shot from me to the garden, but now there was no sign of Reverend Plumley there. "I'm sure he told you all about it. Our vicar is as much a gossip as the old rumormongers who gather for tea at Lady B's in the afternoon. Ivy confided in the good reverend. Just as I'm sure she confided in you. And I suppose she told you what she must surely have told him. She thought people were trying to harm her. Did she mention that?"

I could hardly tell him he was one of those people, so instead, I clutched my hands at my waist and lifted my chin, the picture of a confidence I did not feel. "You believe Ivy was mad," I said. "Just as her mother was."

Islington had eyes the color of storm clouds, and at my comment, they narrowed enough for him to study me with special interest. "You know about that, do you?"

"As I said, Ivy and I corresponded."

"Then you need to consider . . ." He pulled in a sharp breath. "No, let us not be circumspect but let me say it clearly. I hope you understand, Miss Manville, Ivy's mind was troubled. Yes, just like her mother's. Whatever she may have told you in letters."

"You are saying those things might not be true."

"No. I am saying most specifically that a good deal of what she said and what she thought was surely not true. I know, for I was her physician just as I was her mother's, and just like Clementine, Ivy fantasized. She imagined things that were not there and saw evil where there was none. I am certain her mental confusion is what caused Ivy to take her own life. Just as her mother did. It was a sad enough business when Clementine did it. The weight of the memory troubled the village for years. And now, we must deal again with the pain and the guilt. That is why I'm telling you it is best not to discuss Ivy's death with Gerald." He glanced over his shoulder and together, we watched Edith take a cup of tea to Gerald and urge him to drink it. "The poor man is upset enough, especially with all this coming just as he was about to embark on an important business venture in Canada. There's no use adding to his woes."

"I can assure you I would never do that."

"Good." This time when he stepped away it was clearly to put distance between ourselves and our conversation. "Then I wish you a safe trip back to wherever you have come from."

"London," I added automatically.

"Then I wish you a safe trip back to London. I hope for Gerald's sake that will be soon. He hardly needs the reminder of Ivy's former life your presence is sure to stir. Good day, Miss Manville. Goodbye."

I kept my place until the doctor walked away, mulling over these new revelations for many minutes, and I might have stayed there even longer if I hadn't noticed a movement outside the window. A gust of wind rattled the greenery and with it, it looked as if a scarecrow flew by. One dressed all in black.

I watched Reverend Plumley dart toward the front of the house, glancing left and right as if to be certain no one was watching him. Interested, I peeked into the hallway. I was just in time to see Simon open the front door. He looked all around and, certain he was alone, he slipped inside and hurried up the stairs.

My dear papa used to say I was more curious than a cat, and warned me the trait would do me no good. Perhaps he was right. Papa usually was. But that did not mean I could deny the questions that filled my head and my determination to do right by Ivy. I could imagine Papa's advice to me now, could almost hear him saying, just as he'd said time and time again in life, "Leave well enough alone, Vi." Yet, just as I had so many times before, I ignored his words of caution. Checking over my shoulder to be sure no one paid me any mind, I watched Simon gain the first-floor landing, saw him steal down the hallway, and followed.

Chapter 5

I can be excused my impulsiveness. Not to mention such a complete breach of etiquette. Simon had, after all, mentioned a diary, one he was eager to read, and I was certain it was what he was searching for. Nothing else would explain why he moved so quickly, so quietly, unaware that he was being followed.

When I got to the top of the stairs, I stationed myself just behind the wall where hall met landing, a place where I might observe and not be found out. From my vantage point, I saw him go into the room at the farthest end of the hallway and it wasn't until he was inside that I wondered where I would hide when he walked out again and came back toward the stairs. Panic shot through me and my heart slammed my ribs. Surely, I was earnest enough in my pursuit of the truth of all that had happened to Ivy, but when it came to reconnaissance I was the most novice of investigators. With no other choice and no other ideas, I shot forward and dashed into the first room on my left.

When the door closed behind me, I let go a breath of relief. At least, until I turned and spied the woman pressed into the corner of the room between a wardrobe and a brown leather couch. Her attempt at concealment was hardly effective considering she wore a white apron that stood out against the dark green walls. And that her apple-round cheeks were fiery.

"Betty?" I leaned forward so as to better study the girl Edith and I had so recently seen outside the George and Dragon.

For her part, Betty was just as surprised to see me as I was to find her. She gasped.

"Who . . . who are you, then? And what the devil are you doing here?"

Because I couldn't explain, I shot back, "What are you doing here?"

She stuck out her lower lip. "Asked you first, didn't I?"

"And I . . ." I am not at all sure throwing back my shoulders and lifting my chin helped me look self-possessed, but I did it anyway, and tossed my head while I was at it. "I am a guest at the funeral luncheon. You are not. You are not dressed appropriately."

"Neither are you! Not a bit of black on you. Not like the lot of them downstairs, all prim and prissy and acting like they care." She snorted. "And you're no friend of the family, I know as much. What are you doing here in the master's room?"

Gerald's dressing room?

I felt my face color, but etiquette be damned! I was not so much concerned about being found in a man's dressing room and being thought a voyeur as I was worried Betty might raise the alarm. Then I would surely be accused of being a thief and spend the night in what in India we called the chokey. Except, from the way Betty's breast heaved and she twisted her hands together at her waist, I did not think she could risk discovery, either.

I stepped closer and lowered my voice, sharing the confidence to gain her trust. "I am looking for something. And I think you must be, too. I did not see you downstairs so I know you weren't hired to help serve the luncheon. How did you get in here?"

She sniffed. "Up the back steps from the kitchen, a'course. Through the hall there at the other side of the stairway. There are many ways around a house if a person is familiar enough with it."

"And are you? Familiar with this house?"

She pulled a face. "Helps with the cleaning sometimes. When I'm not behind the bar at the George and Dragon. But I'm not so familiar that I can turn up what I'm looking for."

"And that is?"

Betty was not a pretty girl. She was younger than me, and she had bad skin and a large, flat nose. When she lifted her top lip, she looked more a predator than a harmless girl.

"You're searching for something, too," she ventured. "Or are you lookin' for anything you can thieve that might be worth a pretty penny or two?"

The idea was appalling and I immediately defended myself. "Certainly not! If you must know, I am looking for Ivy's diary."

"Ivy!" I do believe if we had been outside, Betty would have spat on the ground. "It's her fault I have to search at all. She's the one what stole from me."

"Did she?" This was interesting, and, eager to know more, I closed in on Betty. "What did she take?"

"Something of mine. And I want it. After all, she's dead, ain't she? She don't need it no more and it's rightfully mine."

"I can help you."

She eyed me uncertainly. "Why?"

"Because neither one of us can chance being discovered. Which means we have to trust each other and we need to be quick about our business. Two sets of eyes are better than one. I will help you look for your stolen property if you will help me locate the diary." I shot a glance over my shoulder. "The sooner we are done here, the better."

"Aye." Betty pursed her lips. "It's a brooch if you must know." As if the piece of jewelry might be there, she touched a finger to her left shoulder. "Sparkled, it did. Like sunlight on icicles. Diamonds and opals, it was."

"The brooch Ivy wore in her wedding photograph?"

"Wore it every single day, she did."

The thought of this girl owning something so precious struck me as odd and I'm afraid my voice betrayed my disbelief. "After she took it from you?"

Betty shot me a look. "She flaunted it, that's what she did. Wore it so I would be sure to see it every time our paths crossed. And now, her being dead, I want it. It's only right."

"She wasn't buried with it, was she?"

I do believe Betty had never considered this, because her face turned ashen and her jaw went slack. "No. No." She shook her head, seemingly trying to convince herself more than me. "He never would'a done that."

"Gerald?"

She did not answer, but glanced around the room. "It's here. Somewhere. It's got to be."

"Then we best begin our search," I told her. "Before someone else gets the notion to come upstairs."

With that warning ringing through both our heads, we started into our work. I searched in the wardrobe. Betty patted down and looked beneath the couch cushions. I took the liberty of looking through Gerald's desk. She had just finished going through his dressing bureau when we heard the door at the end of the hall open and softly close.

I put a finger to my lips and went to the door, opening it but a crack. I was just in time to see Simon dash past, his expression still grim with determination.

"Is that what he's lookin' for, too?" Betty's whisper raked my ear. "That there diary?"

I nodded.

"Well, he ain't found it." She was so sure of herself, I turned to hear more. "His hands." Though Simon had gone down the hallway and up the stairs to the second floor, she pointed as if he were still there. "They was empty. He did not find the book you're looking for. But then—"

"He's a man," I said.

"And a man . . ."

"Wouldn't know where a woman might conceal something so precious!"

Together we slipped out of Gerald's dressing room, past the room next door, which must have surely been the happy couple's bedroom, and to Ivy's boudoir. It was as feminine as Gerald's was masculine. The walls were painted a delicate shade of pink, the furniture was refined and just old-fashioned enough to make me think it must have once belonged to Ivy's mother—a washstand, an easy chair, a couch, a large wardrobe, and a low dressing bureau where, the moment we were inside, Betty began digging through the drawers. When she slammed the drawer shut on the last of them, I knew she'd had no success.

"No diary, either?" I asked her.

She shot a look over her shoulder at me. "You ain't even lookin', just standin' there gawkin', so don't you go criticizing."

Betty was right, so while she went through Ivy's dressing case and her jewel box, I searched the rest of the room, ignoring the places I was sure Simon had already looked—under the bed, between the blankets, in drawers. Instead, I concentrated on all those places where I had hidden diaries over the years. After all, I had a stepmother, and as she was a nosey parker, I'd learned early to be ingenious.

The diary was not tucked in a boot, hidden among Ivy's undergarments, or outside on the window ledge. Nor was it in the wardrobe where Ivy's clothes still hung, neatly arranged. Something else there, though, caught my eye. When I plucked the metal contraption from the wardrobe and held it at arm's length, Betty discontinued her search long enough to give it a curious look.

"It is a Langtry folding bustle," I told her. Then, so she did not think me empty-headed and concerned with fashion, was sure to add, "It was designed by none other than Lillie Langtry, and my half sister has been rhapsodizing about getting one ever since their production was announced. She's shown me the advertisements for it in the newspapers. See." I gave the back of the bustle a poke and it folded up and in. "The springs work to fold the bustle up when a woman sits or lies down. When she stands again . . ." I moved my hand away and the bustle popped back into its original shape. "I hear it is all the rage in Paris."

"Oh, don't that just bang up to the elephant!" Betty's sigh was filled with wonderment. "New, you say?"

"Yes." I considered this and all it meant. "The latest thing. And Betty . . ." I looked at the young woman who stood on the other side of the bustle. "Why would you buy a thing so fashionable and new and exciting if you were planning to kill yourself?"

As if the bustle was on fire, Betty backed away. "You're saying . . ."

"I'm saying it's what I've heard. That Ivy might not have fallen into the millpond by accident but that it's possible she jumped."

She ran her tongue across her lips. "And you're thinking . . ."

"Well, I don't know what to think. Which is why I would like to find Ivy's diary."

"Not here," she concluded with an unequivocal shake of her head.

"Then we must keep looking."

To that end, I put the Langtry bustle back where I found it and we left the room and went up the stairs to the second floor, where I'd seen Simon disappear.

Just as we arrived, me leading the way and Betty behind me, he came out of a room at the end of the hallway and went up another set of stairs there, luckily too set on his mission to glance down the hall toward Betty and me.

"The attic?" I asked Betty, and when she did not answer, I turned to where she was trying to conceal herself behind me. "Is there an attic?"

Betty nodded.

"It would be a clever spot to hide both a diary and a piece of jewelry."

She nodded again.

"Then we must wait for Simon to come back down before we go up to look." I grabbed Betty's hand and together we slipped into a nearby room that looked to be used by guests, and waited. I will admit to discouragement when Simon was upstairs for but a short time. Had he found the diary so quickly? Or had he somehow surmised it wasn't in the attic? Whatever the reason, I would not so easily give up. He went downstairs and then and only then did we slip out of the room. I led Betty to the attic stairs.

"Go on." I urged her to go up ahead of me, but, her knees locked and her eyes wide, she cast a look up the stairs and shook her head.

"I thought you wanted to find the brooch," I hissed.

"That's as may be, but brooch or no brooch, I ain't going up there."

"Why ever not?"

She slid me a look. "You don't know?"

"Really, Betty." When I made an attempt to grab her hand again, she tucked it behind her back along with the other one. "Well, if you won't come along, I will simply go myself."

"But, miss." She darted between me and the doorway. "You ain't afraid? You ain't heard?"

"About . . ."

"Mrs. Clague, a'course. Ivy's mother." She leaned closer and though we were already whispering, she lowered her voice even more. "Mad, you know."

"So I have heard."

"And kept . . ." Betty's eyes shot to the stairway. "They say Mr. Clague never had the heart to send her off to a madhouse so he kept her here. Up there. Where she couldn't hurt no one. They also say . . ." She ran her tongue over her lips. "This is where she done herself in and sometimes her ghost still roams the place, angry at having been locked away and weeping for her sad fate."

I barked out a laugh, then remembered myself and clapped a hand over my mouth. I whispered through my fingers. "Do you believe such nonsense?"

"My gram says it's true."

"Well, it's not. Mrs. Clague is dead. She isn't up there now." Yes, I sounded doughty enough. It was a good thing Betty could not tell it was not phantoms that made my heart suddenly beat an uncomfortable rhythm, my palms slick with sweat, but the incontrovertible knowledge that I was trespassing in a place I did not belong. The only thing that made me step forward was the thought of the diary. That, and the varied stories that I had heard that day.

Ivy's death was an accident.

It was caused by her own carelessness.

She had killed herself just as her mother had.

The theories whirled through my head along with the grim memory that invalidated them all.

Those faces circled in the *Mercury*.

Ghost or no ghost, anguished memories or not, I knew what I had to do. I put a hand on Betty's shoulder. "You'd best leave. I don't know how long I might be up there and—"

"You'll look for it?"

"Your brooch? Yes, I promise."

Without another word, Betty turned and skittered down the hallway.

The coating of dust on the stairway blurred by Simon's footsteps told me this was a little-used portion of the house, and the stairs creaked as I climbed them. They ended at a locked door, but there was a hook on the wall beside it, and a key hanging from the hook. I unlocked the door, pushed it open, and stepped into what felt like a different time and place, a room preserved in amber, looking like it must have looked all those years before, when Ivy's mother was kept there, a prisoner of her own madness.

The attic was a dark, moldering place so different from the light and airy rooms downstairs it seemed impossible I was still in the same house. There was but one window in the tiny room and the gray light of the afternoon filtered through the tattered curtains on it. Beneath the window was a bed, the blankets on it ragged, the pillow flat and nibbled at one end; the only sign of life the room had seen in years was the mice I heard scampering in the walls. There was a single chair next to the bed along with a washstand, and there was a bookshelf on my left.

Of course I had my suspicions about Betty's tale of the brooch and Ivy's thievery. Betty did not seem to be a woman who might own a piece of jewelry so expensive.

But a promise was a promise, and mindful of that, I did a quick search. Nothing there sparkled, certainly not the room's gruesome past, and the sadness of the place sat upon my shoulders like a weight. I gave up my search for the brooch and, once again remembering my own attempts at keeping secrets from Sephora's mother, I turned my attention to the bookshelf.

A Bible; *The Count of Monte Cristo*; *The Hunchback of Notre Dame*; *The Personal History, Adventures, Experiences and Observation of David Copperfield the Younger of Blunderstone Rookery*.

It was clear from the marks in the dust on the shelves that Simon had jostled the books out of their usual spots to look between and behind them, yet I wondered if he had missed the most telling clue of all.

The Personal History, Adventures, Experiences and Observation of David Copperfield the Younger of Blunderstone Rookery was as thick a book as its title was long. And unlike the rest of the room, that particular volume was remarkably free of dust. As if it was often removed from the shelf then carefully returned.

Encouraged, I pulled the book from the shelf and flipped it open. As I suspected, the pages had been hollowed out and a slim leather-covered volume was nestled in the cavity.

I slipped Ivy's diary into the chatelaine bag at my waist and turned to give the sad little room one last look.

It was then I first noticed something like writing on the wall just below the window. Well aware I had not the luxury of lingering, I darted over for a look, pushing aside the curtains to allow light into the room and freezing there as if an icy hand had touched my insides.

The window itself was barred with thick pieces of iron. And the odd marks I had seen?

They were not letters or writing at all, but scratches sliced deep into the plaster. As if someone had been clawing at the window ledge.

Desperate to escape.

Chapter 6

I am hardly the fanciful type, yet I could not contain the images that now flooded my brain.

Clementine Clague, madness overtaking her, her hair in tangles, tears streaming down her cheeks. I envisioned her clawing at the windows and walls, attempting to break loose from her prison.

Was poor Ivy a witness to her mother's misery? Did she hear Clementine's cries in the night? Was she, perhaps, the one who had discovered Clementine's body?

Even those thoughts were not as troubling as the one more germane to my visit to Willingdale—did the same madness that ate away at Clementine afflict Ivy, too? Had she simply imagined that someone wanted to kill her? Was Dr. Islington right? Had lunacy overtaken Ivy and caused her to take her own life?

It was all too awful, all too much to work out there in so dismal a place, and I dropped the curtains and spun away from the sad scene.

A sense of dread settled over me and I raced to put as much distance as I could between myself and the wretched little room. I closed the door behind me, locked it, and hurtled down the stairs, so eager to escape the oppressive atmosphere that I was concentrating firmly on where I stepped and did not look ahead of me.

That is the only thing that explains it, of course.

For when I got to the bottom of the stairs and turned to start down the hallway, I stopped just short of slamming into the man standing there.

I let out a yelp of surprise just as he caught hold of my arms to keep me from falling and after a second or two, the blood stopped whooshing inside my ears, the scene settled, and I found myself face-to-face with Gerald Armstrong.

There I stood, frozen, and I honestly didn't know if it was from fear or mortification. I also could not say if the look that flashed across his countenance was surprise or irritation. I only know his eyes sparked, his hold on me tightened, not so much helpful and comforting as it was controlling.

My reaction was one of pure instinct. I wrenched out of his grasp and stepped back. While I was at it, I straightened my skirt and pulled in breath after breath to still my heart and calm myself.

"You are not hurt, miss?"

His question might be filled with concern, yet I could not help but notice there was a spark of vexation in his eyes. And what eyes they were! Eyes that might make a woman forget herself if she had not just committed the sort of transgression of manners that would call down Miss Hermione's disapproval—and burglary as well.

"I do beg your pardon," I stammered.

"As well you should. What were you doing up there?"

Giggling and blushing would not help me, it was clear. Not this time. Instead, I chose as remorseful an expression as

I could muster. "I was quite lost, I'm afraid, and then I heard a noise upstairs and . . ."

He shot a look up the stairway. "Someone is up there?"

"No. I saw no one. I am afraid my mind might have been playing tricks on me as I am still so shaken by the news of Ivy's passing."

Gerald turned from the attic stairway. He was a tall man and well made. Good features, a frame both muscular and fit that made me think of the many men in London who were all agog about the new fashion of physical culture and regularly exercised at athletic studios.

"I have not had a chance to offer my condolences," I said, eager to keep the subject on Ivy and away from what I'd been up to. As tempted as I was to remind myself my visit to the attic was not in vain, I kept from touching a hand to the bag hanging at my side, to the stolen book nestled in it. "I am very sorry for your terrible loss."

"Thank you." Some of the tension went out of his shoulders, though his questions were still pointed. "But I do not believe we've met. Who are you? And what are you doing here?"

It had been easier to explain to Betty! Now, beneath the careful scrutiny of this striking man and fully aware of the burden of his grief, I scraped my hands against the skirt of my gown.

"I am a friend of Ivy's," I told him. "Come to visit."

"She didn't tell me we were to have a visitor."

"I had no intention of staying. I'm just down for the day and—"

"What did you say your name was?"

"Violet Manville."

I did not think I imagined his quick, sharp intake of breath. "Manville?" As if cataloguing my features, he gave me a careful, studied look. The shape of my nose. The sweep of my forehead. The color of my eyes. "Of the Yorkshire Manvilles?" he asked.

"I'm terribly sorry. I am not acquainted with that particular family."

"No big strapping brother named Angus?"

"I'm afraid not."

"And no father who's made his way in the world thanks to paper factories?"

"No. I have no such relations that I am aware of. My father worked in the Foreign Office and now I live in London with my aunt and half sister."

"Ah." He considered this. "And does this half sister of yours get confused and lost in unfamiliar houses like you do, Miss Manville?"

I would have laughed at the joke if not for his unhappy state. If there was the slightest indication his comment was in jest. "Sephora would know better," I assured him. "She is not one to go off exploring and I'm afraid I just couldn't help myself. It is such a beautiful home."

"Ivy would be . . ." Emotion clogged his voice and he turned away, coughed. He did not turn back to me until he was again fully in control of himself. "My wife would be happy to hear you say that. She loved the house. Her father designed it, you know. As he did so many of the country residences hereabouts. Have you and your sister been here before?"

"My sister? Oh, no! I'm sorry if I misled you. She is not here with me. I came alone to see Ivy."

"And left your sister in London."

"Yes."

"And she doesn't know the family?"

"Your family, sir? No, I'm certain she does not. She's never met Ivy. In fact, I had not seen Ivy in years. We were at school together. Miss Simpson's."

"And between then and now?"

"We corresponded. I knew of her marriage, and I do hope you'll forgive me if I'm being too forward at mentioning it, but in her letters, Ivy told me how very happy she was."

"Yes." He pressed his arms to his sides, controlling a heartache I could not begin to understand. Gerald cleared his throat. "You corresponded frequently?"

"I had a letter from Ivy very recently."

"Did you?" When he turned and started down the hallway and for the stairs, I had no choice but to go along. "What did she have to say?"

"Nothing of import," I assured him, for telling him Ivy suspected someone wanted her dead seemed particularly cruel. "She talked of the weather and the garden. And she invited me to visit."

"Yes, that sounds like Ivy. Always so welcoming. If our paths should cross again, Miss Manville, I would like to read that letter. To have some insight into her thoughts these last days."

He motioned for me to start down the stairs and I went ahead of him, and we did not speak again until we were on the ground floor. "You'll find the other guests still in the parlor." Gerald nodded in that direction before he pinned me with a look. "As it is a large house and as you are obviously not familiar with it, I would suggest you stay there. That way, you won't get lost again. I would hate to see anything happen to you."

He bowed from the waist and strode to the front door

to talk to a man waiting there and I paused in the hallway, debating whether he'd just offered kind advice—or given me a warning.

Considering it, I walked back into the parlor. I was just in time to see Lady Betina Thorn stroll to the corner of the room, look over her shoulder to be sure no one was watching, and pull a silver flask from her reticule. She poured its contents into her teacup. I closed in on her just as she tucked away the flask again.

"Do I know you?" She eyed me when I approached, squinting and the slightest bit unsteady on her feet. "We have not met, I am sure of that."

"We have not. And I am sorry we are meeting now on such an unhappy occasion. I am Violet Manville."

Her eyebrows shot up. "Adelia's niece?"

I allowed myself as much of a smile as was appropriate. "You know my aunt?"

"I do, indeed. She has spoken of you time and again. She was happy to be able to help both you and your half sister when you returned to this country."

"And we are happy to have her affection and support," I told her.

"Ah, Adelia!" Lady Betina's dark eyes sparkled and I wondered if she was aware that when she spoke, a faint odor like peat smoke rose from the whisky on her breath. "Many's the adventure the two of us have had together. How is she?"

"Off to the Continent," I told her.

"With a man, no doubt." Her eyes sparkling with mischief, Lady Betina put a hand on the nearest table to steady herself and leaned forward. "She'll have stories to tell when she returns, no doubt. And when she does, let her know Lady

B is looking forward to hearing them. That's what she calls me, you know, and you must call me that, as well."

"I will," I promised.

"Now, tell me what you're doing here."

I appreciated Lady B's directness. "I was a school friend of Ivy's," I told her. "Come to visit with no knowledge of what had happened to her."

"And walked into this." She glanced around the room. "I'm sorry."

"What can you tell me," I asked her, "about Ivy's passing?"

Lady B's scowl might have been more forceful if she hadn't hiccupped. "Silly girl," she grumbled. "And I'm sorry to say it since she was a friend, but since she was a friend, you must know as much yourself. Featherbrained. Her head always in the clouds." By way of demonstrating, she brandished one hand above her head.

A little too enthusiastically.

Thanks as much to the dramatic gesture as the contents of her glass, Lady B lost her balance and stumbled. I reached out a hand and caught her in time to prevent her from falling, but the liquid in her glass sploshed, spattered, and spilled over both of us.

She squealed. I gasped. All around us, conversations ceased. People turned our way. Lady B's eyes went wide and in that moment, I could fairly see the thoughts that flew through her head. Someone there was surely perceptive enough to divine the real reason for the mishap and soon, word would spread to all of Willingdale of Lady B's secret flask. Her face paled. Her bottom lip trembled, and I knew I needed to act quickly.

To that end, I settled her on her feet then I slapped both

hands to my cheeks. "Oh dear," I groaned, loud enough for the assemblage to hear. "Look what I've done by banging into you when I wasn't looking. Please do accept my apologies." I pulled a handkerchief from my pocket and dabbed at the blotches of liquid on her skirt. "I cannot believe I was paying so little attention. I am so sorry."

"It is fine, dear." With a small, knowing smile, she accepted my ministrations at the same time she looked around and announced, "All is well. No need to worry."

And with that and the firm belief that one clumsy stranger was responsible for the muddle, the company went back to talking.

"Thank you." Lady B mouthed the words.

"Shall we sit down?" I asked her.

"Yes." She latched onto my arm so as to be sure to keep herself upright and carefully put one foot in front of the other, and together we made our way back to the couch where I'd seen her sitting earlier. Once she was seated, I sat next to her.

"Tea," she told the maid who instantly appeared to see what she needed, and when the girl was gone, she told me, "Really, tea this time. I only added a bit of an antifogmatic to mine earlier to chase away the chill of the graveyard. And now, oh my, folks might think I was sozzled the way I swayed and slipped. You saved me a good deal of embarrassment, my dear. I don't know how I can thank you."

"You can tell me what happened to Ivy."

Her eyebrows shot up. "Is that why you're here in Willingdale? You're looking to find out what happened to her? There must be some real reason you're concerned, for I know you could not be a school friend." The look she gave me told me there was no use trying to dispute it and she proved it by adding, "How could you have gone to school with Ivy when you lived in foreign lands with your father?"

Caught in the lie, I tried to stammer out an explanation, but Lady B stopped me by patting my arm. "Your secret is safe with me," she said, "just as I know mine is with you."

As much as I would have liked the counsel of a confidante, I could not reveal all, not without betraying Adelia's secret identity or the shocking content of Ivy's letters to Miss Hermione.

"I didn't know anything had happened to Ivy," I said, neatly avoiding explaining myself. "Not until I arrived to find, as you say, all this. And since I have been here, I have heard any number of stories to explain Ivy's sad end. I have to admit I'm curious as to what really happened."

Lady B frowned. "She was always thinking of herself instead of considering the feelings of others. Always worried about the past instead of looking toward the future. And as I said, more inclined than not to have her head in the clouds. If you ask me, she probably wasn't watching where she was going. That would explain why Ivy tumbled from the bridge."

"Even though the wall there is high enough to prevent such accidents?"

Her gaze snapped to mine. "What are you saying?"

"Only that I would like to know the truth. If you're sure it was an accident . . ."

Lady B snorted. "What else could it possibly be?"

"And she'd had other such accidents?"

"No. Of course not. Except . . ." A thought occurred and Lady B tilted her head. "Now that you mention it, there was the incident outside the church."

"St. Christopher's?"

She nodded. "You've seen it. It's an old building, and

Reverend Plumley is forever telling us he needs more money for upkeep and repairs. That explains, of course, why a loose slate fell from the roof."

I flinched. "It struck Ivy?"

"Nearly," Lady B said. "Certainly frightened her, very understandably. Then there was the runaway hay wagon. Edith Cowles would know more about that. She was with Ivy when it happened."

"Two accidents." I considered this in light of what Ivy had told Miss Hermione. "And the third killed her."

"You are so much like Adelia!" Lady B muffled her chuckle behind one hand. "She, too, would be wondering and asking questions."

I dared one last one. "Did Ivy have any accidents when she was with you?" I asked.

Whisky only goes so far to soften a person's disposition. Perhaps she was stunned. Maybe she was outraged. Or it could be Lady B was simply surprised I, like Adelia, had the cheek to say things that are best left unspoken. She sat up straight. "As a matter of fact, she did not."

"Just inquiring," I assured her at the same time I stood. "It's time for me to be getting back to town."

She snatched at my hand. "I did not mean to sound so . . ."

The word *defensive* popped into my mind, but there seemed nothing to be gained from pointing it out.

Perhaps I didn't need to. Lady B offered an apologetic smile. "You'll remember me to your aunt?" I assured her I would and she added in a softer voice, "And accept my thanks again for helping me out of a difficult situation."

"Happy to," I told her.

By that time, the maid had returned with Lady B's tea, a friend sat down at her side, and I found myself once again standing near that photograph of Gerald and Ivy on their wedding day. This time, I did not dwell on their happy faces as much as I focused on the brooch pinned to Ivy's dress. It was a pretty piece, and valuable, from the look of it. At the same time I marveled a girl like Betty would happen to own such a thing, I wondered how, if that were true, Ivy had managed to steal it.

My head whirled, and rather than confuse it with even more questions, I vowed I'd find out more. Just to be sure I had an excuse for coming back, I reached into my chatelaine for my watch, unhooked it from the chain that kept it from getting lost, and slipped it under the piano.

It made perfect sense, after all, for a woman to return in search of a lost watch.

❧

The weather never did improve that day, and by the time the train hurtled back to London, the fog was thicker than ever. Between it, the quickly failing light, and the smoke of chimneys, stoves, and factories that spread a choking blanket over the city, the darkness was nearly complete. Tendrils of fog wrapped around me as I made my way to the cab stand outside the station. I gave the driver the address of Parson's Lodge, our home in St. John's Wood, and settled myself on the hansom seat that felt as if it was stuffed with stones. We started out, the horse clomping over the cobbled streets, the sound of its hooves echoed by those of the horse and hansom behind us. For a few blessed minutes, I allowed myself to relax as much as I was able in the jostling cab, to clear my mind and relieve my head of the worry that had settled there the moment I walked into the churchyard of St. Christopher's and found myself in the middle of a mystery.

Perhaps it was these moments of repose that sharpened my mind and made me aware of the fact that the hansom behind us slowed when we slowed, turned when we turned. There was little I could see, but I looked out the window nonetheless, at the cab so carefully following our path. I tapped the roof.

"A little faster, please," I told the driver.

He quickened our pace.

As did the cab behind us.

Another tap.

"Turn here."

"As you say, miss," the man called down to me from his seat behind and above where I sat. "But it ain't the way you want to go."

"Turn nonetheless," I ordered, and the cab did.

So did the cab behind us.

I told the driver to turn again, and to make another quick turn after. Each of our moves was mirrored by the cab that followed. All the while, my brain spun with possibilities and plans. Whoever it might be, why he might be following . . . none of it mattered. Not right then and there. I knew only that I had to elude him. The last thing I wanted to do was lead someone so bold to our home at Parson's Lodge. I handed more money than was necessary up to my driver, told him to stop, and bounded from the cab and into the enveloping fog.

Though I dared not take the time to look back, I heard the creak of the other hansom's wheels and the way the horse whinnied. It, too, had stopped.

I looked around to gauge my bearings, but darkness and the eddying fog made it impossible to know exactly where I might be. I hardly cared. I hurried down the road and when

I heard the distinct, sharp sound of boot heels against the pavement behind me, I walked faster still.

Around a bend. Across the road. When the fog that wreathed me swirled on an evening breeze, I saw a scene I recognized. Regent's Park! A breath of relief escaped me. I was still far from home, but headed in the right direction.

Still, my footsteps were being dogged.

I took the chance of looking over my shoulder and grumbled a curse. The fog made it impossible to see more than a black, hulking shape some thirty feet or so behind me. A large man? A woman enfolded in a cloak? I could not tell, and as I did not want to find out, I broke into a run and darted around the first corner I came to.

Here, two villas sat side by side, a garden between them, along with a narrow passageway that led back to a mews. I ducked into the passage and flattened my back as much as I could against a latticework covered with trailing vines. Safe where I could watch the road and not be seen, I did my best to catch my breath.

I listened and heard footfalls heading off in another direction.

Then silence. Whoever was following me had lost the trail.

Whispering a prayer of gratitude, I dashed from my hiding place, reminding myself that I really must be more vigilant. Unfortunately, I was once again focusing on the wrong things, as for the second time in just a few short hours, I did not look where I was going.

I smacked directly into the man who stood between me and the path toward home.

Chapter 7

Sephora

"It is getting late, Miss Sephora."

Even through the miasma of misery enveloping me like a funeral pall, I heard Bunty call to me from the hallway and I knew in a moment or two, she would come looking for me. I would have liked to think I could greet her with aplomb and deal with her as matter-of-factly as Violet always did, yet I knew I had no chance. Violet was a woman of logic, poor thing, and thus able to handle any situation with cool detachment. I, on the other hand, was a creature of fire, of passion, my nature never more in evidence than it had been these past two days when my tears came in unending streams and my heart, my poor heart, felt as if it had been ripped from my body. It had left behind a void, an icy hole, nothing but bitter loneliness within.

No, there was no way I could face Bunty as I was. Not yet. Not until my problem was somehow solved and my soul was once again intact.

Not until my dear Franklin was back at my side.

I dashed tears from my eyes, the better to take one last, quick look at the photograph I held in trembling fingers. Franklin Radcliffe, my heart, my soul, my all. He stood on the beach at

Brighton, the rolling sea behind him. His shoulders were back. His chin (such a well-shaped chin!) was held high. The sunlight sparkled against the lenses of his spectacles and made him look—dare I say it?—like a mythical, magical creature.

"Miss Sephora?"

Bunty's voice was louder now, closer, and moving quickly, I closed the leather case that held the photograph and tucked it back in my reticule where I kept it at all times. I leapt off the couch, stuffed the reticule beneath the cushions, and just before Bunty pushed through the door, I sniffled. Ever so delicately, of course.

Bunty was old, and if she had ever experienced love at all, I was sure she had long ago forgotten how it could make a woman's heart sing. Or plunge her into the deepest depths of despair. That certainly explained why when she looked at where I stood with my hands behind my back and the most innocent of expressions on my face, her own countenance was devoid of even the least bit of interest. Oh yes, I had been successful at hiding my wretchedness. Bunty suspected nothing at all.

"I've held supper thinking Miss Violet would be home soon," Bunty said, and thankfully her gaze remained on me and did not travel to the bulging couch cushions. "But as she has yet to arrive, I thought you might like to eat without her."

Eat? As if a woman could eat when her heart had been wrenched from her body? When her life had spiraled into an abyss where there was naught but darkness and misery? I sniffed. But not in a way that would betray that I'd been crying.

"I can wait," I told Bunty. "I'm sure Violet will be here soon enough. Where has she been all day?"

"I'm sure I can't say," Bunty replied, which was not the

same as telling me she didn't know. "I'll keep the roast warm and you two can have a nice sit-down when she gets home."

I put the back of one hand to my forehead. "I think not. I believe I have a headache coming on."

"Too much of the outdoors." Bunty nodded knowingly. "It is sure to happen when you spend two days out. Yesterday at the Serpentine and today . . . ?"

Rather than provide details, I managed a laugh. I can only attribute my ability to call up this smidgen of levity to the pluck I had inherited from Mama. After all, one's forebears needed a great deal of courage to travel to the other side of the world and make their fortunes in tea. I was lucky, indeed, to take after Elizabeth and her family and not my father's, the unfortunate way Violet had.

"I told you, Bunty. I've been out and about with Margaret. As for the headache . . ." So she was sure to notice how completely piteous I was, I pressed my fingers to my temples. "I will be fine in the morning." This, of course, was a lie. If I did not hear from Franklin by morning, my misery would be more complete and I wondered if I would be able to get out of bed and put one foot in front of the other. "Perhaps you might bring up a cup of warm milk. I'm sure it will help me sleep."

She had just backed out of the room to get said liquid when someone rang the bell.

"Late for a caller," Bunty grumbled at the same time my heart soared.

A caller? It could only mean one thing, one person, and I fluffed my skirts, pinched my cheeks to assure that they were appropriately pink, and prepared myself for Franklin and what had better be a thorough, heartfelt, and poetic apology.

I needn't have bothered.

When Bunty returned, she was alone, and I would have once again let sorrowfulness overtake me if she didn't have a bouquet of flowers cradled in her arms.

"For you, Miss Sephora," she said.

"Of course they're for me." I raced forward to take the flowers from her. "No one would be sending flowers to Violet."

"And who'd be sending you flowers?" she wanted to know.

My laugh has been described by more than one young man as rivaling the ring of crystal. "Ah, when your likeness appears on the Society page there is no telling who may have seen it!"

"It was one picture," Bunty reminded me. "One time. And you wouldn't have been included in it at all if Lord Hatton hadn't taken a tumble from his horse there in Regent's Park, and you hadn't been on the scene to witness it."

"On the scene," I reminded her, "and noted in the accompanying article as Miss Sephora Manville, a fair young heiress who stood by and watched the terrible event unfold."

"That may very well be, but—"

I shushed her with the wave of one hand. I had better things to think about than Bunty's opinion of my moment of notoriety the month before. The flowers were tied with a bow of a distinctive shade of blue that told me they'd originated from Whitby's, one of the most prestigious flower sellers in London. My hand touched the stems. My heart sang.

"You may go, Bunty," I said.

"Really?" Her silvery eyebrows rose. "You don't want me to cut those for you? To get them in water?"

"I can manage," I told her, and the second she was out of the room, I untied the bow, searching for the card I knew must accompany the bouquet. There was none.

This was perplexing, and thinking it over, I stepped back and tapped the toe of one dainty slipper to the floor. Was Franklin being shy? Was he so discomfited (as well he should be) at the fact that he'd arranged to meet me the day before and had failed to keep our tryst that he could not find the words to express his remorse?

Or . . .

It should be noted: this was not my first bouquet from a love-smitten gentleman. I was used to flowers. Armfuls of them. Yet this was the oddest assortment I had ever seen. Pink hydrangea, pretty pink-and-white sweet william, magenta zinnia, nutmeg geranium, delicate blue forget-me-not.

It hit me then, and a smile cracked the façade of my wretchedness. Franklin was as much of a romantic as I was!

Leaving the flowers, I hurried up to my room and rummaged through the dressing gowns, cosmetics, hats, and jewelry spread here and there around it. When I found the prize I was looking for, I took it back downstairs and into the parlor. I put the book on the table in front of me—*The Language of Flowers*—and got to work.

"Hydrangeas." Searching the pages, I mumbled to myself. "Ah, 'thankful for you.'"

This simple message encouraged me, and I went on to the sweet william. *Grant me one smile.*

"I will surely bestow a smile on you when next I see you, my love," I whispered. "I'm sure you have a reason for abandoning me yesterday when we were supposed to meet in the park. I'm certain you are sorry for what you did. These flowers, they prove it."

I went on to the magenta zinnia.

"'Lasting affection.'" I read the words in the book and

nearly swooned. And forget-me-not? "'True love, faithfulness, remembrance.'"

I clapped a hand to my heart so as to keep it from leaping from my body.

And the last flowers, the nutmeg geranium with their pretty white petals and delicate scent? *I expect a meeting.*

"Yes, Franklin, yes!" My happy exclamation sailed to the ceiling. "He hasn't forgotten me," I told myself. "He didn't mean to leave me waiting in Hyde Park all day yesterday for him. He would be appalled to know I went back today because I was afraid I had my days mixed up. Oh, Franklin!" I pressed the flowers to my breast and this time, the tears that welled in my eyes were tears of joy.

It was all a misunderstanding, of course, all some crazy mix-up. Franklin still cared. He still loved me. There must have been some very good reason for him to leave me alone and forsaken.

His mother.

The thought occurred and my mood was instantly spoiled. I set the flowers on the table, plunked into the nearest chair, and crossed my arms over my chest. I knew I should not be uncharitable. After all, Franklin's mother was old, and an invalid besides, but really, if I was to be the most important woman in his life, if I was to become . . .

Happiness bubbled through my sour thoughts. If I was to become Franklin's wife, then we must decide what to do about his mother. And we would. Together. Franklin and I would be together. Always. A sigh escaped me at the thought, one filled with pure contentment. Or at least it would have been if the front door didn't open and bang shut, jarring me from my woolgathering.

Most unusually, this commotion was caused by Violet, who stormed into the parlor.

Even her precipitous entrance, though, was not as surprising as her state of disarray.

Not so much alarmed as I was simply embarrassed on her behalf, I sat up and cast a look over my half sister. Her cloak was open. Her hair was up on only one side, hanging limply over her shoulder on the other. She had a streak of what looked to be soot on her cheek as if she'd just come from a train. And worst of all . . .

I could barely imagine a faux pas so grievous, and my outrage nearly choked my words.

"Violet, you've gone out without . . . without a hat?"

She ripped off her cloak and though Bunty appeared to whisk it away, Violet paid her no mind. She tossed her cloak over the nearest chair, the better to prop her fists on her hips.

"I have just had the most interesting encounter," she said.

"I can only imagine." I rose. Though I am not nearly as tall as Violet, I have for years perfected my posture, and I put all my hard work into best use by holding my head high and steady. "I can only hope it was not with someone of our acquaintance. If you went out looking like that and without a hat besides—"

"Hat be damned!" She gripped the back of the nearest chair. At least she was wearing gloves. "I have just seen Margaret Thuringer's father."

This was not something I expected, but I dared not show my surprise. Violet had an uncanny way of picking up on what she thought of as my failings. I would not give her that satisfaction.

Ignoring both her grim expression and the look of open curiosity on Bunty's face, I swept around the table. "I do hope Mr. Thuringer is well," I said, my words as light as my steps.

"He has a tendency to eat too many sweets, poor dear, and it upsets his system so."

I would have made it all the way to the door and to the hallway beyond if Violet didn't step in front of me. "I don't care a fig for Mr. Thuringer's insides, though considering the way I banged into him as I was walking home this evening, I think perhaps he may be feeling a bit of pain."

"Did you? Run into him?" I gave her an airy laugh. "How very odd. And why were you walking home? Where were you coming from? Why weren't you in a cab?"

"It hardly matters," she insisted. "What does matter is that I was not looking where I was going, but in the other direction. Mr. Thuringer was on his way home from the theater, and . . ." She pulled in a long breath, and the way it escaped her in staccato gasps, I wondered if there was more to the story than Violet told. There was no use asking. Violet was not one to share, especially not with me. We were so different in tastes and temperament, it was not the first time I thought we were sisters in name alone. "We bumped into each other. Literally. As I was grateful to have someone to accompany me home, we passed a few pleasant minutes. We did not, however, talk about Mr. Thuringer's health."

I pursed my lips. It was an expression I often practiced in the mirror, one that had served me well at teas and soirees when there were young men in attendance and I had yet to decide which of them was worth striking up an acquaintance with. The perfect way to show a disinterested sort of interest.

It had no impact whatsoever on Violet.

"In fact," she said, "it was Margaret we discussed."

I saw the truth of the thing then, her narrowed eyes and her clenched lips, and though it was unladylike to even think of a curse much less to whisper it, I could hardly help myself.

Of course Violet heard. She had the ears of a hunting hound. "You told me," Violet said, "that you spent yesterday with Margaret."

"As I did. Watching the boating on the Serpentine and—"

"And yet Mr. Thuringer says Margaret was not out yesterday."

My laugh has been known to melt the hearts of men of all ages. It did not have the same effect on women. Bunty and Violet were living proof. As always, Bunty stood by, awaiting instruction, little impressed with my air of nonchalance. The thunderous expression on Violet's face did not change.

I ignored them both, throwing out the offhanded comment, "Margaret's parents do not know everything she does."

"And yet they might know this," my sister said. "For they certainly know that Margaret has been ill and has taken to her bed. She has been there all week."

I cursed my luck for not being able to come up with a more credible story quicker, and Violet's fortune—was it good for her and bad for me?—for running into Mr. Thuringer on this of all nights. "What I really meant to say—"

Violet did not give me a chance to finish. But then, her gaze alighted on the flowers I'd left on the table and the anger of her expression dissolved. I might actually have been relieved if I did not see the way her cheeks puffed out as they always did when she was thinking. And the way her eyes opened just a little wider as they inevitably did when she came to a realization. If she hadn't pulled one corner of her mouth tight. Yes, exactly as she always did when she was worried.

She rounded the table for a better look, her rock-steady gaze shifting from the flowers to me, and said quite simply, "You know better than this."

"Better than . . . ?" My question dissolved into a huff

of outrage, and really, I could hardly help myself. It was one thing for me to reflect on my relationship with Franklin, on all it meant and all it promised. It was another altogether for a half sister with no fortune, no prospects, and little hope of changing her lot in life to stand there and dare to question my good sense.

I gave Violet the disdainful look she so clearly deserved. "Perhaps if you got your nose out of your books and yourself away from the musty museums where you spend all your time, you would know more of the world outside your head, Violet. Then you might admit it is only natural for a young lady of fair countenance and fine manners to have admirers."

"Yes. But if said young lady"—I did not like the emphasis she put on that last word—"keeps her friendship with certain of those admirers a secret, I must also wonder why. These flowers are not from that army captain who sought to court you last spring. He would not be able to afford a bouquet from Whitby's. Nor are they from that silly boy Hubert Greenstreet, the one you met when Adelia took us to the theater a few weeks ago. He wouldn't have the sense to send a message with flowers."

"A message? How did you—"

"Oh come now, Sephora! Even a man knows better than to send such a mishmash of a bouquet. He requested these flowers very particularly. And I see you have been consulting your *Language of Flowers* to find out what they mean. Don't worry." When I made a move to shoot forward to scoop flowers and book from the table, she stopped me, one hand raised. "I hardly care what message he sends. I do care you lied about being with Margaret, and I suspect you did it because you were with this fellow instead. That kind of secrecy won't do, Sephora. I hardly care if it is proper or not. I do care that it is not wise. I need to meet him. I need to—"

"What? Measure his worth? Decide if he's from the proper family? We are hardly from the proper family, Violet. We have no parents and an aunt who is—"

"Generous and loving." She shot the words at me from between clenched teeth.

This I could not deny; Adelia had been good to us. She was as hospitable as she was kind. I was hardly in the mood to admit it, though, and I didn't have the chance.

"You have money from your mother," Violet pointed out. "And you will come into that inheritance in just two years' time. You're an appealing catch, Sephora."

She did not mean this as a compliment.

I did not take it as one.

My throat tightened. My fingers curled. "You are telling me I cannot judge the merits of a suitor. That only you can do that for me. You're telling me you think a man might be more interested in my fortune than he is in my person."

"It is always a possibility. You don't want to end up being married and miserable."

"Should I be unmarried and miserable? Like you?" If Violet would not listen to reason, perhaps the depths of my emotion would make more of an impression. I slammed a hand against the table. "You do not understand. You cannot possibly."

"I know there are those who would prey on an unsuspecting girl. And I know that a girl, if her head is properly turned—"

"Oh, no!" I pointed one trembling finger in her direction. "Don't you dare say it, Violet. How can you? You cannot be so bold to offer advice. Not after what you did in Calcutta!"

Did I wound her with the comment? I could only hope so. Violet being Violet, she did not give me the satisfaction of seeing it. Her expression unreadable, her movements quick and efficient, she simply turned and walked from the room.

If only it was so easy for my anger to depart along with her. I stood fighting for breath, wishing my mind was quicker and I had said more to hurt her.

"She would be your strongest ally, you know. If only you'd let her."

When I looked up from my grim thoughts, I found Bunty still there, watching me from the doorway. "She wants only what's best for you."

"Shouldn't I be the one who decides what's best for me?" I asked her. "I am not a child."

Bunty gathered Violet's cloak and turned to leave the room. "Perhaps then," she said, "you should stop acting like one. And Miss Sephora . . ." She had the cheek to not try to hide a smile. "You'll want to retrieve your reticule from beneath those cushions. It is sure to make them lumpy."

She closed the door behind her, and it was just as well she was gone because then she didn't hear my screech of frustration.

Bunty, pointing out what she saw as foolishness instead of what it was, a clever ruse to keep Franklin's photograph and Franklin's identity, and Franklin's undying love for me a secret!

Violet, the millstone around my neck! The prying sister, masking her own misery as concern for me. As if that could fool me in the least.

"She's jealous," I reminded myself, and I gathered the book and the flowers and went to the hallway and pounded up the stairs. "She hates to see me happy because she herself is so unhappy. It isn't my fault!" It was a good thing there was no one about to hear me because I snorted. Which only goes to prove how terribly Violet had upset my normal equilibrium.

At the first-floor landing, I shot a look toward her closed bedroom door.

"If you would just try a little harder to look your best," I grumbled. "If you would learn to keep your opinions to yourself and not be such a bluestocking. If you would attempt to be a lady instead of thinking you have to be at the center of things, participating and planning . . ." It was all too much for me. I trembled.

"You're not always right," I muttered. "You do not always know what's best for me. Not the way Papa did. And yet . . ."

And yet, as much as I hated to admit it to myself (and never would to Violet), I so often saw our dear papa's hand in what she did. I heard his voice in her words. I felt the concern he surely would have shown for my welfare even in Violet's overbearing attempts to rule my life.

"Oh dear." It struck me then, my callousness, and it rooted me to the spot. It was one thing to argue with Violet—we had come to learn over the years that was what sisters were for—but the fact that I'd had the temerity to mention our time in Calcutta . . .

I swallowed the sudden lump in my throat even as my conscience pricked, and I hung my head.

Surely even a sister should not be so cruel.

I raised a hand to knock on Violet's door, but knew in that instant I would not have the opportunity to apologize that night. I could not bear to wound Violet further, and when I heard her from inside her room, I had no doubt that is exactly what my presence would do.

I went on my way, and let her cry her heart out in peace.

Dear Miss Hermione,

As women cannot clearly think through problems and are not commonsensical enough to know their own minds, I am fully aware that most of the letters you receive come from the weaker sex. Women are, after all, the ones who need guidance and advice. This missive, however, is an exception and I would not be asking the advice of a mere woman if it were not for the fact that I am totally confounded by my current situation and have nowhere else to turn. I need your assistance, Miss Hermione, on how I might reveal my feelings (they are honorable, of course) to a certain young lady. As she is clearly my inferior, I cannot make my appeal too complicated for she would surely not understand. What shall I tell her?

Yours sincerely,

A Bewildered Suitor

Dear Bewildered Suitor,

The answer to your question is really quite simple. What should you tell the young lady? To look elsewhere for a mate, of course, for you, sir, are clearly not worthy of either her or any other lady's time or attention.

Yours sincerely,

Miss Hermione, who has little patience and no tolerance for such folderol

Chapter 8

Violet

July 1

The letter from Bewildered Suitor and my response to it would be printed in *A Woman's Place*. That did not keep me from adding a flourish to Miss Hermione's signature below the handwritten answer I was preparing to send to the editor of the magazine. Nor did it stop me from adding a bit of extra oomph when I applied Adelia's blotter to the paper. The blotter was a pretty thing, silver with an oak base fitted with blotting paper: decorative enough to belong on the desk of a woman like Adelia, weighty enough to allow me the gratification of a satisfying thwack.

I had just finished with said thwack and set the letter with the others I'd answered that morning when Bunty knocked and entered the library.

"You were out late last night."

Even tightlipped and with her hands clutched at her waist, Bunty did not do artlessness well, and I let her know as much with a smile. It served her right and besides, it was my way of disguising the fear that bubbled in my throat when I thought of how I'd been followed on my way from the railway station.

If I had not so fortuitously run into Margaret Thuringer's father, I am not sure what might have happened, or if I would have arrived home at all.

A shiver skittered over my shoulders and rather than let it upend me, I shrugged it away. "I was delayed," I told Bunty.

"No doubt by the business spoken of in the letter Miss Hermione received. The matter of Ivy and—"

"She's dead, Bunty." I did not mean to surprise Bunty so, yet the news was best told quickly and without elaboration. Bunty swayed on her feet, and I rose from my chair and assisted her to a seat on the settee.

Her voice was breathless. "Murdered?"

"Perhaps," I told her. "There are conflicting stories and I didn't have time to get to the bottom of things. When I return to Willingdale—"

Her sharp tsk cut me off. "You have no business interfering in such things. It could be dangerous. Besides, there is work to be done here. You mustn't forget it. You cannot go traipsing off and not keep your word to your aunt."

I darted back to the desk and lifted the letters I'd written so that I might flutter them in Bunty's direction. "Done! And Adelia was right. It's all very simple and took me no time at all this morning. One letter was from a woman asking the best way to decide which cook she should hire."

"And you—"

"Told her to ignore their references and have each of them cook a dinner, of course. The second letter came from a girl troubled by her complexion. I suggested soap and water and plenty of fresh air and sunshine. The third letter was from an elderly woman who doesn't want her grandchildren to visit because they are altogether too ill-behaved. I reminded her that her home is her castle, and that if the children cannot conduct themselves to her liking, they, like unruly pets, should be kept outside. And then of course there was Bewildered Suitor." My voice soured at the very thought. "I will leave you in suspense as to that one, Bunty. You may read my reply in *A Woman's Place*!" I returned the letters to the desk. "I looked through Adelia's files. She may have had her head turned by Hamish MacGill but she has been, nonetheless, industrious. There are letters from Miss Hermione that have yet to be printed in the magazine and those, along with these I've answered, mean I am well ahead of schedule, and have all the time I need to—"

"Stick your nose where it doesn't belong," Bunty mumbled, forgetting I have excellent hearing.

"Someone needs to find out what happened to Ivy," I told her. "And I have the perfect place to start. Her diary."

She held up a hand, the palm to me as if that might deflect my words. "I don't want to know how you obtained it. Nor do I want to hear what's in it."

"But you do," I told her. "I spent some time reading it this morning and one entry in particular gave me an idea. But I will need your help before I proceed."

She eyed me with what I could only call suspicion.

"It is just for a simple experiment," I told her. "And we have until noon before we need to begin."

"Well, until then . . ." To be sure we had time enough, she looked at the watch pinned to the bib of her white apron. "We need to discuss Miss Sephora."

"Yes." I tapped a finger to my lips. "We need to keep an eye on her."

"And on this young man, whoever he is."

"You have no ideas?"

"None."

"Margaret Thuringer might know."

"And has sworn to keep the secret, no doubt." The way Bunty nodded, so sure of herself, told me she herself had been embroiled in such melodrama when she was young. I felt a small pang of something suspiciously like jealousy: we'd never stayed in one place long when I'd been a young girl, and I'd had no close friends to share secrets with. Fairly new to London and as private as ever, I still didn't.

Bunty went on, pulling me back from my thoughts. "No, you'll get nothing from Margaret."

"Well, we might learn something from Whitby's," I said, and in answer to Bunty's questioning look, added, "That is where the flowers came from, and the clerk there must surely know who paid for and sent them. I'll stop and inquire."

"And if the clerk will not tell you?"

I grinned, happy to have a plan in place for at least one of my problems. "A few bob may loosen his tongue. At least then we would know who this mystery man is. It's not that I object to Sephora having a young man," I was quick to add so Bunty did not think me either petty or jealous. "It's just that the secrecy of the thing . . ."

"Aye." She nodded. "That's what concerns me as well. A young man requesting permission to walk out with Miss Sephora would be one thing. But if she's lying to you about where she's going and who she's with, if she's meeting him on the sly . . ."

Neither of us needed to elaborate. "Then it's settled," I told her. "I will look into the matter of the flowers. And you, Bunty, will meet me at the front door at noon. Dress appropriately, we are going out."

"Out?" She rose from her seat and fluffed her skirt. "Shopping?"

"Hardly. We will post these letters, for one thing. Then we're going to visit the stables at the end of Marley Road. I've sent a message to the proprietor. He'll be ready and waiting for us."

When she passed me on the way to the door, Bunty's sigh was impossible to miss. "You're just like her," she said. "Always some idea spinning around in your head. Yes, just like Miss Adelia."

"I will take that as a compliment."

"As it is meant to be." At the door, Bunty paused and passed a nervous hand over the front of her white apron. "But there is another thing, Miss Violet. About Miss Sephora, about last night and what she said about . . ." She flicked her tongue over her lips. "It was Calcutta she mentioned, I do believe."

"Was it?" If nothing else, sweeping around the desk and back to my chair gave me something to do and a way to keep Bunty from detecting that now, just like then, even the mention of Calcutta made my breath catch and my heart clutch. "I pay little attention to Sephora," I assured her. "If she was blathering on about our time in India—"

"It is none of my business, of course, but it did seem to upset you, Miss Violet."

"Nonsense." I plumped down in the chair behind the desk and made a great show of putting Miss Hermione's letters into an envelope and addressing it to the editor of *A Woman's Place*. "You know how I treasured my time in the Far East," I told Bunty.

"I do. But if Miss Sephora is being mean-spirited—"

"She is not. Or I should say more clearly, she is probably trying to be, but as I said, I pay her no mind. She thinks of herself as a woman, but more often than not, Sephora acts like a child." The tall-case clock in the hall rang the hour and I listened, counting out the eleven chimes. "You'll be ready at noon?" I asked Bunty.

She knew she would get no more from me and simply nodded.

It wasn't until she left the library and closed the door behind her that I let go a long, shaky breath and slumped back in my chair. It was bad enough that Sephora had—quite contemptibly—brought up Calcutta, but worse now that Bunty had caught a whiff of the gossip. It was not as if I was ashamed of anything that had happened in Calcutta, nor did I regret a moment of it. It was simply . . .

I pressed a hand to my heart and refused to cry as I had the night before. Then, Sephora had caught me unawares. Now, I reminded myself, I was in possession of my emotions. My tears were spent so long ago, it was a wonder I'd had any left to shed after our confrontation in the parlor. I was a different person now than I had been in India, and not simply when it came to my mystery persona of Miss Hermione! I was older, more mature, better able to understand myself and control my life than I had been back in Calcutta, and to prove it, I held my breath and slid open the top drawer of the desk.

It had been a good long while since I'd looked at the photograph and, for each and every day of that time, I'd congratulated myself for resisting its magnetic pull. Now, five years removed from Calcutta, the pain was not nearly as bad as it had been then, the longing not as sharp. I had grown so used to the emptiness that occupied the place where my heart once resided that I no longer felt the pangs. It was Sephora's cutting words that brought it all back to me, Sephora's callousness that made me search through my belongings the night before for the case that contained the photograph. I'd slipped it in my pocket that morning before I came down to the library and I'd tucked it in the drawer where I might study it in private even though I knew it—and I—was better off with it stowed away permanently.

Still, I could not stop myself. My heart beating double time, I opened the red leather case.

I touched a finger to the image that looked back at me, to his prominent jawline, his dusky skin. To his coal-dark hair and his eyes, always so bright with wit and intelligence. The years slipped away and I swore I could smell the scents of tuberose and night-blooming parijat. The heat of Calcutta caressed my skin. And Ash was there, as he had been in my father's garden, his white linen shirt gleaming like the moonlight that bathed his face, the taste of pomegranates on his lips.

"Ash." The name escaped me on the end of a sigh. "If only . . ."

My words were fragile and pathetic enough to remind me there was no changing the past. Ash and I were once in love. We intended to marry. My dear papa gave us his blessing, but when his superiors at the Foreign Office caught wind of the news, it was another story. As intrepid as the British are, they are, for the most part, not bias free. As it turned out, Ash's family had prejudices against me every bit as unbending. Our wedding was canceled before it was ever officially announced, and in the years since, I had learned to let the past go. To prove it, I snapped the leather case closed.

Now, as I had done a hundred times since Calcutta, I steadied my shoulders, schooled my breathing, and reminded myself that some things were not meant to be.

Telling myself not to forget it, I put the photograph in my pocket and vowed I would return it to the very bottom of my traveling trunk where I would shut it away forever. Like the memories. The tenderness. The passion.

It was just as well that at that moment, I heard a rapping on the library door. It forced me to rise and leave my reveries behind.

I knew it was not Bunty, for she would have knocked and entered. Carefully, I opened the door only so much as to poke my head out and found my sister looking back at me.

But not for long. She moved to her right, the better to try to see around me and into the library.

I moved to my left.

She slid in that direction, and I countered by moving to my right.

Sephora glowered. "What are you doing in there?" she wanted to know. "You spend hours locked away in the library when you know it's supposed to be forbidden to us. That is Adelia's private room."

"It is my private room now," I told her, and just to prove it to her, I slipped out of the library and locked the door behind me. "I have Adelia's permission to use it."

"Why would she give you such permission and not me?" I had the feeling Sephora would have stomped one slipper-clad foot if she thought it would get her anywhere.

"What is it you want?" I asked her.

She pulled her gaze from the door and back to me but only for a moment before she stared at the tips of her silk slippers. "I wanted to say . . . about last night . . ."

An apology?

That would have been as uncharacteristic as it was uncomfortable. I had no need to take the chance of my emotions bubbling to the surface again, no desire to expose any hint of weakness to my sister, who would surely latch onto it and use it to her advantage.

I breezed around her and to the stairs and stopped there, one hand on the bannister. "If you're talking about confessing what you've been up to when you claim to have been with Margaret, I will give you my full attention. If you wish to waste my time with other things . . ." I put my foot on the first step.

"You're such a Mrs. Grundy! Always worried about what's right and what's proper." Sephora's gaze snapped to mine. "At least when it comes to me. When it comes to yourself—"

"You have no idea." My voice was calm, yet I do believe even Sephora had the sense to know she was treading dangerous waters.

She backed up a step and lifted her chin. I wonder if she knew that it trembled the slightest bit. "I may have been young when we were in Calcutta, but I know what I heard. People talk."

"Ah." The single syllable was not the protest she was expecting, and it stopped any further outburst from her. I proceeded up the stairs and when I arrived at the first floor, I looked over the bannister at her. "That is something it's best for you to learn now," I told her. "You see, Sephora, you cannot always believe what you hear."

ൽ

Horses power our metropolis.

Hay powers our horses.

As modern and as sprawling a city as London was, it was not hard to arrange for horses, a hay wagon, and a driver. They were waiting for us at the stables when Bunty and I arrived. In my original message to the owner of the establishment, I had mentioned what I had in mind, and he (a brawny man by the name of Porter) had clearly never had such a request from a young lady of supposed proper breeding. Porter had apparently spread the word far and wide. In addition to the driver of the hay wagon, a crowd had gathered there in the wide, cobblestoned stable yard—groomsmen and stable boys, a coachman or two along with various denizens of the neighborhood, laboring men and women, who chatted and whooped and called out as if it was a country fair and not the scientific experiment I had hoped for. For the day's expedition, I had chosen a lightweight pale blue dress in cotton lawn and a straw hat with a wide brim, and in the sea of dark working-class colors, I stood out like a particularly flamboyant flower.

The crowd did not hold this against me, particularly as before we got started, I paid the driver for his services and offered a particularly generous baksheesh to Porter, who tugged at his forelock, grinned at me, and to the delight of the crowd, showed off the sovereign I'd placed in his palm.

Prepared, I stepped back to Bunty's side.

"This is your experiment?" She sized up cart, horses, and the crowd, which looked to be getting larger by the minute. "What's happening here? What's this man there in the cart going to do?"

I signaled to the cart driver that I was ready to begin and he turned the cart and headed out of the stable yard and into the street beyond. The final steps of the experiment would be conducted right where we stood, but for that to happen, his horses needed to gain some speed and that could not be done in the enclosed courtyard.

Together, we watched them clomp away, the hay wagon and its shaggy load swaying behind.

"That's simple, Bunty," I told her. "He is going to run me down."

"What!" She latched onto my sleeve, not trying so much to stop me from leaving her side as she was hoping to keep herself upright. "Miss Violet, what on earth are you thinking? You cannot possibly—"

I shrugged her away as gently as I could so that I might produce Ivy's diary from my pocket. "It is right here on a page marked 'May the thirteenth,'" I told her, opening the book to the appropriate page. "This is where Ivy talks about how she was in Colchester with Edith Cowles on a market day. They were walking along just as a hay wagon rumbled by. According to Ivy, the wagon was on the road as it should have been, and she and Edith were walking to the side, well away from danger. And yet, Ivy was nearly killed by that wagon."

"What you mean is . . ."

"Remember, Bunty, Ivy had reason to suspect Edith. It's why she included her in that list of suspects she sent to Miss Hermione. The incident with the hay wagon must be the reason Ivy was suspicious of Edith. I simply want to see if it's possible, if Edith might have pushed Ivy in front of that wagon. All you need do, Bunty, is help."

"By pushing you?" She reared up to her full height (which was not all that tall) and sent a glare of epic proportions in my direction. "I will not," she said.

"It is perfectly safe, and really, that's not at all what I'm asking you to do." I said this with all the confidence I could muster, though truth be told, the sound of hoofbeats out on the street, of the hay wagon drawing nearer, sent my heart clattering to the same rhythm. "According to the diary, after the incident, Edith insisted that Ivy stumbled. She was pulled from the brink of disaster by a stranger."

The hay wagon appeared, rumbling toward us, the sound of the horses' hooves louder than ever. "There has to be a reason Ivy suspected Edith. Now pay attention, Bunty. I'm going to pretend to stumble and we'll see if that might be enough to put me in harm's way or if Ivy needed a little help"—I gave the word the twist it deserved—"to fall in front of the wagon. Are you ready?"

I didn't wait to see if she was. The wagon approached. The crowd surged forward for a better look, hushed with anticipation. I walked along casually, watching the wagon, waiting for the right moment to begin the experiment.

With the wagon yet six feet from me, I staggered and fell to my right, directly into its path.

Just an instant later, my arm was grasped, tugged. Hard.

A moment after that, the wagon whizzed by and there I was, derriere to cobblestones.

The crowd cheered and clapped. Bunty did not join in their merriment.

She stood over me, her blistering scowl testament to her opinion of the proceedings. "Miss Violet, you are as mazed as a brush!"

Since Bunty's fists were on her hips, she offered no assistance with getting me to my feet, but luckily, there was no lack of help from the men around me. Once upright, I faced Bunty's blistering anger.

"You call that an experiment? I call it daft. It's a good thing I moved as quickly as I did to pull you out of the way of that cart. You think you can just flounce around, acting as if you're falling when—"

"Bunty." The way I pinned her with a look stopped her tirade, but I dared not say more with so many people crowded around us. Instead, I brushed off my skirt, and since my hat was askew, I righted it atop my head, then took Bunty's arm and stepped to where I could not be overheard.

"I was not acting," I told her.

Bunty's mouth fell open, but I did not give her a chance to start again into scolding me. Instead, I glanced over my shoulder, assessing the people in the crowd of thirty or so, looking for any face that might be familiar, sinister.

I swore they were strangers. All of them.

"I kept my head throughout," I told Bunty. "So you must know I am neither overdramatizing nor imagining. I know what I felt. Bunty, just as the wagon neared me, someone reached out from the crowd and pushed me."

Chapter 9

July 4

Three days removed from the incident, I should have been far enough detached from the panic I'd felt when the hay wagon hurtled toward me to have put the fear behind me. Still, as I waited outside the A.B.C. tearoom, I could not help but back away from the curb when a cart rumbled by.

Had I been pushed into the path of the hay wagon there in the stable yard? This, I would swear to.

Had Ivy been pushed on a market day in Colchester? As the woman who might have been the victim in that particular instance was not alive to tell me, that was a more complicated question. To find its answer, I would have to depend on Ivy's diary. And a conversation with Edith Cowles.

I did not have long to wait to begin. Exactly at three, as we had previously arranged, a hansom stopped nearby and Edith alighted. Not without incident, it should be noted. But then, her skirts were wide. The packages she carried were many. Her bustle was large. The cab door was not. The driver had no choice but to get down from his high seat and assist his passenger to the ground.

"Miss Manville." She saw me waiting nearby and was talking even as she approached. "It is good to see you. I cannot tell you how auspicious it was to receive your invitation to come up to London today. I have been meaning to do some shopping." She raised both hands and the packages wrapped in paper and tied with strings that dangled from them. "You provided me with the perfect opportunity."

"After all that shopping, you must surely be hungry." I led her to the door of the tearoom and stepped back so that Edith—and her bustle—could get into the building before I did. But as she took her first real look at the establishment—its bright lighting, its neatly dressed female employees, its tables filled with women chatting and sipping tea—she froze.

"Are you sure about this?" Edith looked over her shoulder toward me at precisely the time I side-stepped my way around her back-end encumbrance to stand at her side. "All these women here? Unchaperoned? I am no bumpkin, I know things are different here in the city than they are in the country, but really, is this proper?"

"Proper and too long in the making." I wound an arm through hers to escort her to where an A.B.C. employee, a woman in a neat gown and a white apron, waited to show us to a table, and once we were seated, I told Edith, "There should be other places a woman is free to go without having to have a man accompany her, don't you think?"

"Not the theater, of course," Edith said, sucking in her bottom lip and pulling back her shoulders to underscore her statement. "Or . . ." Her face flushed a color that did not complement her pea-green dress. "You certainly don't mean pubs!"

She was so earnest, I couldn't help but laugh. "And why not? A woman may get thirsty, much like a man. Shouldn't she be able to quench that thirst?"

It was just as well Edith didn't have a chance to answer; I knew what her answer would be. A server arrived and we placed our orders—tea, cucumber sandwiches, an assortment of sweets. When I offered to pay for the lot of it since I was the one who suggested the outing, some of the starch went out of both Edith's shoulders and her attitude.

The softening of her demeanor gave me the perfect opportunity to ask, "How are the people of Willingdale?"

"You mean . . ." As if anyone in the crowded tearoom knew us or cared what we had to discuss, she glanced around and lowered her voice. "You mean Ivy. You mean the repercussions of her . . . well, you know."

"Her death, yes. As I recall, the vicar was quite upset."

"He takes his duties to his flock very seriously."

"Dr. Islington, however, was not."

"Really?" Edith considered this. "You must surely be mistaken. He knew the family, was physician to Ivy's unfortunate mother. I can't imagine he wouldn't have sympathy for all that happened. Unless . . ." Her eyes popped open, her voice was breathless. But then, the whiff of scandal will do that to some people. "What did he tell you? Does he think Ivy took her own life?"

"I hardly think a man of Dr. Islington's status would say as much to a perfect stranger," I replied with the aplomb of a seasoned liar, and when our tea arrived, I made a great show of pouring, adding milk to mine, and stirring. "And Mr. Armstrong?" I asked.

Edith had been about to take a sip of tea and she stopped and set her cup on the table. "As you can well understand, the poor man is distraught. I am comforted by the thought that Gerald will recover." A tiny smile played its way around her lips and she must have thought it was inappropriate to talk so of a man newly widowed because she did her best to hide the expression behind a taste of her tea. "He is quite resilient. I say this with some authority, Miss Manville. You see, just a bit more than two years ago, it happened to me. The death of my husband."

I had been about to take a bite of a cucumber sandwich and, in my shock, dropped it on my plate and sat back. "I am so sorry! I had no idea."

"No, of course you didn't. I bear my burden well." She did indeed, for in spite of being in the midst of a discussion about her late husband, Edith bit into a sandwich with gusto. "And the two of us, married less than a year at the time."

"That's awful."

"You cannot imagine." She dabbed a serviette to her lips. "William's unfortunate passing left me with the burden of running the mill."

"The one in Willingdale?"

She nodded. But then, she had a full mouth. She chewed, swallowed. "I have had to find a man to take on the responsibilities of operating the business for me, of course, and I'm happy to report he is competent enough. I have to neither think about the mill nor worry about the day-to-day chores that keep it running. My only concern is its profits. But all that hardly matters, you asked about Gerald. I suppose that is my way of saying I fully understand his situation and I know that someday, he will find his way to happiness again. In the meantime, I have offered all the assistance and sympathy I can."

"He is fortunate to have such a caring neighbor." At this point, with the way Edith eyed it, I feared for my own cucumber sandwich. I was peckish and knew Bunty would not serve dinner until eight. I could ill afford to give Edith the impression the sandwich was unwanted, so was sure to take a quick bite, before asking, "How did they meet? Gerald and Ivy?"

I don't believe I imagined it. Edith's top lip did stiffen the slightest bit. "He bought a property in Willingdale and had come to live in our part of the world after a lifetime of traveling for business. You may have heard it at the luncheon, he had plans still for a journey to the wilderness of Canada. He said he had no real taste for going once he was a married man, but that his business interests dictated it. It must be difficult, don't you think, to be a man and have such burdens?"

"And Ivy was going to accompany him when he went abroad?"

"Certainly not." She jiggled her shoulders and, her tea finished, she poured a second cup from the pot on the table. "It is hardly appropriate for a woman to travel to such uncivilized—" Edith remembered herself and what I'd told her of my background and drowned her apology under a long sip of tea. "It was apparently a very lucrative business opportunity and Gerald felt he had no choice. Ivy told me when he returned, their fortune would be assured."

"Exciting, indeed. Did Ivy say what the business was?"

"Ivy was a well-bred young woman. She knew better than to ask Gerald. She knew her husband would handle it. You have not . . ." As if she'd just realized I was some strange species of insect she'd never clapped eyes on before, Edith's gaze raked me up and down. "You have not been married, have you? It's quite apparent."

There was no use reminding her that not every marriage was one-sided. Instead, I ignored her question and returned to the matter at hand. "And you were saying, about Ivy and Gerald? About how they met?"

"Well, yes. Of course." There was but one cucumber sandwich left on the serving plate and after the briefest of glances designed to determine if I would challenge her for it, Edith snatched it up. "As I said, he came to Willingdale."

"And met Ivy on his arrival."

"Well, no." After a bite (it was a large one), she set her sandwich on her plate. "In fact, Ivy was not in the village at the time. She had a . . ." Edith thought about it. "An aunt, it was, I believe. In Durham. The woman was elderly and frail and Ivy went north to care for her. No, in fact, Ivy did not meet Gerald until she returned the next winter. By then he'd been in Willingdale some time."

"And that, then, is when they met and fell in love."

Edith's smile was stiff around the edges. "They married soon after."

"And that was . . . ?"

"February of this year."

"And how soon after that did the accidents begin to happen to Ivy?"

Edith's gaze snapped to mine. "How did you—"

"We corresponded," I told Edith, seeing no need to inform her that my detailed knowledge actually came from Lady B's passing remarks and Ivy's own diary. "And naturally, Ivy mentioned the unfortunate incidents."

"Naturally." Edith clenched her teeth around the word. "But I doubt she took responsibility for them as she should have. I told you, Miss Manville, Ivy was a clumsy girl."

"Is her own gawkiness the reason she was nearly run down by the hay wagon?"

She had just swallowed the last of her sandwich and Edith coughed and put a hand to her chest. She sat back, emptied her teacup, took a deep breath. "That was nothing." She waved a hand at me.

"Ivy thought enough of the event to mention it to me. She said she might have been killed had not some stranger come to her rescue."

"Well . . ." Edith cleared her throat and controlled a smile. "I am hardly one to dispute the facts. I was the one who called out for help so I suppose I had no small part in saving her. But surely, it's nothing one friend wouldn't do for another."

"It was a market day and you were in Colchester."

Edith blinked rapidly. "My goodness, she did provide you with details, didn't she?"

"And there were many people around?"

"A good many."

"Yet you were the one closest to Ivy when she stumbled?"

"Stumbled? Is that what she said? I will tell you this much, it happened very quickly and so it is difficult to remember all of the incident as clearly as I would like, but no, I would not say Ivy stumbled. It was more as if . . ." Thinking back to the day, Edith narrowed her eyes and I knew when she came to some realization about the event, because she sat up, her jaw tensed. "When she flew into the road, it was more as if her feet were not touching the ground."

I thought back to my experiment three days before and imagined I had looked much the same when I was pushed. "You mean to say she may have been jostled by someone in the crowd?"

Edith grinned with delight when a plate of cakes was delivered. She served herself a piece of Victoria sponge, took a bite, and licked her lips before she bothered to say, "That's as may be. Ivy may very well have been pushed. But there is another possibility. Perhaps she jumped."

❧

I was not sure how much I had really learned from Edith at the A.B.C., or how much more she might be able to tell me about Ivy, but I was not quite willing to give up. When we finished our tea, I asked if she would like to stop at Whitby's with me. She was delighted at the prospect of spending more time in our great metropolis, and together we ventured to a street of prosperous shops. A haberdashery, a dressmaker, a watchmaker. Whitby's stood in good company.

Outside the shop, we stopped to admire buckets of dahlias in breathtaking colors, and pots of white Chinese primrose that reminded me so much of the ones we'd grown when Papa was stationed in Hong Kong, I vowed to order some and have them sent to St. John's Wood where they could be planted in Adelia's garden.

Inside the shop, the air smelled of musky greens and delicate flowers. I breathed deep and was surprised to see Edith smile. She did not seem the type who would enjoy the sensual pleasures of the place as much as I did.

"Flowers are indicative of good character and healthful tastes, don't you think?" she asked, and examined a vase of pretty pink dianthus. "I daresay the poorer classes do not adorn their homes with such."

"I daresay they cannot afford to," I told her, but quickly turned my attention when a man—mustachioed and neatly dressed—emerged from a back room.

"Good afternoon, ladies." He tipped his head. "May I help you choose a bouquet?"

"Yes, indeed." Edith flounced past me. "But only if you think it will travel well."

"We will wrap the flowers for you. Is it roses you're looking for?" He waved a hand toward overflowing vases. "We have Niphetos." He pointed toward a white rose with a strong fragrance. "It means *falling snow* in Greek," he informed us. "Very popular, they are, with ladies of the better classes, like yourselves."

"Then I must have some," Edith told him. "And these?" She sniffed a bouquet of yellow roses.

"You have excellent taste," he told her. "That is Isabella Sprunt, another of our most popular flowers."

"Six of each," Edith said. She chose her flowers and the man left to wrap them, and, I noted, she did not bother to ask the cost. Which made me wonder how profitable the mill in Willingdale might be.

"And you, miss?" he asked me when he returned and presented the bouquet to Edith. "Is it flowers like these you're looking for? Or perhaps you'd like to send a message to a gentleman with flowers, eh?"

I did not return his smile. "That is exactly what I'd like to speak to you about," I told him. "A bouquet delivered four nights ago to a Miss Manville at Parson's Lodge in St. John's Wood. I need to know who sent them."

"Well, I can't really say, miss."

"But you must keep records." I sidled up to the front counter and peered over it, hoping to see a ledger or order book. "You certainly know where the flowers are to be delivered so you must know who purchased them."

"Be that as it may, miss—"

I had no time or taste to play a polite game of back-and-forth.

I opened my purse and pulled out a coin, and though I'd told Bunty I would offer only a couple of bob in exchange for the information I desired, I knew by the stateliness of Whitby's, by the quality of the flowers and the cleanliness of the shop, that this man would be little impressed by a few shillings. Instead, I held up a sovereign. He was not as delighted by the coin as was Porter, the stable owner, but yes, he was intrigued enough. His dark eyes lit and the clerk ran his tongue over his lips. "A Miss Manville, you say?"

"Yes." I turned the coin in my fingers so that it caught the light and flashed. "Sephora Manville. It was a seemingly random bouquet, but we both know that is unlikely. It was meant to send a message. And I need to know who that message came from."

He glanced again at the sovereign, then disappeared into the back room.

"What an odd request," Edith commented.

I paid her no mind. In fact, my full attention was on the clerk when he reemerged, a ledger in his hands.

"Manville . . . Manville . . ." He looked through the book and spoke under his breath. "Ah. Here it is!" He set the book down on the counter, the better to point to Sephora's name.

I craned my neck for a better look. "And the sender?" I asked him.

He skimmed his finger across the page. "That would be . . . oh."

When his expression fell, I pushed forward to read the entry myself.

"William Shakespeare?" My question was as pointed as the look I shot him.

"I believe the customer came late in the evening," he stammered, "and one of the younger clerks was on duty."

"One of the younger clerks who had never heard of William Shakespeare."

"Or who did not dare to question a customer," the man told me.

It was hardly helpful, but never let it be said that I am not a woman of my word. I ordered Chinese primrose to be sent to Adelia's and before we left, I set the sovereign on the counter.

Outside, I shrugged off my annoyance.

"It was not what you wanted to hear from the clerk," Edith commented, and I reminded myself that though she seemed harmless, she was, after all, observant enough. And one of the people Ivy thought wished her dead. It would be a mistake to underestimate Edith.

"It was hardly helpful. William Shakespeare." I pulled a face. "Who would have the cheek to leave that name?"

"Someone with a sense of humor?"

"Someone who does not want to be found out." The realization hardly pleased me. "No matter." I sloughed off my disappointment. "For now, what matters is that we find a cab for you and send you on your way."

While Edith balanced her bouquet of roses along with all her packages, I hailed a cruising hansom.

"I am so glad I visited," she said. "Perhaps we will see each other again."

"Oh, I am sure of it." The cab stopped and the driver climbed down to help his fare with her parcels. "You see," I told Edith, "I have misplaced my watch." By way of demonstrating, I patted my pocket. "I am sure I had it when I went to Willingdale and I haven't seen it since. I'm very much afraid I may have dropped it at the Armstrong house while we were there for the luncheon."

She was about to step up into the cab and she paused, looked my way, frowned. "You mean you're going back? To Gerald's?"

"Well, it seems the most logical place to start my search."

"No. Do not bother." She got into the cab and settled herself, then leaned out the window. "I will inquire as to whether your watch has been found. I will let you know. It's the least I can do."

"And very kind," I told her as the cab drove away. I waved at the same time I wondered. Was her offer simply polite? Or was it designed to keep me well and truly away from Willingdale, and anything I might discover there about Ivy?

Chapter 10

July 6

"She had nothing to do with it, Bunty." I refolded the letter from Baden-Baden I'd been reading and tucked it back in its envelope, picturing as I did my aunt at the spa there. Lingering in the hot springs. Taking in the commanding views of the countryside from Hohenbaden Castle. Marveling at the Geroldsau Waterfall. "Adelia has answered the letter you so kindly posted for me last week. I gave her a brief description of all that's been happening and asked about her friend, Lady B. She tells me that on the night of June twenty-seven, the night Ivy died, Lady B was here in London. In fact, they had dinner together." I had just finished breakfast and I sat back in my chair and smiled. "I am glad to hear it. I like Lady B."

Bunty had already loaded my breakfast dishes onto a tray and she paused before she left the room. "And yet, we cannot ignore the fact that Ivy singled her out as suspicious."

"I do believe that's because Lady B was upset about some land Ivy refused to sell. According to Adelia . . ." I set a hand again upon the letter that had arrived only a few minutes earlier. "Lady

B has a temper that flares in a moment and is gone just as quickly. Ivy must surely have seen the worst of it. But by the time Lady B discussed the land sale with Adelia, my aunt assures me there was no malice in Lady B's recounting of the details."

"Well, that's a good thing, then." Bunty continued to the door.

"It certainly helps narrow the field of suspects."

Bunty pursed her lips. "If you ask me—"

Fortunately, there was no time for her to—again—let me know she was less than happy about my determination to investigate Ivy's death. Sephora marched into the room.

"Have you thought more about it?" she demanded of me.

I sighed. But not so loudly that she could hear it and thus take it as a sign of my surrender. "We talked about it earlier," I reminded her.

"Yes, and you said I could not accompany you today when you go out. But Violet . . ." Here, a harumph. "Why not?"

The fact that Sephora challenged me with the question should certainly have ruffled my feathers.

Strangely, though, rather than feeling anger, I found myself realizing for the first time that though she does it often, Sephora does not do petulant particularly well.

Or perhaps I had seen her attempts at piqued, peevish, and cheeky so often, I was simply immune.

The raised chin?

Hardly daunting.

Fists on hips?

Not nearly as formidable as she thought.

The narrowed eyes?

When I had the chance, I would be sure to tell her the expression made her look both shortsighted and silly.

I stood and stepped around her, but she would not be put

off. She backstepped, her slim body a blockade preventing me from getting to the hallway and so, to the front door.

"You're not going to answer me?" she wanted to know.

I set my straw hat on my head and pulled on my gloves. "I cannot answer you. I do not know what you're talking about."

"I'm talking about exactly what I've been talking about since first thing this morning." She stuck out her bottom lip. She should have known better. The tactic was not particularly effective. I couldn't help but wonder if she knew it was also not attractive. "You said you were going on a journey today. To some village. Willing . . . something."

"Willingdale," I told her. "And as I recall, when I told you I was going, you said you wanted to come along. And I told you, Sephora—"

"That I could not. That I must stay here while you are out having . . ." As if the very thought was too much for her, she sucked in a long breath to steady herself. "Adventures!"

Sephora hardly ever takes me by surprise. This, however, came so out of the blue, I couldn't help but laugh. "I never said any such thing. In fact, I told you—"

She opened her mouth to speak, but I did not give her the chance. I held up a hand.

"I told you, Sephora, you cannot come along because you have not been invited. I am going to visit a friend."

"That cannot possibly be true," she wailed. "You don't have any friends!"

Her words caused me to think back to when Bunty had known that Sephora's friend would keep her secrets. To the regret that stabbed me at the time when I realized I had no such intimate connections. It was too profound a concept to be considered on an early afternoon in the entryway of a home in St. John's Wood.

"Don't be ridiculous," I said, as there was no time for me to be philosophic. "Of course I have friends. There's Mr. Taylor for one."

"The attendant in the Indian gallery at the British Museum? Honestly, Violet, you may see the man more often than most anyone else since you are always and forever visiting the museum, but he is hardly a friend. Besides, he is at least eighty years old. I mean a real friend."

"Mrs. Cunningham, then," I told her.

Lips pursed, she nodded. "Oh yes, that white-haired woman who haunts the museum reading room just as you do. Just because you sit in the same library as Mrs. Cunningham, your noses pressed in your books, does not make her your friend."

"It hardly matters what you think, Sephora. I am off today to visit a friend." Even when I eyed her, she did not budge. "That is, if you will kindly move away from the door."

"But I could come along." She danced a few quick steps across the herringbone pattern of the parquet floor. "Now that Bunty is watching me every moment of every day and insisting that when I leave the house, she must come with me, my life has descended into endless boredom. Endless!" She emphasized the tragedy of it all by throwing back her head. "Going out with you, it will save my life. Don't you see? I'll have a chance to breathe some fresh air. And me coming along will help you, too. It will give you someone to talk to on your journey and once we get there—"

"*We* are not going." I hoped the ice in my voice conveyed the proper message. After all, I could not tell her that I was returning to Willingdale to investigate a murder, no more than I could reveal that my mission there began thanks to the fact that I was, at least for the foreseeable future, the de facto Miss

it before anyone else in the village. I confessed that I was in love with Gerald. That he was in love with me. I told Simon to prepare for a wedding, and that Gerald and I were determined to be married as quickly as we could. And Simon . . .'"

I well remembered reading the passage and now, just as it had the night before, it made me uncomfortable. I squirmed in my seat.

"'It was so unlike him,'" Ivy wrote. "'Simon, who is always so kind and so mild-mannered. Simon who has for years known my mind and shared my secrets. Simon . . .'" Here, just like in the letter Ivy had written to Miss Hermione, Ivy's handwriting grew sloppier, more frenzied. Just like I had the night before, I had to hold the book closer, then take it to arm's length to make out the words.

"'Oh, I have never seen Simon look the way he did. His face, usually so gentle, turned a vivid shade of red. His eyes bulged and—I barely dare write the words—he banged a fist on the nearest table. I can hardly bring myself to write what he said to me. He said . . .'"

Here, the words were smudged and I had no doubt it was because, as she wrote them, Ivy's tears fell upon the page. "'His voice was grave. His words were hushed. His expression hardened and his eyes . . . there was none of the easy friendship I had always seen in Simon's eyes before. They were as cold and as lifeless as stones.'"

This was not my story, I was simply reading Ivy's words, yet my voice wavered with emotion. Ivy's desperation, her shock and sadness, vibrated through each frantic line on the page.

"'How can being in love with Gerald be terrible? It is quite the most wonderful thing that has ever happened to me. This, I told Simon of course, but he would have none of it.'"

Here I had to flip a page and though I knew what the next lines of the diary said, they still struck me as they had when I first read them, like a fist to the stomach.

"'Simon swore right there in St. Christopher's with God as our witness, that I would live to regret my decision to become Gerald's wife.'"

I closed the diary and wondered as I had the night before if Simon's reaction to Ivy's news was related to the accident that happened outside the church, with the piece of roofing slate that nearly crashed down on Ivy's head. That, and Simon's response to Ivy's blissful news, must certainly be why Ivy suspected him.

When the train arrived at the station in Willingdale, I disembarked, but did not, as I had the first time I visited, search out a cart. I knew St. Christopher's was located close by and besides, it was a glorious afternoon. A few minutes' walk would clear my head and, hopefully, help me prepare the words I would say when I spoke to Simon. I was just getting them sorted in my head when I heard a sprightly voice call from behind me.

"Violet, wait! Don't walk so quickly."

No! It could not be!

I knew who I'd see even before I turned, but even so, I could not help but groan when my suspicion was confirmed. "Sephora, what are you doing here?"

Grinning, she hurried to where I stood. "The same as you, of course," she had the cheek to say. "I am out for the day. Visiting friends."

"You have no friends in Willingdale."

"Neither do you. Which makes me wonder why you've come all this way. It's positively . . ." She looked all around and shivered. "Rustical."

"It's a lovely little village," I insisted. "And you have no business being here. How did you find me?"

"I slipped out of the house and followed you, of course. While Bunty was busy talking to the butcher's boy at the back door. I was so very clever. Like the heroine of a rollicking novel! Bunty will be cross, but really, Violet, Bunty works for us, does she not?"

"She is in the employ of Aunt Adelia."

"Who is far too kind a person to ever begrudge me a day out. Really, Violet, admit it. Adelia would be the first to recognize the unfairness of all you and Bunty have put me through. We are creatures of passion, Adelia and I. She would understand. You cannot possibly."

"I understand that you have no business here."

"But I do." She lifted her chin. "I'll meet your friends. Unless they're bookish like Mrs. Cunningham. Or stodgy like old Mr. Taylor. Then I'm quite sure I don't want to meet them." She had the nerve to smile.

"You cannot stay." I whirled and kept walking. "You must . . ." I stopped, turned, pointed back to the station. "You must get on the next train and go back to London."

"Certainly. I'll go back as soon as you do. Until then—"

"Until then, you cannot simply stand in the middle of the village green and wait for me."

"Of course I won't. I'll come with you."

"But as I said . . ." My patience was at its limit and I curled my hands into fists and wondered what I might do next. As fate would have it, the decision was made for me when a trap came by. It was pulled by a stocky brown pony and it had but a single passenger. She saw me and told her driver to stop. I wasted no time approaching Lady B.

"Good afternoon!" She leaned over the side of the cart so

we might converse. "How lovely to see you. But what are you doing here, Violet?"

"I am in search of a missing watch," I told her, and as it was half true, felt no guilt whatsoever. "I do believe I might have dropped it at the funeral luncheon."

"I'm afraid you won't be getting it back today. I was just with Gerald Armstrong and now that our business if finished, he told me he is going to Colchester to meet with his solicitor. Another day, perhaps."

I thanked her for the information, glanced back at my sister, and waved her forward so that I might make the introductions. "This is my half sister, Sephora," I told Lady B. "And as I hoped to have a conversation today with the vicar, I didn't anticipate her coming here to Willingdale with me."

"Ah." Lady B nodded. She understood. But then, she was a friend of Adelia's, and I knew my aunt did not suffer fools gladly. Of course Adelia's friends would be as quick and as bright as she was. Lady B crooked a finger. "Come closer, girl," she called to Sephora.

Since the cart was a pretty one and Lady B was obviously a woman of quality, Sephora was only too happy to oblige.

"I am a friend of your aunt's," Lady B told Sephora, "and you, I understand, are looking for a way to keep yourself amused this afternoon."

For all her faults, Sephora's manners are impeccable. When she wants them to be. "Why yes, ma'am," she said, the picture of propriety. "I had hoped to stay with Violet and visit with her friends, but she is disinclined to include me."

"Well, I am one of those friends." Lady B signaled to her driver, who got down and opened the door of the trap. "And we're going to spend some time getting to know each other.

Will you join me at my home for light refreshment, Miss Sephora?"

Sephora blushed. She always delighted at the chance of spending time with Society people. With the driver's help, she stepped up and into the trap. "You're coming, too?" she asked me.

"I will be along," I assured her. "I have some things to attend to first."

I was saved from explaining any more when Lady B told her driver to continue on, and even before they drove away, I heard her pepper my sister with questions. "What's the weather like in London today?" Lady B wanted to know, and "Wherever did you find such a lovely lawn fabric for your dress?"

Thick as thieves before they'd gone one hundred feet, and I was free to go about my business. To that end, I walked to St. Christopher's and, once there, pulled open the oak door of the church.

It was cool and dark inside and it smelled of incense and candle wax. The church was old, solid, and plain, yet the stained-glass window behind the altar (an image of none other than St. Christopher himself if I was not mistaken) caught the outside light and scattered it in rainbows through the nave. Red across the pews. Blues and greens in the aisle. Yellow splashed across the wall to my left.

There was no one about, and I found myself wondering what vicars did all day when they weren't in church praying. Would Simon be out visiting the sick? Or perhaps he was helping a farmer bring in a crop as an act of charity.

Still wondering how I might locate Simon, I stepped out of the church and into the graveyard. On the day of Ivy's funeral, the graves had worn a gray pall of fog and mist, but this afternoon, the sky was bright and the sun illuminated the stones as well as the words etched upon them: names and dates, sentiments of love and longing. I was reading one such epitaph when I heard a sound carried on the breeze and, curious, I wound my way through the churchyard to follow it. It was hushed and lonely, a stark contrast to the gentle light and the softness of the afternoon. A sigh. A moan. The cry of a small animal. Or . . .

I ventured through the graveyard and around to the back of the church and found Simon Plumley, his back to me, kneeling on the ground next to freshly disturbed earth, his head in his hands, his shoulders rising and falling to the rhythm of the sobs that wracked him. There was as yet no headstone to mark the spot, but I recognized it well enough. I had been there before.

It struck me then, all Ivy had said when she talked in her diary about their encounter the day she'd told Simon she would marry Gerald, his reaction. It could only mean one thing.

Simon had been in love with Ivy.

Considering this new revelation and how it might change my planned conversation with Simon, I backed away. It would do me no good to surprise him in a way that would embarrass him, so I rounded the church, and came toward Ivy's burial place from the other direction. As I anticipated, Simon couldn't help but notice me long before I was close enough to see the tears I knew stained his cheeks.

He turned away to scrub his hands over his face, then stood.

"Miss Manville!" He waved and called out. "It is a surprise to see you. What brings you again to our little corner of the world?"

"Just a quick visit," I told him, keeping my distance until he wiped a handkerchief over his cheeks, coughed away the tightness in his throat, pulled a hand through his hair. When he was done collecting himself, I took a dozen steps closer, my eyes on the mound of dirt at the vicar's feet. "I thought as I was at a disadvantage the last time I was here, I would return and pay my respects to Ivy."

"Of course." He stepped away from the grave. "I have just been saying a prayer for her immortal soul. She was . . ." His shoulders rose and fell. "She was a good friend, and is sorely missed in the village."

I walked to his side, careful to keep from stepping on the newly turned earth, gathering my thoughts and my courage. Somehow, planning this conversation back in London had been simple enough. Yet now, faced with asking awkward questions of a man who had strong feelings for Ivy and who, I could not help but think, may have killed her because of them, I found myself struggling to find the words that would not offend too greatly and still help me obtain the information I needed. Perhaps a direct approach was best?

"Do you believe Ivy was happy?" I asked Simon.

He nodded. "By all accounts, certainly."

"And so, you are quite sure she did not take her own life?"

As if I'd punched him, he flinched and stepped back. "You don't think . . . You can't possibly . . . Who is spreading a rumor so vicious?"

"Just rumblings. At the funeral luncheon. I hardly paid them any mind, but on thinking about it, I felt I must find out the truth. I knew you were the person who would give it to me."

He didn't reply, simply backed away and gestured for me to follow.

I did. Around and about a path bordered with marking stones, farther from the church and finally, outside the stone wall that surrounded the graveyard.

We were in the square shadow of the church here, the gloom made deeper still by the overhanging trees. The ground beneath my boots was slick with moss. There was no breeze, and yet I found myself shivering with sudden cold.

"There are eight of them." Simon motioned at the ground around us. "Those who over the years received a verdict of felo-de-se at the time of their deaths."

I knew the term. "Felony to self. Suicides." Here, the headstones were small and close one upon the other. "Ivy's mother is . . ."

"Here." Simon pointed to a plot not as overgrown as was the rest of the sad compound. "Ivy came each week and tended it. And I . . ." His voice caught and, so as not to embarrass him, I pretended not to notice. "I will do the same for Clementine Clague. In Ivy's name."

I looked back the way we came. "What you are telling me is that if there was any real evidence that Ivy might have taken her own life—"

"She could never have been buried in the consecrated ground of the churchyard. And of course, you were there at the funeral. You know she is. That should calm your worries as to the cause of her unfortunate death."

"But then, how did she die?" I asked, but the vicar was not listening. He had bent his head in prayer and I joined him. It wasn't until we were finished and he led the way back onto the grounds of the church that I asked again, "Tell me how she died."

"Surely you know. You heard the story. The same story I heard. She slipped. She fell into the water of the millpond and drowned. It is such a pity." His gaze grew vacant. "She seemed so happy of late."

"Was she?" I watched for his expression to betray some emotion other than the sadness that sat upon him like a cloud. "I heard she was looking for advice, that she was not comfortably settled into married life."

"Really?" Thinking, he pursed his lips and, vicar or not, reverend or layman, even Simon could not control the tiniest smile of self-satisfaction that played its way around his lips. Whether or not he was a killer, he had surely been jealous of Gerald and the marital bliss he shared with Ivy. "She never told me," he said.

"Even though she considered you a dear friend."

This time, he did not try to hide a bittersweet smile. "She was kind."

"And Gerald?"

It took him a moment to realize what I was asking. "Are you saying . . . do you mean, was Gerald kind? Was he good to Ivy? Yes, as far as I know. Though if you ask me . . ." He caught himself on the verge of gossip and swallowed whatever else he might have said.

"If I asked you . . . ?" I encouraged him with a look. "You know something about Gerald?"

The reverend's lips pinched. "I know he has been out with Lady B today. Looking at a bit of land Lady B is interested in purchasing from him."

"You do not approve."

"It is not my place."

"Yet I see you have an opinion. Why would you care if Lady B buys Armstrong land?"

As if he was ridding himself of a burdensome secret, Simon huffed out a breath. "For some time, Lady B has had her eye on a bit of land left to Ivy by her father and thus wholly owned by Ivy. Until the time of her death, of course. Then Gerald inherited it and the rest of Ivy's fortune. The land is on the shores of a pretty little lake that borders Lady B's own property, but according to Lady B, the view of the lake afforded from Ivy's land is more scenic than what she can see from her own land. She has had her sights set on building a folly there."

I remembered what Lady B told me at the funeral luncheon, that Ivy was always thinking of herself instead of others.

I ventured a guess. "Ivy refused to sell."

"Lady B is rather used to getting things her own way. She was quite angry when Ivy refused her offer. The way I heard the story, Lady B then offered even more money, but Ivy would not budge. That place on the lake where Lady B wants to build, it is where Ivy and her mother would often walk together. Ivy said it had too much sentimental value, that she didn't want to see Lady B erect some ridiculous folly just to amuse herself. She would not sell."

"And now Gerald has."

"I've been told he is seriously considering it," Simon growled. "Ivy has not been dead a fortnight and . . ." He bit back the rest of what was surely a tirade against Gerald, and had I been politer and less interested in the drama that had apparently swirled around Ivy, I would have left it at that. Instead, I dug for more information and, eager to weigh Simon's memory of the event against Edith's, I asked, "How did they meet?"

Simon snapped away from his dark thoughts. "Gerald and Ivy?" He made a small, futile gesture with both hands. "He showed up here in Willingdale out of nowhere and swept Ivy off her feet."

"Yet I've heard it wasn't really out of nowhere. Is it true, Gerald was already living here in Willingdale when Ivy returned from Durham?"

"Yes, she was there caring for her aunt. But then, that's the kind of person Ivy was. Always thinking of others."

"And where, exactly, is the nowhere Gerald came from before he settled here?"

This, he had to think about. "Kent, I believe," Simon said. "That is, originally. He's spent his life traveling for business, or so I'm told, and when he decided to settle, he came here. There was a time . . ." Across the churchyard, a woman and two young children with flowers in their hands entered through the gate and walked to a grave marked by a tall white monument.

Simon stepped closer to the church, farther from them. He lowered his voice. "There was a time I thought Gerald might have married Edith Cowles. She's a widow, you know, and when Gerald first arrived here, he seemed much taken by her."

"Then Ivy returned."

"Yes."

"And Ivy and Gerald fell in love."

"Yes."

"How did Edith feel about that?"

Simon pressed his lips together for a few long moments before he said, "She never looked particularly happy when she saw Ivy and Gerald together. Even here in church. One Sunday, Edith actually moved her place, from the second pew closest to the altar, to one farther back. I thought little of it until I realized Ivy and Gerald had come in and sat in the third pew. It struck me that Edith didn't like being in such close proximity to them."

"And how did Edith react at the news of Ivy's death?"

"That is a peculiar question. Do you think . . . ?" A sudden change came over him. His eyes gleamed. He stood at attention, looking nearly hopeful. That is, until he remembered himself.

As if it might make me forget the momentary excitement that had shown in his eyes, Simon cleared his throat. His brows dropped low over his eyes. "Really, Miss Manville, I believe we have overstepped the boundaries of ordinary conversation and we are starting into a subject we should not be discussing." He gave me a curt nod and stepped toward the door of the church.

I was not about to let him get away so easily. "What about the accidents then?" I asked him, following. "The ones Ivy had been having?"

Praying either for guidance or for patience, he closed his eyes and I fully expected to be dismissed. Instead, Simon stepped back, opened the church door, and moved aside so that I might walk in first.

"Come," he said. "If we are to talk about this, we must do it privately."

Chapter 11

In the time since I'd last stepped inside, the sun had moved across the sky and now instead of a church filled with the glowing colors of the stained-glass window, St. Christopher's was a place of shadow. Stone and slate. Unlit candles. Pockets of darkness like small creeping creatures where nave and transept met.

His boots tapping the stone floor, Simon proceeded up the main aisle, checking to be sure we were alone. Convinced, he slipped into a pew. I sat down beside him.

"What did Ivy tell you?" he wanted to know. "About the accidents?"

"Simply that they'd happened. She wondered if perhaps they were her own fault. It seems her mind was always on Gerald. On pleasing him. On taking care of him. On being the good wife she believed he deserved. With her mind so engaged, Ivy thought she might not have been paying attention to the world around her as much as she should."

"I do believe she was very much mistaken about that."

I considered his words and what they meant. "Are you saying . . . ?"

"That the accidents were no accidents? I cannot tell you

how I've prayed for guidance, Miss Manville. How I have questioned my own thoughts, my own intentions. Yet no matter how much I pray, I always come back to the very same place. The very same conclusion. It is my belief someone was trying to kill Ivy."

Surprised to find a person whose suspicions mirrored my own, I sucked in a breath.

"Do not pretend the thought has not crossed your mind." He bent a kindly look in my direction. "For that explains your interest in pursuing the matter. Your questions about Ivy have more to them than simple curiosity. Just as your demeanor tells me you are more than simply an idle woman with empty hours on her hands and nothing else to do but follow the latest gossip. Tell me, truthfully, Miss Manville, what is it you are looking for?"

I did not have to consider it. "Justice for Ivy."

He nodded. "Then we are of one mind. As I said, I was concerned about the accidents. Ivy was surely spirited, but in spite of what I'm sure you've heard from others, she was not careless. After hearing about the accidents, I became so worried that I . . ." Color rose in his cheeks. "I had taken to following Ivy. From a distance, of course. She never knew. I thought I might keep an eye on her."

"But you did not follow her the night of her death."

He didn't need the reminder. He let go a breath that sounded as if it came from his very soul. "One of our congregation was ill and I was obliged to sit at his bedside and pray with him that night. I cannot tell you how many times I've regretted it."

So Simon had an alibi! I would confirm it, of course, but for now, he needed neither assurance nor patronizing. "You did what you had to do. What you're supposed to do."

"Yes, I've told myself as much. And yet I cannot help but wonder if I might have helped. If I could have . . ." He hung his head and his voice choked with tears. "Perhaps I am guilty of the sin of pride for thinking that I might have made a difference."

"Or perhaps you're simply a good man who cannot abide the suffering of others."

He lifted his chin and the small smile that twitched at the corners of his thin lips told me he appreciated my encouragement. Even if he didn't quite believe it.

"As soon as I heard about Ivy's death, I wondered if it might have been—" He lowered his voice. "I wondered if it might have been murder. I haven't dared to even speak the word to anyone but you. I was relieved when I heard you were making inquiries." He sent me a sidelong look because he knew I would ask for an explanation. "Gossip travels fast in a village. I hoped you'd learn something and share your findings with me. In the meantime, I sought to do what I could." He cleared his throat. "I must confess something to you and I hope you don't think less of me for it. At the funeral luncheon, I slipped away from the crowd and went in search of Ivy's diary."

It was not easy keeping my voice level and my expression neutral, but I could not reveal the truth, not until I better understood Simon's motives. And checked his alibi. "Did you find it?"

He shook his head. "I had hoped something Ivy said in it might give me a clue, some inkling of what might have happened, of who might have . . ." His words dissolved in a sob.

I gave him a minute, then asked, "Who do you think might have killed Ivy?"

"It is wicked of me to speculate," he said.

"And yet if we do not speculate, we might never find the truth."

"Yes." He wasn't agreeing with me so much as he was trying to convince himself. "I have, of course, considered it. Over and over." He ran his tongue over his lips. "Did Ivy tell you? About Lady B wanting to buy her land?"

"In fact, I heard the story from Lady B herself," I told Simon.

"Ah." He wasn't surprised. "When it comes to conversation, Lady B is not one to hold back."

"Perhaps she has no secrets to keep." Now that I'd heard from Adelia and knew Lady B was in London on the night Ivy died, I knew this to be so. Otherwise, I would not have entrusted Sephora to her care that afternoon. Yes, Ivy suspected Lady B. It was why she circled Lady B's picture. Yet it was a relief to know, whatever Ivy suspected about Lady B, it couldn't have led to murder.

"Ivy had no accidents that involved Lady B that I know of," I told Simon.

"That is true."

"Then are you saying Lady B might have been so angry at Ivy for refusing to sell the land that she decided to kill her?" It seemed improbable, yet perhaps Ivy believed it.

"I do not think it a strong possibility," Simon admitted.

"And if I told you I know for a certainty it cannot be true?"

He let go a breath filled with relief. "I have always liked Lady B. I am happy to hear it, and I never thought it was likely, but as you said, we must consider all possibilities."

He was right. So I moved on to the most obvious. "And the hay wagon incident?" I asked him. I was sure he knew the story.

He considered my question before he asked, "Ivy never said Edith pushed her, did she?"

"Do you think she did?"

Simon scraped a hand through his hair. "The thought has crossed my mind. As I mentioned, Miss Manville, before Ivy returned to Willingdale, I fully expected Edith and Gerald to marry. I believe that's what Edith expected, too."

"Her husband, the miller, was dead by then?" I asked.

"Yes. In fact, William died only a month after Gerald arrived in Willingdale." Simon shook his head. "Such a terrible tragedy. William was a robust man and though he was older than Edith, he was certainly not in his dotage. How he mistook rat poison for the sugar for his afternoon tea is a mystery."

I knew of the man's death, but not the cause. I sucked in a breath. "That's awful."

"Yes, it was, and you'll hear many around here say it is also suspicious. Not that the authorities ever believed it enough to do more than simply question Edith about the circumstances. They were satisfied, so the rest of us must also be even though it is hard to forget how smitten Edith seemed the moment she met Gerald. She started keeping company with him soon after Will's death, and though many looked askance at it, we did our best to put our suspicions aside. Those kindlier souls said if Gerald could bring some happiness to Edith, well, it might have been a bit soon after Will's death, but who are we to judge?"

"They became friends, Edith and Gerald?"

"Yes, I believe that is how it started."

"And you did say Edith wasn't happy to be in Ivy and Gerald's company. She was jealous?"

"Perhaps with good reason."

"Gerald had made promises?"

He shrugged. "There was talk, though nothing official was ever announced. After all, Edith was still in mourning."

"And was Edith jealous enough to look for revenge?" I asked.

He considered this. "Is that what Ivy said?"

"She did not."

"Or . . ." Simon sat up straight. "Do you think it might have been someone else? May the good Lord forgive me, but lately, I look at everyone in Willingdale with mistrust. From my place at the altar, I've studied the people in the pews and, God help me, I wonder where each of them was the night Ivy died, what grudges they might have held against her. It is not a good way to live, especially for a vicar. I shouldn't be so suspicious."

"I have no such compunction. I am happy to be suspicious enough for the both of us."

As I'd hoped, my statement brought a smile to his face, at least until I asked, "Other than Edith, who had reason to want Ivy dead?"

Simon bowed his head and I wasn't sure if he was considering all the information we'd shared or praying. I only knew that after a few long minutes, he turned in his seat, the better to look me in the eye.

"Gerald."

I sat back, surprised. "You don't think . . ."

"I told you. About Gerald selling the land to Lady B. It's his now Ivy is dead. As is her fortune. He can do anything he likes with it. All of it."

"But surely a husband would not kill his wife for something as insignificant as a parcel of land."

Simon slid along the bench to the side aisle, then got up

and walked toward the altar. "There is a great deal of darkness in people," he said. "A man in my position hears things."

Because I didn't want to miss a word, I rose and followed him. "Things about Gerald?"

"No." From the way he hung his head, I couldn't help but think he was honestly disappointed to admit it. "But think about it. He came to Willingdale seemingly out of nowhere. He won Ivy's heart and now he is selling her land. I cannot help the dark ideas that enter my brain. Over the years, I've heard stories; stories about wives who hated their husbands and husbands who wanted nothing more than to get rid of their wives."

"But you have no reason to suspect Gerald to be one of them."

"No." He ran a hand along the back of one pew. "I wouldn't even mention it except . . ."

"You were in love with Ivy." I spoke the words so that he didn't have to.

Simon's cheeks flushed a color that matched the bloodred of the stained glass behind him. "Is it so obvious?"

"I saw the way you looked at her photograph at the funeral luncheon. I heard your voice waver with emotion at her grave. It was an easy assumption."

His shoulders rose and fell. "If a stranger knows as much, I suppose I am the laughingstock of all Willingdale. So be it." He shrugged off all discomfort. "Ivy and I grew up together. We were friends. I always thought Ivy—"

The name shivered in the air around us, the whisper of a ghost.

Ivy.

Ivy.

Ivy.

Hearing it, Simon pulled in a rough breath. His arms pressed to his sides, he swallowed hard. "Did she tell you how I felt about her?"

"It would explain why you're jealous of Gerald."

"You must believe me, Miss Manville, I prayed Ivy was happy in her new life. I am, in fact, the one who joined Ivy and Gerald in holy matrimony."

"That must have been difficult," I said, with real pity for the man.

He didn't need to answer. His gaze strayed to the altar and the arrangement there of white roses and purple hollyhock. "It was one of my duties as vicar of the parish."

I thought of Simon's picture in the *Mercury,* of the circle Ivy had drawn around it. "There are those who would say an unrequited lover may have had reason to cause Ivy's accidents."

He sucked in a horrified breath. "Never! She didn't think that, did she?"

I didn't have the heart to tell him she did or she would not have singled him out in her letter to Miss Hermione.

Simon puffed out a humorless laugh. "If I was to arrange such accidents in the hopes of killing someone, don't you think it would have been Gerald?"

"You did tell Ivy she would regret marrying him," I noted, as gently as possible.

He hung his head. "I am afraid my emotions got the better of me."

"And what of the accident that befell her right here at St. Christopher's?"

A sob escaped him. "She came to see me," he confessed, "that Sunday after evening prayer. I'd been avoiding her. I was not sure I could control the emotions that roiled in me when we were together. But that evening, I had no avenue of escape. After the service, I came out of the sacristy . . ." He glanced that way and motioned the way he'd walked. "Down the aisle. There she was, waiting for me in the back pew. She told me she was sorry our friendship was not what it once was. And I . . ." He twisted his hands together. "I told her it was only natural, she now being a married woman. She said she hoped we might find some common ground, that we might talk now and then."

"And you?"

"It was the most difficult thing I've ever done in my life, but I knew I had no choice. I knew what I had to do. I told her that I was always ready to listen to all the members of my flock and that with her marriage to Gerald, that was exactly what she was. Just another member of the parish. She grew angry." Remembering it, Simon's expression settled into a mask of regret. "She told me she didn't want to be treated as just another of my parishioners, that our past friendship had earned her more than that." A tear slipped down his cheek. "What if there was something she needed to tell me? Something about the accidents that had been happening to her? Something about what troubled her?" He rubbed his hands across his eyes. "What if I could have helped?"

"She never said?"

He shook his head. "They were the last words we ever spoke to each other."

"And when Ivy left the church, one of the slates from the roof crashed down nearby?"

Simon's eyes clouded with the memory. "Yes, and that was surely no accident. Come!" He took my arm. Together, we walked to the back of the church and the stairs that led to the bell tower and we began our climb.

The steps were stone and narrow; they spiraled up and past the chamber where three massive bells hung. There was a door opposite the largest of the bells and it led out to a porch that ran along the perimeter of the church roof. We stepped onto it and, after the gloominess of the church, the sunlight strained my eyes. Squinting a bit in the glare, I could see over the wall that surrounded the porch to a portion of the graveyard and beyond that to the road that led to the village green.

"You see here," Simon pointed, "both the porch and the wall are paved with slates. The church is old, and difficult to keep in a good state of repair. But we do our best. Here." He stepped back to allow me nearer to the wall. "Take hold of one of these slates. You'll see it is fastened firmly in place.

"But here . . ." Simon stepped aside and pointed to a spot where most of a slate was missing, only its edges left behind. "You see what I see, don't you, Miss Manville?"

I surely did. "A slate has been forcibly pried from the wall," I said.

"And it is no coincidence," Simon pointed out, "that from this very spot, a person might easily see the path that leads from the church, the way Ivy and I walked out."

I held up a hand to stop him at the thought. "You were with Ivy when it happened?"

"Right at her side. And you can see what all this means, can't you?"

I did, yet putting it into words made my blood run cold. "This, like all else that befell Ivy, was no accident at all."

Chapter 12

Sephora

July 8

"I was simply the most brilliant thing!" I tittered and was fully justified in calling up a blush. After all, the tale was true enough and I was only too pleased to recount it for my enthralled audience of one. "I slipped out of the house. Just like that. And followed Violet to the train station and from there, all the way to Willing . . . Willing . . ." Thinking, I bit my lip. "Willing Something!"

I might have known Franklin would never let a little thing like a memory slip dull his admiration for me. From his place on the park bench next to me, he offered a smile as warm as the morning's sunshine.

"Brains and beauty." He dared to lean closer so he might touch his hand—ever so gently and ever so properly—to mine. "As long as you went through all that trouble, I do hope you had a good time in Willing . . . Whatever!"

He was so clever, I couldn't help but laugh. "I had luncheon with a woman of quality, Lady Betina Thorn. I'd hoped to stay for tea, too, but Violet came back from wherever she'd been looking as bright as a thundercloud." I did not even try to hide the moue that said exactly what I thought of the conclusion of our excursion to Willing . . . Whatever. Why bother when my pique was genuine? And when a young man liked nothing more than watching his sweetheart show a bit of sauciness?

"Violet insisted we come home," I told him, eager for Franklin's sympathy. "And so we did. And though I was cross about it for all our train journey, once we arrived, I was very glad we stayed no longer." Here, I allowed my pout to dissolve into the most adorable of smiles. "Otherwise, I would not have seen your message waiting for me on the table in the hallway, not until this morning, anyway, and I would have spent another miserable night wondering when I might see you again. Oh, Franklin!" Had we been in private and not in Hyde Park, I fear I might have thrown my arms around him as a way of displaying my overwrought emotions. "When I waited for you the other day and you did not come to meet me—"

"My darling, please forgive me." He pressed my hand in his. A tingle sparkled up my arm. My heartbeat quickened. "I am only too sorry for the pain I caused you. I knew you would be clever enough to interpret the message I sent with the flowers, and I hoped that would assuage your fears. I was so pleased we were able to arrange this meeting today. I daresay you used the same ingenuity to make it out of the house this morning, sight unseen, as you did yesterday when you followed your sister? She has not . . ." He craned his neck and looked all around. The Italian Water Garden was nearby and there was no one there except a strolling couple, a soldier in a scarlet coat with a woman on his arm. A pathway meandered from the trees on our left and disappeared far to the right, and only one man was on it, an elderly clergyman with his nose pressed in a book.

"Your dreadful sister and that harpy of a housekeeper you told me so much about, they didn't follow you, did they?" Franklin wanted to know.

He was so romantic, as eager as I was to keep our tryst a secret! I nearly swooned.

"I don't think they've discovered I'm gone yet," I told Franklin, and it made me so happy to think how clever I'd been. "When I made my escape Bunty was busy in the kitchen and Violet was shut up in the library, though what she does in that musty old room, I cannot guess. I slipped out just as the maid-of-all-work arrived." My smile disappeared and my lips thinned. "I cannot for the life of me understand what Aunt Adelia is thinking. She doesn't want a maid to live in. Can you imagine it? She has a girl come every morning. I cannot say I approve, for I believe when a maid lives in, she feels more responsibility for the family's welfare. Don't you agree?"

He turned in his seat, the better to look my way, and the lenses of his spectacles winked in the light. Franklin is quite the finest-looking man I have ever laid eyes on! His chin is strong and noble, shown off most handsomely by his mutton-chop whiskers, narrow at his temples and broad and round near his lower jaw. Behind his spectacles, his eyes twinkled with affection and tenderness. That day he was dressed in a black frock coat, striped trousers, and a black top hat.

Ah yes, Franklin had breeding, taste, and sense. He would make the ideal husband.

"I fully agree," he said. "A live-in maid is a must for any proper household."

Was I surprised knowing we were of one mind? I was not!

Lovers are linked by more than hearts, or so I'm told. Oftentimes, their minds work in union.

"At least one maid," he added for good measure. "In fact, when I marry . . ."

Poor Franklin. He had not meant to mention a thing so private, so momentous, as the possibility of establishing his own home and family. With his own, darling wife.

The tips of his ears reddened. "You will forgive me, dear Sephora. I shouldn't be so forward as to talk of the future. I cannot help it. The thought of a lifetime . . . with you . . ." Here he gave my hand another tender caress. "It is all that brightens my days. With Mother being so very ill . . ."

I fluffed the skirt of my gown and wondered if Franklin knew it as the gesture so many women used to show when they were not happy with the direction in which a conversation had turned. Somehow, I managed to keep the irritation from my voice. "Your mother takes up a good deal of your time."

"Alas, yes." Upon his sigh, those broad shoulders of his rose and fell and I found it hard to keep my mind on my vexation and not let it wander to the musings that tickled and tempted me—what it might feel like to have his strong arms around me. What it might taste like when his lips touched mine. How infinitely joyous it would be when our hearts beat as one.

I am sure when I fanned my face with one gloved hand, Franklin thought my lace-edged parasol was not sufficient to keep the heat of the morning sun from my face. It was just as well he was in the middle of another apology for his mother's pitiful behavior.

"As I have told you before," he said, "Mother is quite old and very frail. It is the reason I have never introduced you to her. Her heart would not take the shock of knowing I have found a woman who has replaced her on the pedestal where I have always kept her."

He had the tongue of a poet!

My heart beat with such fury, I thought I might faint. What he said was practically a proposal of marriage, but it was unladylike to give in too quickly to so blatant a proclamation.

It wasn't easy, but I kept myself to the topic at hand. "If your mother continues to come between us . . ." My silk purse was on the bench and I fingered it, gaining courage from the feel of the frame with Franklin's photograph inside it. We could be honest with each other, open, and I could bring up such a sensitive topic. After all, he had honored me with his photograph and I had given him one of me. This was more than a simple flirtation.

"I was so concerned when you did not meet me the other day, so worried that something had happened to you. And now you tell me you could not meet me because your mother took poorly and you could not leave her side. I understand you are a good and loyal son, but you must remember, Franklin, I have feelings, too."

"What's this?" His eyes flashed with annoyance and I tensed.

That is, until Franklin threw back his head and laughed. "You are showing some mettle, indeed, my darling. How I do admire you for it!"

"Do you? Really?" Emboldened, I dared to suggest, "Perhaps your mother would see me the same way. If only I could meet her . . ."

"Soon," he assured me. "When she convalesces. We will arrange a tea."

I liked the sound of it. "And my family? You'll call to meet Violet?"

He wrinkled his nose. "From what you've told me about her, I doubt it would be a pleasant experience."

"She can be civilized. Upon occasion. And though I doubt she has a heart lurking beneath her stony exterior, once she meets you, I know, I simply know she will realize what a good and proper gentleman you are. Then she cannot possibly object to our . . ." Did I dare to say it? I fluttered my eyelashes. "Our courtship."

"I should like nothing better. In fact—"

Whatever else Franklin might have said was lost in his gasp of surprise. But then, I could hardly blame him. We had been so caught up in our conversation, neither of us had seen a young man in rough clothes appear before us as if out of nowhere. He had bushy eyebrows and a narrow forehead, large hands, and thick, dirty fingers. While we were still gathering ourselves, the lout snatched my purse from the bench and ran down the path as if the hounds of hell were on his heels.

"Franklin!" I clapped a hand to my heart. "That man, he has taken my purse."

His eyes sparking fire, Franklin pushed himself off the bench, watching the ruffian. "Your purse and all the money in it."

"I care not about the money. Your photograph is in that purse. I cherish that more than any amount of money on this earth."

He darted a look at me before he clapped his eyes to the quickly disappearing form of the ruffian. And then Franklin did the most splendid and the most remarkable and the most romantic thing imaginable.

He took off running after the thief.

"Oh, Franklin!" I cannot say if my exclamation was one of admiration or a warning. Yes, he was as brave as a hero in a novel. But he must be cautious! Surely a man who would so boldly take a woman's purse was capable of any amount of wickedness.

My heart pounding, a tight ball of panic wedged in my throat, I hurried to the middle of the path, but the thief and Franklin had rounded a corner and disappeared into the trees and from here, I had no sense of what might be transpiring. I obviously could not go after them, for that would not be proper, so instead, I stood wringing my hands and sobbed, praying Franklin would return unharmed, and with the precious photograph.

Minutes passed. The sounds of my distress attracted something of a crowd. The soldier and his darling who had been walking along the water. The clergyman who had passed us by only a short time before. A group of young boys dragging their kites who obviously did not understand the gravity of the situation and hooted and called out as if they were at a raucous sporting event.

My stomach clutched and my head spun. My vision was so clouded by tears, the scene in front of me turned into a poorly painted watercolor, a mingling of sepia and walnut accented with patches of green and blotches of blue sky. The pathway was a blur through the center of it all.

It was empty.

"Someone must call for help," I pleaded with the people around me. But they too (except for the raucous young boys) were stunned by the events and stood rooted to the spot, watching as I was for Franklin to return.

Finally, there was movement on the pathway and Franklin appeared!

My knees grew weak and I fell back against the gallant soldier. He passed me off to his lady love who put a comforting arm around my shoulders to keep me from falling to the ground when Franklin stumbled forward.

The legs of his trousers were coated with dust. His tie was askew. There was a band of blood on his forehead.

"Franklin!" Heedless of the impropriety of such a show of emotion, I broke from the ministering grasp of the woman and rushed ahead. I arrived at Franklin's side just as he pitched forward. Fortunately, the soldier and the clergyman were not far behind for (as I may have mentioned) Franklin is tall and well made and I would not have been able to keep him on his feet. The soldier hitched an arm around Franklin and assisted him to the bench where so very recently we had shared our hopes and dreams for the future. The woman produced a handkerchief and dabbed it to the wound on Franklin's head.

It was naught but a small injury, but really, what did that matter? Franklin had been bloodied in the name of love! I took the handkerchief from the woman's hand so I might tend to Franklin's needs. It was the least I could do for a man who had proved his devotion to me with such gallantry.

"Are you terribly hurt?" I asked him.

He passed a hand over his forehead and then pressed it to one of the muttonchops on the side of his face and I saw there was a smudge of dirt there, as if the ruffian had cuffed him. "I am . . ." As if it was the first he realized we were not alone, Franklin looked at the people gathered around us. "I am grateful for help," he said, ever the gentleman. "I will be . . ." He pulled in a breath. "I will fully recover and be fine once I have had a chance to sit and regain my strength. But my darling . . ." When he looked my way, I dropped down on the bench next to him. "The thief was too quick and strong for me. Your purse, I am sorry to say, is gone."

"It doesn't matter." The wound to his forehead had

stopped bleeding and I gave it one more gentle dab before I sat back. "My purse . . . nothing in it . . . nothing is as important as your welfare. Thank God you were not hurt more seriously."

How he had the courage to smile, I cannot say, but that is exactly what Franklin did. At the strangers who had come to our aid and who, now that they knew Franklin would recover, dispersed. At the boys who, realizing the excitement was over, had gone back to their play. At me. Oh, how Franklin smiled at me, his expression so filled with regret, it tore at my heart.

"It is fine," I assured him, and now that we were once again alone, I pressed my hand to his. "I have other purses. And you can have a new photograph made for me. I only hope when that awful ruffian looks inside my purse and finds the photograph, he remembers how you nearly bested him." I dared to touch a gentle hand to muttonchops, but when Franklin winced, I drew it away. He and the thief must surely have engaged in fisticuffs and he wished to spare me any more distress; he did not want me to know how much pain he was in.

Brave hero that he was, he smiled. "I promise you a new photograph, and soon."

"Not too soon. You must rest and recover. We will find a cab and I can accompany you home."

"No need." He pushed off the bench and how he managed it, I do not know. I can only say it was a statement of his courage. He stood tall. "The incident is done with, and I am fine."

I rose to face him. "You're sure? If you are feeling the least bit unsure on your feet—"

"How can I feel weak when I know I have your affection and devotedness to support me?" He brushed my cheek with one finger. “I will accompany you to a cab, Sephora, so that you might get home and rest. After what has happened, I am sure you need to lie down. I will return home on my own. But Sephora . . .” He caught my hand in his. “Let us not wait to see each other again. We must be together again soon. Such a terrible event makes a man appreciate the preciousness of life and of all he loves. Let us see each other here again.”

“Tomorrow?”

His lips thinned with disappointment. “I cannot. But the next day—”

“Yes.” I nearly burst with joy. “Same time?”

“Same time.” He offered me his arm and together we left the park and he hailed a cab and waited until I was in it. I had no doubt I looked as beggarly as a fishwife when I hung my head out the window so I might keep my gaze glued to my hero as we drove away. Only the promise of another meeting lifted my mood.

“Two days,” I whispered.

Two days until I would see Franklin again.

ஓ

But alas, I did not.

Two days after the criminal happenings in Hyde Park, I waited in the agreed place at the agreed time.

But Franklin did not come.

He did not come the next day, either. Or the day after that.

It wasn’t until the fourth day as I sat on the same park bench where only so recently Franklin had all but declared his love, that the terrible truth revealed itself to me.

Dear Franklin, who always thought of me first and who refused to let my mind be troubled, had been wounded more seriously in his heroic effort to save my purse than he revealed.

Even now, it was possible he was confined to his bed. Or incapacitated. He might even be . . .

I dared not let the dark thought invade my mind, and I shook myself to be rid of it and watched raindrops fly from my shoulders. I had been so lost in my reverie, I hadn't realized it had started raining, and as I had left the house so hurriedly in an effort to get to the park, I had brought along neither a cloak nor an umbrella.

I pushed myself from the bench and dragged down the muddy pathway toward the road, my heart as heavy as my footsteps.

Two cabs passed me by, no doubt because the drivers looked me over and decided a woman so waterlogged was not a reliable fare. A third took pity on me and as we made our way back to St. John's Wood, questions bounced along in my head to the rhythm of the horse's hoofbeats.

What had happened to my dear Franklin?

How would I find out?

What could I do?

Who would help me?

The cab had already stopped in front of Parson's Lodge when I jostled myself back to awareness. Though I am usually disinclined, as was my mother before me, to believe that any amount of thinking is good for a proper lady, I must say my moments of reflection had apparently had a positive result.

I had an idea!

I paid the driver and tore into the house, and ignoring Bunty's exclamations of "Why, Miss Sephora, whatever has happened to you?" and "Miss Sephora, let me help you with those wet garments," and "Miss Sephora, you know better than to be out in the rain," I raced up the stairs and to the privacy of my bedchamber.

There was someone who could help.

For the first time in four days, I felt what might actually be hope, and as I peeled off my wet clothing, I hummed a merry tune.

One person would assist me in finding my dear Franklin. One person was capable of assuring me of his health and his continued love for me.

And I knew . . . I grabbed for my dressing gown and, once enfolded in it, I raced to sit at the desk near the window . . . I knew exactly how to get in touch with her.

Dear Miss Hermione,

I am the most wretched of women! My sweetheart (the kindest and most handsome and the most considerate of men) has disappeared and I am sore afraid he may be injured or was somehow made insensible by an attack he recently endured in the name of my honor. Perhaps—dare I say it?—his fate is even worse.

I am so overcome with worry and emotion, I have not slept nor eaten, and I can barely keep myself on my feet. I must find him and so set my mind at ease regarding his fate. But, Miss Hermione, I do not know where to begin to look. I was told he lives with his sickly mother somewhere in the London environs, but other than that, he has given me no indication of where to start my search.

I am desperate, Miss Hermione. I am despondent. He has my love and soon, very soon, I'd hoped he would ask for my hand. I must find him or I will surely perish from a broken heart.

Yours ever hopeful,

A Heartsick Miss

Dear Heartsick Miss,

He is the most considerate and the kindest of men, and you have no idea where he lives? What does this suitor of yours do, materialize out of nowhere when he is inclined to see you?

Really, Heartsick Miss, you are using neither your logic nor your intelligence in this matter and it is that more than anything that infuriates Miss Hermione.

You want to find this man? Given what you've told me about him, I am sorely pressed to reason why, but if that is your chosen course, I would suggest you do the only commonsensical thing.

Gather your wits, woman, and look for him! Start where last you saw him and work backward. Remember every little thing he told you about his business and his acquaintances. As for his sickly mother . . . I will not add to your worries, Heartsick Miss, but will simply say that when you discover the whereabouts of your paragon, you will surely be writing to me again.

Sickly mother, indeed.

Miss Hermione

Chapter 13

Violet

July 14

"It really is quite absurd the predicaments people get themselves into," I told Bunty, who was standing next to my desk, waiting for the answer to Heartsick Miss's letter to be put in the envelope with the others I'd written that morning so she might post them to *A Woman's Place*. "Imagine any woman tolerating a relationship such as the one she describes."

Bunty pursed her lips. "They say love is blind, but if you were to ask me, I'd say it is deaf and dumb, as well. There is no telling how a woman might act when she's in Cupid's throes."

"Well, Cupid should be kinder, especially to those who lack for intellect, as this woman surely does." I put the envelope in Bunty's hands, then brushed my own together, satisfied my morning's efforts in the name of Miss Hermione meant I had the rest of the day to dive into the mystery that occupied me so. "I spent last night reading more of Ivy's diary," I told Bunty.

One corner of her mouth pulled tight. "You'll go blind reading late into the night as you do."

"Aren't you going to ask what I discovered?"

She clutched the envelope at her waist. "If I do, it will only encourage you."

"Not so." I removed Ivy's diary from the top drawer of the desk. "I have found all the encouragement I need right here. See." I flipped the pages to the place where I'd stopped reading the night before.

Bunty bent closer to peer at the passage. "It's just as I said, you'll go blind. My goodness, her handwriting is atrocious."

"Indeed." I smoothed a hand over the page. "That's why it's taken me so long to make my way through the diary. When Ivy was flustered or excited, she wrote with passion and a great deal of speed, just as she did in her last letter to Miss Hermione. See, here . . ." I pointed to page after page where both the date Ivy had written at the top of the page and the entry below it were neat and legible. But then, look here," I instructed Bunty, flipping a few more pages. "You know what these scribbled lines mean, don't you?"

She wrinkled her nose and searched the page again. "I cannot say," Bunty admitted. "I cannot read a word of it."

"Think, Bunty. When Ivy was emotional, her writing deteriorated. And here, her writing is nothing more than a wretched mess. That means when Ivy wrote this she was . . . ?"

Bunty slapped the envelope to her thigh. "She was agitated."

"Exactly. And it wasn't until I was finally able to decipher her words that I could determine if her agitation was from a good cause, or a bad one."

"And you determined what?"

"I determined, Bunty, that on the day she made this entry in her diary, some . . ." Again, I consulted the date written on the page just to be sure. "June eight, Ivy received a letter from a woman named Sally Gwinn, who lives outside of Oxford at a place called Hollyhock House. Ivy does not say who this woman is and from that, I've concluded they must be old acquaintances. Because otherwise, you see, Ivy would have said something like Sally Gwinn was 'a woman I once met at Lady B's,' or 'a friend of my mother's.' But she doesn't. She simply uses this Sally Gwinn's name, which means Ivy has no need to remind herself of their association. She wasn't expecting to hear from Sally. See here." I pointed. "In regards to receiving the letter, she says it was 'a delightful surprise' to find it with the morning's post. But later, here where the writing is smudged and barely legible, she talks about getting in touch with Sally. 'I must learn more,' Ivy says. 'I must know the truth.' And see here, she has marked the page with the stub of a train ticket. She says she must learn more and she did not write to Sally, she went in person to Oxford to talk with her and learn the truth."

"The truth about what, do you suppose?" Bunty asked.

"We have no way of knowing. I looked ahead in the diary and what I do find odd is that after Ivy goes to Oxford"—I rippled the pages of the diary—"there are blank pages. Dates written at the top but no entries from June ten until an entire week later. It's confounding. And it's why I've written to Sally." That letter, too, was already in an envelope, and I retrieved it from my desk and handed it to Bunty. "In my letter to Sally Gwinn, I've told her I am a friend of Ivy's and I'd like to know what they discussed when Ivy visited. And when I have Sally Gwinn's answer . . ." I pushed back my chair and stood, preparing myself to finally say aloud what I hoped for, somewhere in my bones. "Perhaps that will shine a light on Ivy's murder."

"Murder? You're sure?"

"Absolutely. There are so many secrets in Willingdale, so many people who are not willing to tell the truth. Those accidents Ivy spoke of were surely not accidents. It's no wonder she thought someone was trying to kill her. Someone was, and that someone finally succeeded. All we need do now is discover who that someone actually is."

"And you think writing to this Gwinn woman will help?" Bunty weighed the envelope in one hand. "I can't say I agree, but I suppose it doesn't hurt."

"And little victories like these, Bunty, are why it is so important for me to keep poring through Ivy's diary." I am not one for dramatic gestures, but I had to admit to feeling some pride at that moment, and I swept out an arm to take hold of the diary. Instead of wrapping my fingers around it, though, I smacked a hand against it and knocked it from the desk. The slim volume went airborne, flipped, flapped, and landed facedown on the carpet.

I bent to retrieve it so Bunty didn't have to, and saw it had landed so that the last page and the inside of the back cover were exposed, as was the endpaper pasted there, marbled in watery blue, earthen brown, and pale yellow.

"Do you see that?" I asked her.

She glanced from the paper to me. "Fancy paper such as that, it's a common enough thing to see at the back of a book."

"It is, and of course I hadn't seen it—I've been focusing on Ivy's entries, not on the physical diary itself. But Bunty, look at this." I flipped the pages so as to expose the inside of the front cover and the endpaper there.

Bunty gasped. "The paper there. It's green."

"Yes." I ran a hand across the page. "Marbled, too, but in greens and golds with bits of red added. A different paper from the back of the book. And that"—I looked at Bunty—

"is not common at all. In fact, I would go so far as to say I've never seen it."

"Whatever can it mean?" she wanted to know.

"I haven't the slightest idea." I dropped back into the chair behind the desk and with a wave, instructed Bunty to bring another chair over so she might sit next to me. I turned up the light on the paraffin lamp on the desk and looked closely at the brown-and-blue-marbled endpaper.

"Look. Here." I pointed and Bunty leaned nearer. "This corner," I told her, touching a finger to the place. "It is pulled back the slightest bit. Do you think . . ." I looked toward Bunty.

"Could this brown-and-blue-marbled sheet be pasted over the original one, the twin to the one at the front of the book?"

"If the original there at the back was damaged, I suppose. Elsewise, why would Ivy bother?"

"Why, indeed. It is almost as if . . ." I smoothed my hand over the inside back cover of the diary and my words dissolved in a breath of surprise. "There is something thin beneath the paper," I told Bunty, and grabbed her hand so that I could whisk her fingers over the spot. "Ivy has pasted the new endpaper over the old endpaper because there is something sandwiched between them."

Her silvery eyebrows raised, Bunty sat back. "But what could it be?"

To my mind, there was only one way to find out.

In the time since I took over the role of Miss Hermione, I had brought some much-needed order to Adelia's library and so, of course, to her desk. Where there were once piles of papers, there were now orderly stacks. The mementos, trinkets, and yes, the bar of carbolic soap had been removed.

I had, however, kept the ancient Roman *pugio* I'd found beneath a linen handkerchief. A dagger makes for an efficient letter opener, and besides, I rather liked the slick metallic sound it made when I pulled it from its brass scabbard. I used the tip of the *pugio* to gently loosen one corner of the brown-and-blue endpaper, then slid the blade of the knife along one vertical side of the paper.

"There you have it. It's coming away," Bunty crooned, but I refused to be distracted by the admiration that saturated her words.

Instead, I concentrated on the task at hand and slipped the dagger along the bottom horizontal edge of the marbled paper. With it thus loosened, I was able to bend the paper back to expose what was nestled between it and the original green endpaper beneath it.

"And look at that, will you!" Bunty clapped a hand to her heart. "You were right. There is something there."

"More than one something." I carefully removed the newspaper clippings that had been hidden and fanned them out, the better to show them to Bunty.

She groaned. "Not more newspaper articles. Who is Ivy accusing now, the Archbishop of Canterbury?"

I knew she meant to be amusing, but I did not laugh. I was too busy looking over the bits of paper.

"They are all obituaries," I said.

Bunty sobered. "Friends of Ivy?"

"I suppose they must be. Yet . . ." I shuffled through the death notices. "Yet they are all men. And see here, they all died in foreign lands. This one in Australia. This one in Africa. Here is one who died at sea and another who, my goodness, he was on an expedition to the Arctic when he perished. That is certainly remarkable. If they were Ivy's friends or acquaintances, why would she keep their death notices hidden?"

"You don't suppose they might have been her lovers?"

Such a scandalous accusation shouldn't have made me laugh, yet I could not help myself. "From what I've heard of Ivy's life, she scarcely left Willingdale. And though she did attend Miss Simpson's Academy, she would have been much too young then to have a lover. And see here . . ." I looked over the obituaries. "These men lived nowhere near Willingdale. This one was from Edinburgh, this one lived in Cornwall. This one . . ." I glanced over the clipping. "He was from Wales and this last one, Reginald Talbot, lived here in London. I doubt very much Ivy would have had a chance to meet any of them. Unless they were friends of her father's."

"Which still doesn't explain why she would hide their death notices." Bunty pointed out exactly what I was thinking.

"It does seem odd, doesn't it?" I set the clippings back in the diary, but not before I wrote down the most pertinent information contained in Reginald Talbot's.

"You're off again." I was grateful Bunty caught on so quickly. I didn't have to explain.

"It says here he had a widow," I told her. "One Marguerite Talbot. And if Mrs. Talbot still lives on . . ." I consulted the obituary one last time. "Lilac Lane, then she may be able to explain Ivy's connection to her husband."

"If she still lives there," Bunty conceded. When I moved forward and toward the door, she stepped back. "But what if it's something you shouldn't be asking about, Miss Violet? Some scandal as I've suggested and this Mrs. Talbot will be hurt by your questions? Or what if it's something sinister?"

I opened the door and shooed Bunty out to the hallway so I might lock the library behind me. "I hardly think there is anything sinister lurking in a place called Lilac Lane," I assured her. "Now if you'll be so kind as to step outside and hail a cab for me, I will get my hat and . . ." I glanced up the stairway. "Sephora isn't up and about, is she? I can't have her following me again as she did the day I went to Willingdale."

Her hand already on the doorknob, Bunty looked back at me and shook her head. "Locked up in her bedchamber. Has been these past days. Says she's not feeling well."

As if I could see her up there and somehow assess her health and the truthfulness of the story she'd told Bunty, I looked again up the stairs. "Should I look in on her?"

"I will do it directly when I get back," Bunty told me. "And then I'll take her up some soup. You go." She stepped outside. "Do what you have to do. Only, Miss Violet, you will be careful, won't you?"

My straw hat was hanging on a peg near the door, and I clapped it on my head and pinned my chatelaine securely to my side. "Of course I will be careful," I assured Bunty. I did not bother to explain about my pistol.

ꕥ

Lilac Lane was a narrow street in a remote corner of Bayswater in the west of London. As I arrived, a gaggle of children played in the road, three skinny cats streaked by, a sleeping dog opened one eye to assess me then went instantly back to his slumbers.

There was not one lilac bush in sight and I began to second-guess my glib remark to Bunty about how a place with such a name could never be sinister.

Here, the summer sunshine barely penetrated the pall

of smoke that hung over the neighborhood. The street was chockablock with sturdy brick homes that stood side by side like soldiers at attention. The years had eroded any remarkable features they might have once had just as they had faded the paint on their front doors. Many of the homes, I noticed, had "Rooms to Let" signs in their front windows.

Marguerite Talbot's was one such home and when I knocked, the door was answered by Marguerite herself, a middle-aged woman with unruly brown hair who wiped her hands on the apron she wore. I believe she was anticipating a potential lodger because she was smiling, at least until she saw a lone female on her doorstep. I introduced myself and asked if I might have a few minutes of her time.

This, Mrs. Talbot had to consider. "I've a stew on the stove and six lodgers who will expect it not to be burned when they sit down to dinner this evening," she said.

I promised not to keep her long enough for her stew to burn.

Still, she hesitated and I sighed with relief when she finally stepped back and waved me into a small parlor where there were two threadbare but comfortable-looking chairs, a shelf of books, and a Chesterfield sofa, tufts of horsehair escaping from the tears in its upholstery.

"What can I do for you?" Mrs. Talbot asked.

It was hard to come up with a plausible fiction to explain my presence so I opted for the truth. "I've come about your husband," I told her.

Marguerite's bottom lip trembled, her knees gave way. She sank down upon the sofa. "Reggie? Why? He's been dead these five years now."

"Yes, I know. And I'm sorry if asking about him has brought up sad memories. But I am in something of a quandary and I hope you can help. I've discovered your husband's obituary among the possessions of a late friend, and I'm trying to understand why she might have kept it."

Marguerite, it seemed, was not one to let grass grow under her feet. She caught on quickly; her face shot through with color. "What are you saying exactly, miss? For if you are implying that my Reggie and this friend of yours—"

"Nothing of the sort." I hadn't been invited, but I sat in the chair nearest the small window that looked over the street. "In fact my friend was little more than a girl when your husband died. I cannot think how she might have known him." Though I didn't know if it was true, I did know I had to put Marguerite's mind to rest. "I would be surprised if they had ever met at all."

"And yet, this friend of yours, she had the notice of Reggie's death? The one from the newspaper five years ago?"

"You can see why I am curious." I settled myself as comfortably as I could in the sad little room and with the woman who looked as if her soul had fled her body years before. "I thought perhaps you might help me make sense of this little mystery."

She clutched the arm of the sofa with one hand. The other, she put to her throat. "Oh, how I do miss him. Every single day."

I leaned forward. "Tell me about him."

She did not answer me, simply pushed to her feet and left the room and I heard her footsteps on the stairs. A minute later, she was back, a framed photograph cradled in her hands. "Reggie," she said, and passed the photograph to me.

Reginald Talbot had a dark, bristling beard and a bushy mustache. Other than that, it was hard to say what he looked like for he was wearing what we called a "planter's hat" in

India, what most people know as a pith helmet. It was pulled low on his head, shading his eyes and making it nearly impossible to see much more of his face than his nose. And all that facial hair.

I might not have been able to learn much from it, but I knew its value to her, and I handed back the photograph with all due respect.

Clutching it to her heart, Marguerite took her seat again upon the ancient Chesterfield.

"He called me *mainnsamee.*" Her smile was bittersweet. "It's a word he learned in Burma and it means *princess.* He was there you see, in Burma. Reggie was a doctor."

"Was he?" It seemed a singular detail.

"Treated the English planters, he did. That is, until his own health suffered because of the climate. That is why . . ." In an instant, her expression changed and I saw a glimpse of what Mrs. Talbot once was, younger, more carefree, in love.

Her eyes sparkled and the lines at the corners of them disappeared. She smiled. "That is how Reggie came to be here in London, and that is when we met. He had recuperated much of his strength by then, but he could no longer practice medicine. I didn't care. I had a sizable income, you see, left to me by an uncle who had no children of his own. Looking at me now . . ." As if she'd never seen the room before, her gaze wandered the tiny parlor, the tired furniture, the spot on the ceiling where the paint was peeling.

She cleared her throat, and it seemed now that someone was asking, she was eager to speak about the past. "Reggie and I moved into a lovely town house near Portman Square and though we were never blessed with children, we had much to fill our days. I gardened and helped out at All Souls with charity work. Reggie had his club and friends there, and he passed the time of day in discussions with them. You know, the way men of quality do."

Though I wondered why men of quality had nothing better to do, I knew better than to ask.

"We were very happy," Marguerite went on. "Until . . ." She set the photograph down on the floor next to her so that she might clutch her hands together on her lap. "He had an acquaintance. In Burma. The man owned a rice plantation and he convinced Reggie that investing in it was a wise decision."

"You didn't agree?"

"As Reggie's wife, it wasn't my place to agree or to disagree," she told me, her voice not as sharp as it was mournful. "I knew Reggie would do the thinking for the both of us. That is, after all, how successful marriages work. There was another thing I knew as well. The city atmosphere was slowly eroding Reggie's health. If the investment in the rice plantation was successful—and Reggie was sure it would be—we would have enough to retire to the countryside."

"And was the investment successful?"

As if a cloud overshadowed her, Marguerite shivered. "Reggie knew he must assess the situation himself before he invested all our money, so he decided on a voyage to Burma. I wanted to go with him, but he explained that such a journey is fraught with danger and uncomfortable as well. He sailed without me. On the *Koning der Nederlanden*."

I remembered reading about the incident in the newspapers. My blood ran cold. "The ship that . . ."

"Sank in the Indian Ocean. Six lifeboats were launched. Three were never found. And to this day, their disappearance remains a mystery. Reggie's . . ." Her voice broke. "Reggie's was on one of them."

I hated to mention it, but had to know the whole of the story. "And your investment?"

Marguerite cleared her throat. "Reggie was not one to trust banks. I know that sounds foolish, but I could not fault him for it. He had seen his father's fortunes dissolve, you see, thanks to nefarious financial practices on the part of his banker. The troubling state of affairs marked Reggie's mind for life. It is the reason he took the money with him rather than have it wired to him once he arrived in Burma. So you see, Reggie was careful and considered. I am sure Reggie took the money into the lifeboat. What happened to it after that . . ." Her voice faded.

"You loved him very much." I was stating the obvious but could think of nothing else to say in the face of such grief. "You miss him."

"He was so attentive. So attractive! I doubt you can imagine it seeing me now, but we made a handsome couple." She barked a laugh that contained no humor. "Once Reggie was gone, once the money was gone . . . well, I make do. With lodgers and taking in some laundry, I make do."

I stood. "And I have taken up enough of your time." It seemed a better way to end the interview than by dwelling on how far Marguerite's fortunes had fallen; she did not seem the type who would appreciate pity. "I am grateful for all you've told me."

"But it hardly helps, does it?" She rose and showed me to the door. "Unless your friend was once in Burma . . ."

"She was not."

"And unless she knew another of the victims on the *Koning der Nederlanden*."

"That is certainly a possibility." I did not mention the other three obituaries and how I doubted any of those men had a connection with the doomed ship. Marguerite had told me all she could, and more than I had any right to expect, but still I had no answers. I stepped outside. "I will look into it. And if I learn anything that throws light upon your husband's fate, I will be sure to let you know. Thank you, Mrs. Talbot."

I was already in the road when I saw her twitch as though she was touched by fire. She hurried to join me in the middle of Lilac Lane.

"I've just had a thought and, as it happened a month or more ago and seemed to have no significance, I'd put it out of my head. Then again, perhaps it still has no significance. There was no mention at the time of Reggie's obituary."

"But . . . ?" I waited for more.

"Well, I'm just thinking of the day someone came around asking about Reggie, wanting to know more, just like you do. That friend of yours, the one with the clipping, her name wasn't Ivy, was it?"

Chapter 14

"She was there, Bunty! She went to Bayswater. Just as I did." I breezed into the house and was talking even before Bunty had a chance to ask how my day's adventure had gone. "Ivy was there. In Lilac Lane. She went to inquire after Reginald Talbot."

Bunty took my hat and gloves. "That hardly makes any sense."

"Exactly!" I plucked the key from my chatelaine, unlocked the library door, and marched inside. After all I'd heard from Marguerite Talbot and a hot and bumpy ride home in a hansom, I should have wanted to do nothing more than flop onto the couch, take off my boots, and relax. Instead, I told Bunty, "Tea, please," and sat down at my desk, feeling more energized than ever.

When she arrived with a tea tray in her hands (when I spied the seed cakes on it I realized I was starving), I told her to sit, poured tea for us both, and went back to doing what I'd been doing, searching through Ivy's diary.

"She does mention a trip to London," I told Bunty. "I read the passage earlier in the week and Bunty, I've been such a simpleton. Here!" I bit into a seed cake, took a gulp of tea, and pointed at the page. "She talks of going to Mrs. T's, and I thought nothing of it. When she mentioned a trip to town, I just naturally assumed Ivy had come into London to do some shopping, that this Mrs. T. was a dressmaker, perhaps, or a milliner. That will teach me to make such discriminatory assumptions about my own sex. She was not in town shopping, she was here investigating, just as I was. Ivy did not know who Reginald Talbot was any more than I did."

"But . . ." Bunty's forehead creased. "Why would she have his obituary then?"

"Why, indeed." I wolfed down the second half of the seed cake and reached for another. Bunty, it must be noted, makes excellent seed cake. "That is the question that has had me baffled all the way home from Bayswater."

"And the answer?" she wanted to know.

"I have no idea." I hated to admit it, but there it was. Ivy must have found some missing link between those men that made their obituaries worthy of secretly saving. I, so far, had not. I finished my tea, poured a second cup, and sobered, admitting to myself I had gone down a blind alley. "Mrs. Talbot told me she gave Ivy much the same information she gave me. Reginald was a fine man and she loved him very much. He was lost at sea. So was her fortune."

"A pity, that."

"It is. She takes in lodgers now; she seems to make the best of it, but she must be a shell of her former self."

Bunty sipped her tea. "And how does that help us in finding out what happened to Ivy?"

"It doesn't. Not a whit. And yet it is curious that Ivy never wrote about the conversation in her diary. She came all the way here to talk to Mrs. Talbot, learned as little as I did, went home, and didn't make note of it."

"Because it did not help her."

I tapped the desk with impatient fingers. "I must look through the diary more carefully and see if there's any indication she went to Wales or Edinburgh or Cornwall."

"To see the widows of the other men spoken of in those obituaries?"

"What is their connection?" I wondered. "Except of course . . ." I had seen the information earlier, and had noted it, but somehow, it never struck me as particularly odd until that very moment. "They all died abroad."

"And you said as how Ivy's husband was planning a trip out of the country. Do you think it's possible Ivy collected these death notices as a way of pointing out to her husband that his trip might be too dangerous?"

I hadn't thought of this and, not for the first time, I congratulated myself for being wise enough to take Bunty into my confidence. She was as shrewd as she was intelligent.

A thought hit and I paged through the diary to an early passage. I showed the page to Bunty. "Ivy talks about Gerald's planned trip to Canada. She says he is not nervous and he should be because of what happened to his friend, Jack Trembath."

"Trembath? The name is familiar."

"As it should be. Listen here, Bunty. Here is an entry from Ivy's diary from the day of May seven." I cleared my throat and read. "'I am such a fool! So awkward, I wonder how dearest Gerald ever loved me at all. Do I ever stop to think before words fall from my lips?' Here, Bunty, the ink is smeared. Ivy had been crying again. 'Today as I was searching for a glove I was sure I had last night and could find nowhere, I ventured into Gerald's dressing room and found there on his dresser, of all things, an obituary for one Captain Jack Trembath, a man from Cornwall who died the most unfortunate death in the wilds of the Arctic.'"

Bunty sat up. "No wonder the name rang a bell. His is one of the obituaries you found."

I nodded, and kept reading. "'As Gerald had never mentioned Captain Trembath to me, I thought the death notice an odd thing for him to have and at dinner, I mentioned it to him. Oh, how I offended him! I never meant it. Yet his cheeks grew dusky and his hands clenched into fists. He asked . . . dare I write it? It breaks my heart to replay the scene in my head. He asked how I had the brass to poke through his possessions, when it became a wife's business to question her husband. I told him I had no such intent, that I'd found the obituary and simply assumed . . .'

"More staining of the page here," I told Bunty. "In fact, an entire line is so smudged, I cannot read it. But then she goes on here. '. . . a friend from Gerald's school days so that when Gerald saw the death notice in the newspaper, he was naturally interested. Oh, how foolish I felt. How awful! I as much as accused the dearest of all men on earth of keeping secrets from me and I am so ashamed, my heart feels like it will burst. I do not know why I am acting this way, why my brain is so mixed up. I refuse to think . . . no. I WILL NOT . . .' She's written those last three words all in capitals, Bunty, and underlined them as well. 'I will not even think of my dear mother. But I must know how to repair this terrible mistake. I must change my ways or I am sore afraid dear Gerald will fall out of love with me.'"

I turned the page and kept reading. "'Yes, I know what I must do. Where I can turn for comfort and advice. I must ask Miss Hermione.'"

I set the book down with a satisfied thump. "Soon after,

she first consulted Adelia. Simon did tell me Ivy had been worried, distracted. She was concerned about this fuss with Gerald. It does not explain, though, why she kept Captain Trembath's obituary, or who these other men might be whose death notices she also hid away. I suppose after finding the captain's, she might have collected the others and produced them as a warning, to show Gerald how much she was worried about his trip abroad. But how did she collect the notices? Especially one like Talbot's which is five years old? And why hide them again?"

"Maybe this Mr. Armstrong was still angry and didn't want his wife offering him advice and a warning. Perhaps she hid them because he threatened to cast the clippings into the fire."

"But once she'd shown them to him, he may as well have destroyed the clippings. They were no more use to her."

My sigh and Bunty's overlapped.

I drowned the sounds of discouragement beneath another sip of tea and turned to questions that had been niggling at me since we'd found the clippings: Did they relate to Ivy's own death? And if so, how? It hardly seemed possible. Ivy was a young woman killed on English soil. These were men—all men—who'd died in foreign lands. Only one possibility came to mind. "There is one curious fact about Reginald Talbot," I told Bunty. "He was a doctor."

She had nothing to say in reply, which is why I was obliged to add, "We have another doctor involved in this conundrum."

Bunty caught on. She set her teacup on the desk. "That one in the village."

"Yes, Dr. Islington. One of Ivy's suspects. Islington and Talbot might have known each other. But still . . ." I drummed my fingers against the desk. "I suppose the only way of finding out more is to go back to Willingdale."

Bunty frowned, the expression easy enough to interpret. She was our housekeeper, but Bunty also felt responsible for Sephora and myself. The warmth that tangled around my heart at the thought made me pay all the more attention when she said, "Not today, it is late. And not tomorrow, from the look of the clouds." She glanced out the window as if to prove it. "There are storms coming, and no mistake."

"Then I will wait. And read more of the diary. There are answers in this book, Bunty. Just as there are answers in those death notices. There must be. And I will find them."

July 18

Not for the first time, I was grateful for the speed and efficiency of the British railway system. After three days of driving winds and buckets of rain the likes of which I hadn't seen since summer monsoon in India, I was anxious to finally get out of the house and eager to get to Willingdale as soon as I possibly could.

It is important to point out, however, that just because I was in a hurry did not mean I was careless, determined as I was to balance my responsibilities: before I left the house, I made sure Sephora was safely in her room. As she had been closeted there for any number of days, I will also admit (reluctantly since she'd been known to dramatize before) that I was concerned about her health. When questioned, she assured me she was fine and merely spending time relaxing and reading, with none of the usual hysterics that accompanied her playacting. As if to demonstrate, a package of book serializations arrived that very morning from Hatchards in Piccadilly. I had no doubt Sephora had sent off a message requesting the latest (and the most sensational) romantic claptrap imaginable. I also noticed the newest copy of *A Woman's Place* waiting for her on the hall table and though I itched to stay and see how she might react to Miss Hermione's latest advice, I had neither the time nor the luxury. I left her to it, confident she was so immersed in her reading, she would not follow.

As happens so often after wicked weather, the day was clear and glorious. Puffy clouds floated over the railway station. Sunshine spilled over the village. I breathed in the refreshing air and walked toward the village green. Yes, I planned to interview Dr. Islington about any connection he might have to Reginald Talbot, but first, a visit with Gerald Armstrong was in order. After all, I had my lost pocket watch to inquire after.

I had made it only as far as the George and Dragon when I saw a familiar person step out from the pub. Before she could hurry off, I intercepted Betty.

"It's you, is it?" She gave me a squint-eyed look. "Come to cause more commotion?"

"Have I? Caused commotion?"

"You kept me from finding that there brooch. Got in my way, you did."

It was hardly true, but I wasn't about to argue. "And you still haven't found it?"

The way she pouted should have been answer enough, but Betty added a disgusted snort. "Hid it, Ivy did, just so as I couldn't have it."

"She was very good at hiding things."

The reminder made Betty eye me with sudden interest. "That there diary? You found it?"

This was not a confidence I was willing to share. What I had done in pocketing the diary essentially amounted to theft, and I knew better than to admit it. Besides, I might need Betty's assistance, or at least her recollection of events in the village. It was to my benefit to keep her thinking of us as allies. Surely identifying Ivy's murderer was more important than the pang of conscience I felt at misleading Betty. "If I did find the diary," I told her, "there might be some mention of the brooch in it. Then we might be able to discover where Ivy concealed it."

"And you'd tell me?"

Instead of answering, I offered a smile. "Walk with me."

We went on together in silence and we were nearly to where the path split and one portion of it headed to the mill, when I asked Betty, "Do you know much about Dr. Islington?"

She sucked in a breath but I could not tell if it was because she was surprised by my question or outraged that I had the cheek to ask it.

She stopped, the better to study me. "Why're you asking?"

"I have met what might be a friend of his," I said, lying in a way that should never be done in a quaint village on a summer morning. "A certain Reginald Talbot. He, too, is a physician, and he told me both he and another doctor once worked together in Burma, perhaps ten years ago. His recollection is foggy at best, but he thought that man might be Dr. Islington."

Betty wrinkled her nose. "I don't think so."

"Because . . . ?"

"Because he lives here is why. Dr. Islington, I mean. Always has since I've been alive."

"You would know? If he had gone away for a year or two?"

"I am nineteen years of age," Betty informed me. "My sister, Cass, is eighteen. My brothers, Bob, Harry, and Dickie, are sixteen, fifteen, and fourteen. Then there's little Lucy who is twelve and she was born in the year when old Grandad Pete died of the cholera. The year after that, Granny Dottie—she was a witch, you know, and had med'cines people came from miles around to get, but did not have any she could use as to cure herself—Granny Dottie died of consumption. And then there was Minnie, of course, just a year or so before. Kicked in the head by a horse. Imagine that. And there was Kate and—"

"And what you're telling me"—I stopped her before I drowned in the history of the entire population of Willingdale—"is Dr. Islington attended all these people?"

"Oh yes, I remember him being there. And there's more, if you don't believe me. Kate and Agnes and Susan, too. All looked in on by the doctor. So you see, he could not have been out there in . . . what did you call it? . . . Burma? He couldn'a been in this Burma place on account of what he was here."

"And busy." I considered what this meant in terms of my investigation and must admit to being disheartened. If Drs. Islington and Talbot were not connected in any way, what was Ivy's interest in Reginald Talbot?

"A'course . . ." Betty threw out the word in way clearly meant to be casual and just as clearly told me there was more here than met the eye. My interest was piqued, and I looked up from a morose examination of my shoe to find her with a sly grin on her face. "He's never too busy when it comes to the ladies, if you take my meaning."

I thought I did, but wanted to be sure. "Are you saying—"

"That Dr. Islington has an eye for the skirts? He does, miss. I can tell you, he does. He had his eye on Edith Cowles once. Before she poisoned her husband."

Seeing my surprise, Betty squealed with laughter. "You didn't know!"

"Well, I heard he was dead, but—"

"But how does a man who's been takin' care of himself all through forty years finally marry Edith and not a year later, ladles rat poison into his tea instead of sugar? Just after that lovely Mr. Armstrong comes to live in the village? Oh yes." She nodded sagely. "Folks around here, we've been talking about it since it happened."

"Edith does not seem the type to be a murderer," I said, even as I reminded myself that Ivy had thought of her as a suspect. "Is there any proof?"

"Does there need to be? No sooner had Edith put poor ol' Will in the ground than she set her sights on Gerald—" Here Betty remembered herself and cleared her throat. "That is, Mr. Armstrong."

"And you think . . ."

"Ain't just me thinking it, it's folks here all around."

"But not the authorities."

She pursed her lips. "Which don't mean that's not what happened."

That much was certainly true.

I considered all I'd learned about Edith since the day I met her. And I considered something else as well—if what Betty said was true, Edith was plucky enough and vicious enough to commit murder. She'd killed her husband and set her sights on Gerald. Once Gerald turned away from her, it would have been natural in her eyes to plan the murder of the woman who was her rival. Ivy must certainly have heard the rumors about Edith and William, and she knew Edith was jealous of her relationship with Gerald. When the incident with the hay wagon happened, it was only natural for Ivy to suspect Edith.

I had to learn more, and Betty seemed just the one to apprise me. "There was talk," I said cautiously, "of Edith and Gerald marrying."

Betty made a face. "What she was wanting, no doubt, but not what she got."

"What Ivy got instead."

She shot me a look. "Ivy didn't deserve him."

"Why ever not? They were very much in love, from all I hear. Ivy had breeding. And a good income. She had a lovely home, and standing in the village. Why didn't Ivy deserve Gerald?"

Betty grumbled, shook her shoulders, and stomped away.

Shocked by her outburst as I was, I did not hesitate. My legs are long enough that I was easily able to follow. "What else can you tell me, Betty?" I asked her. "About Gerald or Ivy or Dr. Islington?"

She stopped and spun to face me, her cheeks a vivid red, her eyes flashing. "Is it dear, sweet Ivy you want to know about?" She sneered. "You think she was quite the lady, don't you? You know she was mad, just like her mother? If you don't believe that, then you ain't heard about the time she attacked Dr. Islington."

Betty was full of surprises, and this one seemed even more significant than the last. I shook my head in wonder. "I can't imagine . . ."

"Well, imagine it! Happened maybe six weeks ago. I ran into Ivy that morning. She was all aflutter, anxious to get to the train station for what she told me was an important journey."

I thought about Ivy's diary entry. Sally Gwinn? A train ticket to Oxford? Or was it her trip to London to see Marguerite Talbot that excited Ivy so? "Did she say where she was going?"

"She did not, but I can tell you this much, saw her later that day, after she comed home from wherever it was she went. There I was standin' on the green talking to Rob Cranley, him what works over at the newspaper. And there comes Ivy from the station, looking like she would explode. Trompin', that's what she was doing, not walking, but trompin' like every one of her footsteps was meant to pound into the earth and send out a warning."

"Did you speak to her?"

Betty raised her eyebrows. "Didn't dare go near, but I kept an eye on her right enough. And where did she go? Right to Dr. Islington's surgery. A minute later, all we could hear was yellin' and screamin'."

"Him or her?" I asked, and Betty didn't need to consider it.

"Just her to begin with, then his voice joined in like thunder."

"What were they yelling about?"

She pouted. "Couldn't hear all'a it. But I saw her go in. That's the God's honest truth. And I heard the commotion. Ivy sayin' something about the doctor being treacherous, about him being evil. Him tellin' her whatever it was, she was imaginin' it and she needed to calm down and that she was actin' just like her mother did, right before that father of hers locked the missus in the attic."

"That seems quite an accusation."

"Heard it with my own ears, I did. And Rob, he was listenin', too, but had no want to learn any more. He hightailed it out of there, and as there was no one else outside the surgery, well, I had to find out what was happenin', don't you see? In case the doctor needed assistance."

More likely so that Betty had a story to tell at the pub that evening. Not something I mentioned and instead simply said, "Oh?"

She nodded. "I went up there to the window and looked in. And there was Ivy on one side of the doctor's desk, her hair all hangin' down like she'd been pullin' at it, and her eyes bulging, and her face all a'fire. It was as if . . ." Betty swallowed hard. "She looked like a madwoman and no mistake."

"And what was the doctor doing?"

"Just sittin' there, at least when I first looked. Then Ivy, she said something about how she knew the truth and him, he jumped out of his chair. That's when Ivy . . ." Betty demonstrated, waving her arms through the air. "She swiped at the desk, scattering the papers that was there and some of them she caught up and threw right in the doctor's face."

If nothing else, Betty was a skilled storyteller. I could picture the scene and I groaned; if Ivy hadn't been mad, she had certainly been angry. "That's awful. And then what happened?"

"Ivy, she raced around the doctor's desk, that's just what she did. And she pummeled him with her fists. He had to fight her off and I could tell as how he was tryin' not to hurt her, him being brawny and her just a woman. Finally, he had no choice. He took her by the shoulders and pushed her away." Betty demonstrated, straightening her arms, pushing at the air. "That's when Ivy, she turned on her heels and ran and I . . ." Betty lifted her chin, daring me to question her bravery. "Well, I just scampered away as fast as I could, didn't

I? I mean, who wouldn't? What right-thinking person would want a madwoman after her?"

"This is certainly most interesting," I admitted, thinking not just of Betty's dash to safety but of the entirety of her report. "Do you know what resulted from the incident?"

"Saw Mr. Armstrong there at the surgery just a bit later," Betty said. "Imagine he was offerin' the doctor an apology."

Or Gerald was consulting Dr. Islington as to the state of Ivy's mind.

The ramifications of and meaning of this scene, though, was not something I had a chance to deliberate. Not right then and there, as Betty proved by interrupting my thoughts.

"After that, ain't nobody saw Ivy in the village. Not for at least a week. She even missed coming to the fete. We wondered, of course. We wondered if she was locked up in the attic just like her mother had been, and when he was asked, Mr. Armstrong, he said as how Ivy wasn't feelin' well. But she recovered, she did. She was out and about again eventually. But tellin' you all that . . ."

Betty wiggled her shoulders and scraped the toe of one rather shabby boot in the dirt, looking much like a nervous student who'd been told to speak in front of the class.

"That is why what else I has to tell you is so very strange."

"I doubt there could be much stranger," I ventured, but Betty would have none of it. She kept right on.

"See, I saw them together. I mean, after all that, you'd think it would never happen, that they wouldn't want to speak much less stand there side by side. But there they was, the two of them." She pointed toward the millpond.

"The two of—"

"Dr. Islington. And Ivy. Oh, yes! Saw the two of them standing on the bridge there. Can you imagine that he would dare go near her again? Or that she would dare to look the man in the eye after what she done? But no, there they were. It was just after dark."

"If it was dark, how do you know it was them?"

She looked at me as if I had cabbage for brains. "I'd know him, of course. Anyone would know him on account of how we all see him striding through here day and night."

"And her?"

"That were the night of the strawberry moon. Big and full it was."

"And in its light, you saw her face?"

"Didn't need to. Saw my bloody brooch is what I saw, pinned to the shoulder of her dress as usual, glowing and sparkling in the ruddy moonlight."

"Why would Ivy and the doctor be out here in the middle of the night, talking to each other after the awful row they'd had?"

She clicked her tongue. "You swells are all alike. Acting like you're more clever than the rest of us. Truth is, you're always askin' the wrong questions."

"Did I? Ask the wrong question? I wondered if you knew why Ivy and the doctor were meeting but I should have asked—"

Perhaps Betty was right and I did have cabbage for brains.

The truth of the matter struck and I sucked in a breath and hoped to redeem myself in the name of swells everywhere. "I should have asked when you saw them together."

"Aye." She gave me a wink. "For that would do you more good than wonderin' what the two of them might be nattering about."

She turned and walked away.

I scampered behind, irritated with myself and determined

not to let her leave on so tantalizing a note. "So tell me, Betty. When did you see Ivy and the doctor on the bridge together?"

"I told you, the night of the strawberry moon."

"And that would be very helpful if I had a calendar in front of me and knew when that full moon of June occurred, but since I do not?"

"Ruddy swells," Betty grumbled, and continued on. "If you knew what was what, you'd know what night that was. That was the very night Ivy died."

Chapter 15

My pocket watch would have to wait.

My head spinning with the possibilities of all I'd just heard and all it might mean, I left Betty and headed off to find Dr. Islington's surgery. The search did not take long. His office was located in a sturdy brick building nestled between a tailor's shop and a rather shabby bookstore. Two steps led up to a black front door with a polished brass plate beside it. In the highly reflective surface, I saw my own image, head tipped, considering how such a plaque seemed more appropriate for a Harley Street physician than for a village doctor. I wondered if it had been presented by a grateful patient. Or if, rather, it said something about Dr. Islington's opinion of himself.

The door to the surgery was locked and when I knocked, no one answered.

"Drat!" I spun from the door and reconsidered my options.

They were few. I would have to settle for a talk with Gerald.

I retraced my steps and crossed the village green. There was a monument at one corner of it, a stone marker erected in honor of those men of the village who had fought in the Crimean War. As it was artistically rendered, I could not resist a closer look. Slowly, I circumnavigated it, admiring the carving on the memorial and considering the suffering of all those who go to war. When I rounded the back side of the monument I realized that from this very spot, between houses and past a shop with baskets of vegetables in front of it, I could just make out the bridge over the millpond where Ivy had spent her last moments.

With one hand, I shaded my eyes and squinted for a better look. There was a man standing on the bridge, a fellow with wide shoulders. The way he stood, with his feet apart and his chin raised, made me think again of the military men immortalized nearby. This was no soldier, though. I knew that much in an instant. Betty was right. He was easy to recognize, even at a distance. Before he could elude me further, I raced off to intercept Dr. Islington.

Fortunately for me, the doctor did not move. He stood just at the place where a tangle of undergrowth on land met the stone surface of the bridge. He was as still as the monument upon the green, his arms at his sides, his gaze on the millpond below. Sunlight sparkled against the water like the glint of fire upon steel. It ricocheted back at us, glancing against the silk band that circled the doctor's bowler, flickering against the watch chain that hung from the pocket of the green waistcoat he wore under his gray jacket.

At the sound of my sudden approach (I feared the speed at which I moved left me gasping like an old draft horse), he turned and his eyes widened.

Was it surprise I saw there? Or wariness?

There was neither in his bland greeting. "Miss Manville." He put a hand to the brim of his hat. "I hadn't thought to see you here in Willingdale again."

"Need to . . ." I hauled in a breath. "I need to talk to Mr. Armstrong about a missing watch."

"Well, you won't find him in today," the doctor told me. "I have it that he made a trip into London. Finalized a sale for a bit of property to Lady B, you see, and since there was no small amount of money exchanged, Gerald himself wanted to put the notes into his banker's hands."

"Then I suppose I am obliged to come back another day," I said. "Until then . . ." I had been so busy bucketing along so as to speak to the doctor, I had not had time to think exactly how I might approach what I wanted to discuss with him so I simply said, "Ivy attacked you."

He turned from me, the better to watch a barren branch when it tumbled over the dam and splashed into the millpond, and I cursed the timing and my luck. I had no chance to see his expression to gauge if I'd caught him off guard.

"I have no idea what you're talking about," the doctor said.

"I'm surprised, as it happened but a short time ago."

"And she attacked me, you say? That's preposterous." He huffed and grumbled below his breath. "Really, young lady, I have no idea how you get these things into your head, but this is simply not true."

"There were witnesses."

He darted me a glance. "Who?"

"It hardly matters." I, too, could act as if we were discussing nothing more important than the weather. Both hands flat, I leaned against the bridge parapet and looked for all the world to be as engrossed in watching the gurgling water as he pretended to be. "That person remembers the incident well, especially as Ivy had been traveling that day."

He sniffed. "Ivy never traveled."

"Ah, but she did. Twice recently, in fact. On the day in question, she went to your surgery directly from the station."

"Did she?" He let out a long breath and I wished I could say if it was one of surrender or simply of frustration. "What else did this spy of yours tell you?"

"I imagine my spy"—I gave the word a twist to let him know I did not approve of his use of it—"is hardly the only one who knew what happened. The way I heard it, your voices were raised. I imagine half the village heard you. Ivy saying she'd learned the truth. You denying any wrongdoing."

"As I deny this absurd incident ever happened."

"She flung the papers from your desk at you."

"She would never have dared."

"Not normally. Ivy was a level-headed young woman. She valued her place in the community, and more than anything, she cherished Gerald and all he meant to her. She wouldn't dare risk bringing embarrassment down on his head. And yet . . ." I skimmed a hand over the brickwork. "And yet, she confronted you. And that, Dr. Islington, tells me Ivy cared very much about the matter at hand."

He marched a few steps further onto the bridge before he turned back to me. "Which was?"

Damned if I knew, but I couldn't let on. I did my best to put on an air of nonchalance, closing the distance between us in slow, easy steps. "She had just left the station, and that narrows our options considerably. I do believe it is possible she may have come to see you directly after a trip she made to London to inquire about a certain Dr. Reginald Talbot."

Even Dr. Islington was not so good an actor as to pretend the look of sheer bewilderment that caused his mustache to droop and his eyes to widen. And that told me a great deal.

"Not London, then. And this Dr. Talbot?"

He sniffled. "I have no knowledge of anyone of that name."

"And you yourself have never been to Burma?"

He did not answer the question. He didn't need to. His sour expression told me all I needed to know. It also answered the question about where Ivy had been.

"Oxford, then," I said, and the doctor winced. "Ivy had just arrived back in Willingdale after visiting Sally Gwinn, and what happened on that visit upset Ivy so much, she confronted you as soon as she was able."

Dr. Islington sucked in a quick breath. "You cannot know that."

"I do."

"Then whatever you think you know . . ." He slapped a hand against the stone parapet. "You've been lied to."

"You shoved Ivy there in your surgery."

"I never laid a hand on her."

"And Gerald came to see you after. It must have troubled him greatly to hear what happened and I doubt Ivy was the one who told him. After all, she would hardly confess her erratic behavior to a man whose opinion she valued above all others. That proves someone else saw what happened, because that someone reported it to Gerald. My question for you is, did he come to you to apologize? Or to beg for your help? For treatment? Ivy wasn't seen again in the village for another week."

"And what are you implying by that?"

I shrugged, and though I hoped it looked a casual gesture, it was, in fact, a bit of a stall. I was far out of my ken. "Perhaps you gave her something to calm her?" I thought about the blank pages in Ivy's diary, the lost week, and wondered if it had any connection to the circle Ivy drew around the doctor's picture. If he had given her something strong, too strong . . .

My blood ran cold, but I had not the time to dwell on it.

The doctor sniffed. "If I did, well, it really is none of your business, Miss Manville. There are many acceptable treatments for hysterical women."

"Hysterical women like Ivy. And her mother, too, I venture."

I cannot say how he closed in on me so quickly for I swear, I never saw the doctor move. I know only that the next moment, his face was just inches from mine, his breath hot against my cheek. "You'd better keep a rein on your tongue, young woman, or you will regret it."

When he took a step forward, I took a step back, closer to the parapet and the swirling water below. My throat dry and wedged with panic, I'm not at all sure how I managed it, but I laughed. "You could always declare me just another hysterical woman."

"Indeed." His eyes narrowed, his hands bunched into fists, he took another step toward me and I had no choice but to fall back yet again.

Even in full retreat, I pretended at a spot of courage. "All the rancor between you and Ivy makes me wonder how you could talk to her again so casually." My back knocked against the bridge parapet and I let go a small gasp of surprise. But even then, I was not done. "You met her. On this very bridge."

He froze.

"That . . ." His breaths came in deep gasps. "That is not true. Yes, I attended Ivy a number of weeks back. She was unwell for some days. But after that, I never saw her again."

"Not here? On the night of the strawberry moon?"

I did not say it—I could not with such flimsy proof—but the doctor knew exactly what was implied. He reared back, raised his hands, and in the one moment I had to think, I was sure he was going to take hold of me.

Panic bunched my stomach. My blood surged through my veins, the sound of it furious enough to drown out even the rush of the water so dangerous and so nearby.

I scrambled to get hold of my chatelaine and the pistol inside it so that, if nothing else, I might intimidate the doctor, but before I could, the doctor pulled in a long, quivering breath. His eyes wide, he looked down at his own hands, and perhaps he realized the enormity of what might have happened. He backed away.

I was not fooled by his withdrawal. Nor was I intimidated by the fire that flashed in his eyes. I reached into my chatelaine for my pistol, but before I had a chance to draw it, a voice called from the nearby shore.

"I say! Is that you, Miss Manville? Dr. Islington? What's happening there?"

Both of us gasping for breath, Dr. Islington and I turned to find Simon hurrying our way.

Dr. Islington stepped farther from me.

"Poor Miss Manville was careless and nearly toppled into the pond," the doctor said, and though I knew that much was technically true, I gave him no credit for reporting the facts without including the cause of my near-tumble. "When I came to her aid, I'm afraid she misunderstood my intentions. She thought I was attacking her!"

At this mockery, my shoulders shot back. I had not realized my hat was gone and my hair was disarranged, and I scooped a curl of it away from my face.

"I say, Miss Manville, you are quite spirited," the doctor said. "No doubt you would have been game enough to strike a blow to defend yourself."

"No doubt." I grumbled the words and shot a look at Islington that I hoped sent the message I meant it to. He might fool the vicar with his rubbish of a tale, but I knew what had just happened, and it was not some chivalrous attempt to save me. I'd struck a chord with talk of Sally Gwinn, and the doctor's reaction spoke volumes about motive and motivation.

When he closed in on us, Simon's black jacket flapped around him. "Do either of you need my assistance?"

"No. No." Dr. Islington waved him off, righted his hat (which had been knocked askew in our melee) and walked away. "I'll be fine. I assure you of that." He shot a look in my direction. "Oh yes, I will be fine."

When he turned from the doctor to me, the vicar's long, thin face accordioned with concern. "And you, Miss Manville?"

"Does he always lie so?"

Simon turned to look where I was looking but by now, Islington had rounded a corner and was gone. "Was he lying? He is one of your suspects, isn't he? And if that is the case, I have no doubt he was lying about—"

"Ivy. He claims they never had words. Did you hear the story?"

The tips of Simon's ears turned red. "The inclination to gossip is not one of the character traits the Lord admires."

I leaned against the parapet and watched as my straw hat (new this summer and rather handsome) swirled in the water below, dipped, and was dragged under.

"It is not gossip," I told Simon, "if it is the truth."

He came to stand at my side. "They fought. It is one of the reasons I have always wondered if the doctor was involved . . . that is, if the doctor might have been responsible . . . I mean, if the doctor could have—"

"Murdered Ivy?"

He was relieved he didn't have to speak the damning words himself.

"And then what happened, after their row?"

He took his lower lip between his teeth. "Gerald asked the doctor to treat Ivy and . . . well, there are those who say the doctor may have administered that treatment with a rather heavy hand."

"Was he trying to kill her?"

Simon blanched. "I wish I knew."

"Ivy learned something when she visited Oxford," I told him. "And whatever it was, it was something that made the doctor want to silence her."

"Oxford." He considered. "How odd. I do believe that is where Sally Gwinn now lives."

I knew now that I could trust the vicar with a bit more of the puzzle. He was with Ivy when the slate crashed down from the church roof, after all, and he sought to find out the truth, just as I did. More importantly—so much more importantly—he loved Ivy. Thanks to the way he reacted to her marriage to Gerald, she might have suspected him, but I was happy to say, thanks to a casual mention I'd made to the stationmaster when I arrived in the village and his assurance that yes, Simon had been with an ill man the night Ivy died, I no longer did.

"That is exactly where Ivy went," I told Simon. "To see Sally."

His eyebrows rose. "Curious."

"Who is she?" I asked.

"Sally was Ivy's governess. Years ago, of course. She lived there at the house with the Armstrong family and when Ivy's mother was taken ill, I do believe she helped care for her."

Curious, indeed.

"It's all beginning to make sense," I told the vicar, though I could not yet say where the information I'd gleaned was leading. "Sally must have told Ivy something about the doctor, and whatever it was, it upset Ivy. My finding out about her visit to Sally certainly made him angry. He has quite a temper."

"And you think he killed Ivy because of whatever Sally told her?"

"I cannot say, and what I think hardly matters. What I *know* might. Only I'm afraid I don't know much. Not for certain."

"Perhaps this will help." He reached into his coat pocket and drew out an envelope. The way he clutched it, I could see little more than the penny lilac with the picture of our monarch stuck in one corner.

"What is it?"

"Another piece of the mystery, I suspect," he said. "It is odd enough that Ivy traveled to Oxford to see Sally Gwinn, but then this! It came in this morning's post." He turned the envelope to allow me a better look and I saw that it was addressed to Ivy.

"And to the vicarage!" Astonishment rang through my voice.

"That is what I cannot fathom," he admitted. "Why would anyone be writing to Ivy but sending the letter to the vicarage?"

"Who is the sender?" I asked.

"I haven't opened it. I didn't think I should. I was just on my way to give the letter to Gerald. He is, I think you would agree, now the proper owner of it."

"And yet . . ." I considered the letter in the vicar's hand. "There must be some reason the writer thought to find Ivy at the vicarage."

His eyes lit with something like hope. "Another bit of mystery!"

"And only one way to find out more about it."

For a man of the cloth, he caught on quickly to my less-than-honest proposition. I knew from the set of his chin that his resolve was firm, but when he handed me the letter, his hands shook.

I had no such compunctions. I slipped a finger along the envelope flap and drew out the single sheet of paper inside. My heart thumped and my voice caught.

"It is from Edinburgh," I said.

This, of course, meant nothing to the vicar. But then, he did not know about Captain Jack Trembath or Reginald Talbot or of the other obituaries so cleverly hidden inside Ivy's diary. He could not possibly know one of them belonged to a certain Mr. Dunstable Corvey of Edinburgh who had died just three years previously in the wilds of Africa.

I scanned the lines written on the page. "It says here that Mr. Dunstable Corvey's wife died earlier this spring," I told the vicar. "The person who has written this letter is a cousin, tasked with distributing Mrs. Corvey's estate and her belongings."

"That hardly makes any sense," the vicar announced. "Why would this stranger from Edinburgh not only write to Ivy in care of the vicarage, but actually think she might care about the wife of a man who died in Africa?"

"But you see here, it does make sense." I read aloud: "'I am sorry I cannot help you further with your inquiry.' Don't you see, vicar, Ivy is the one who initiated the correspondence. She wrote to his wife to inquire about Dunstable Corvey and she gave the address for the woman's reply as the vicarage. She did not want her husband to know about the letter."

Chapter 16

I now had more than just one mystery on my hands—the row between Ivy and the doctor, why Ivy wanted to keep her communique with the widow in Edinburgh a secret and so gave her address as that of the vicarage, and what she might have learned from her former governess, Sally.

I did not include the attack on my person by the doctor in this list because in my mind, there was no mystery there. Whatever had happened between him and Ivy (and could I believe Betty as to all that had unfolded?), the doctor was more than reluctant to talk about it, and his temper got the better of him, and nearly of me. Would he have flung me over the bridge parapet and into the millpond? As much as I liked to think not, I could not forget the look on his face as he closed in on me there on the bridge. There was surely mayhem in his eyes and I fear, in his heart, and it made me wonder, could he be the one who had followed me on my return from my first visit to Willingdale? Or the person who pushed me in front of the hay wagon? Why?

Unfortunately, I had little opportunity to think further about any of this. The fine and glorious morning on which I had visited Willingdale, confronted Dr. Islington, and received the curious letter from Simon had dissolved into a gray and dismal afternoon. By the time I got back to London, rain battered down. And I, without a hat or umbrella! No doubt Sephora would deplore my sartorial bumbling.

I arrived in St. John's Wood soaked to the skin and chilled to the very bone, and in spite of a long, hot bath, Bunty's fussing over me, and a bowl of her very good chicken broth, by nightfall I found myself confined to my bed, sneezing one minute and falling into a deep and troubled sleep the next.

Rather than being gone the next morning, my illness was worse. The next few days passed in a blur as Bunty ladled tea into me and, at some point during that time, I remember Sephora popping in. She had the newest issue of *A Woman's Place* in her hands and she seemed especially excited, but I couldn't concentrate, much less make myself care. Even while she chattered, my eyes drifted shut, my body demanded rest.

I burrowed into the blankets and reminded myself the world would not notice my absence for but two or three days. After all, what could possibly happen in so short a time?

Sephora

July 23

Gather your wits, woman, and look for him!

Miss Hermione's advice to Heartsick Miss in the latest edition of *A Woman's Place* rang through my head, infusing me with all the zeal of a medieval crusader, propelling me forward as, head high and shoulders back, I marched through Hyde Park.

Start where last you saw him and work backward.

Encouraged by her words, by the very fact that the wisest and most illustrious woman in all of England (aside from Her Majesty, of course) had taken the time from her important and interesting life to try and help me escape the frightful gloom that enveloped me, I closed in on the very bench where only two weeks before (it seemed a lifetime), Franklin had all but declared his love for me.

I prayed he would be there.

Alas, the bench was empty, and seeing it, my swagger liquified, my bottom lip trembled.

"Oh, Franklin!" I moaned, and sank onto the bench, setting a loving hand on the spot Franklin had once occupied. "What has become of you?"

Remember every little thing he told you about his business and his acquaintances.

"Yes," I told myself, fighting to be as resolute as a heroine in a novel. "Yes, I know, Miss Hermione, I know you are right. I must think. I must concentrate."

To that end, I set my hands on my knees, palms up, and closed my eyes. It appeared a rum way of getting to the heart of the matter, yet I had seen Violet sit just so many times, lost in her thoughts, quiet and focused. To me, it seemed a sure way to bring on sleep, but when Violet finished with this silly ritual, she was energized, and always had something to say. About something.

Like it or not, I told myself, this must be the way to have thoughts, and thus convinced, I pulled in a breath and let it out slowly.

Just as I'd seen Violet do. I calmed myself. Focused my desires. Concentrated on the questions Miss Hermione advised me to ask.

What had Franklin told me about himself? He'd talked of his mother, of course.

Even in my state of supposed serenity, I felt my lips thin.

He'd spoken of his mother's advancing years, his mother's delicate constitution, his mother's devotion to her only son and his to her.

My lips pressed even more and I popped one eye open and grumbled. In doing so, I frightened a young nanny wheeling a baby in a pram nearby who quickened her steps and eyed me with what was certainly dread. I fear I could hardly blame her. In the time since I'd last seen Franklin, I had barely eaten and hardly slept. When I had looked at myself in the mirror that morning, I was dismayed. There were gray smudges beneath my eyes. My hair had lost its shimmer. The rose-colored blush had fled my cheeks.

I had best find Franklin—and soon—or he would barely recognize me once I finally did.

To that end, I tried again to concentrate.

Club.

The word tickled at the edges of my consciousness, and something that felt nearly like hope rose in me. I thought harder.

Club.

What did it mean?

The answer zipped through me like a flash of lightning, and I sprang from the bench.

Yes. Franklin had once mentioned going to his club. A place in . . . I forced my mind back to the conversation . . .

It was somewhere in clubland, surely, but was it Piccadilly? Or St. James's Street? Pall Mall?

I screeched my frustration and cursed myself for not having paid more attention. Yet how could I? When I was with

Franklin, all thoughts flew from my head. All I could do was stare into his warm and loving eyes. All I could imagine was what our future lives would be. Together.

A tear slipped down my cheek and I dashed it away with one finger. There were three fellows coming my way down the path that led from the copse where Franklin had disappeared as he raced like a knight in shining armor after the ruffian who stole my purse. Rough fellows, by the looks of their soiled clothes and the sounds of their raised and raucous voices. I could hardly let them encounter a lady who was not at her best.

I turned slightly so as to hide any trace of my misery and glanced their way only as they proceeded by, and that is when my breath caught and my heart pounded.

One of them was a brawny lad with bushy eyebrows, thick fingers, a shock of dark hair that looked as if it had seen neither comb nor shears in a year's time.

The brute who attacked Franklin!

Miss Hermione had given me no advice on what to do in an instance such as this, and I admit, my head spun. There was no constable nearby. There was no man in the vicinity who might assist me. What was a proper lady to do?

With a good deal of trepidation but without a moment's hesitation, I started off after them.

I followed the fiend and his companions out of the park and watched them loiter across the road until an omnibus rumbled in our direction. One of the men broke off from his companions and walked away. The other two (including the one who attacked Franklin) reached into their pockets and pulled out their pennies.

I could not let this monster disappear so easily! I, too, took my fare from my purse, and when the bus arrived, I let the two men board first (no gentleman would ever have allowed this and that only confirmed my thoughts as to their low character) and watched them climb the curved staircase to the open second deck. Rather than appear too obvious, I took a seat on the first level. There, between a clergyman and a woman whose arms were filled with parcels, I kept a careful eye on the stairway, watching and waiting for the men to disembark.

I could not let Franklin's assailant escape.

The bus jolted forward and the corner of a package in the lady's arms poked my cheek. I squeezed closer to the clergyman. The woman spread herself more comfortably and I was jabbed by what was most likely the beak of a goose, all wrapped in brown paper.

I cannot say how many times we jerked forward and slammed to stop after stop as we made our way further into the heart of the great city. I only knew that after ten minutes, I no longer recognized the streets the bus traversed. Another ten minutes and I was totally and completely lost.

My resolve, though, was firmer than ever. Franklin would have been proud!

The clergyman had just nodded off and his head landed on my shoulder when I heard a scramble on the stairs and a voice call to the driver to stop. The two men hurtled from the bus.

I lost no time in following them, unconcerned when the clergyman's head snapped up, his breath caught, and his eyes popped open. It was just as well I moved as quickly as I did, for just as my feet touched pavement I saw the two men round a corner and disappear into a narrow passageway between two buildings. I can hardly be faulted for hesitating while I peered into the gloom. I was jolted from my paralysis of fear only by the thought of Franklin's eyes, his gentle touch, the glowing examples of his heroism.

I swallowed my trepidations and stepped into the alleyway, wondering as I did if Franklin's dear mother would have done as much for him.

Thus fueled by righteousness and love, I followed a path that twisted and turned, a dank corridor closed in on each side by moss-covered walls. When I finally saw daylight again, I breathed a sigh of relief.

That is, until I stepped out and into another world.

Here, the sky was thick with choking smoke and the gutters ran ankle-deep with muck. The buildings themselves, battered and beaten, looked to have given up all hope, leaning against one another as if that alone kept them from toppling. Children with dirty faces and tattered clothing scrambled around me and one of the urchins had the brass to pull at my skirts with his filthy hands and ask for a penny. I ignored all of it, my gaze on a ramshackle building with a crooked door and a faded sign above it that declared it the Hound and Horse. I was just in time to see the ruffian and his companion go inside.

As a woman alone, I could not follow, and I glanced around for a place where I might wait and watch the pub door.

Across the way was a lodging house. The woman who stood on the front stoop, her hair hanging down and her dress pulled down so as to reveal one shoulder, did not look to me like a reputable landlady. Behind me was a laundry where dirty water cascaded from the back courtyard and into the street. A man with a monkey on his arm paraded by and a crowd of children even dirtier than the others I'd seen followed him and cheered.

"Hey! Watch where yer going!" A woman holding a basket of rotted fruit bumped me aside. "Takin' up the way. Standin' there gawkin'."

There was another woman walking beside her and she let out a laugh. "Swells ain't got no sense comin' here. Unless you're not lost, darlin'." She poked her chin in the direction of the woman across the way. "I hear Meg's always lookin' for fresh girls, and a sweet one like you ought to bring a pretty penny!" Cackling, they continued on their way.

Panic climbed my throat. So fearless and determined such a short time before, I felt my knees tremble and my insides bunch. I did not belong there.

Desperate to find my way back to the safety and cleanliness of St. John's Wood, I searched for the passageway that had disgorged me into this nightmare scenario. But there was so much noise from people calling back and forth, and horses nickering, and carts rumbling, it made my head spin. I whirled and ran smack into a drunkard singing a song about a mermaid and I jumped back and brushed at my clothing as if that alone could wipe the memory of this horrible place from my mind.

My eyes clouded with tears, I continued on and raced into the first passageway I found.

It was a dead end. And there was a dead rat in it.

One hand covering my nose to tamp the stench, I went back the way I came. Or at least I meant to. Somehow, I followed a wrong path and turned in a wrong direction. Instead of the street, I found myself at another intersecting passageway, this one darker and more foul-smelling than the first.

"No, no, no!" I did not know if I was trying to convince myself not to lose heart or if I needed the reminder that the situation in which I found myself was not possible. I was a woman of some status, after all. A woman of some small fortune. I did not belong here. But I didn't know how to get out.

No sooner had the thought occurred than a bottle rattled against the pavement. A loud eructation followed. Three feet from me, something moved in the deeper shadows of a doorway and a man stepped into my path. He was a large, bald fellow and he had a patch over one eye. He looked me over, grunted as if he could not believe his single good eye, and grinned.

The man spat on the ground. "Well, ain't this my luckiest of days."

I stepped back.

He lurched forward.

"Yer lost, I'd wager. Don't you worry. Ol' Bob, he'll help you." Moving faster than a man of his size should have been able, he closed the distance between us and before I could protest or move, he wound his arm through mine. He smelled of whisky and fish and stale tobacco. "Let me guess, my little lady, you come here on a mission to save our souls. Am I right? I can always tell the likes of yer type. But now, here you are and you've gotten yourself all turned around." He patted my head.

I recoiled.

Bob tightened his hold on my arm.

I wanted to scream, but my mouth was dry, my throat filled with sand. I considered pushing him away and making a run for it, but he was a large man, and my knees were weak. And I was a lady, after all. The word had never before made me feel so defenseless.

I trembled.

Bob laughed.

He gave me a tug that nearly pulled me from my feet. "Ol' Bob will take you home with him. That's what he'll do. Oh yes, my fine young lady, you and Ol' Bob, we'll share a drink, get to know each other and then—"

"I really don't think so, Bob."

Where the other voice came from, I couldn't say. How it penetrated the terror inside me and robbed me of my breath, I do not know. I only know that on hearing it, Ol' Bob went rigid.

"Ain't none of your business what's happening here," Bob growled.

"I think it most probably is." A second man stepped from the shadows and into an anemic shaft of sunlight that cut between the buildings that hemmed us in.

He was clean-shaven, his cheeks sprinkled with freckles the same cinnamon color as his hair. He had a narrow chin, a long nose, and a truncheon in one hand.

Another ruffian!

I sucked in a breath of horror.

At least until the details of his clothing registered: dark jacket with brass buttons down the center of it.

A custodian helmet with a badge at the front.

A constable!

"Off with you, Bob!" When the constable raised his club, Bob released his hold on me and ran.

I swayed and would surely have crumpled onto the filthy pavement if the constable did not rush forward and catch me in his arms.

"There you go, miss, not to worry." He steadied an arm around my shoulders and held me tight to his side, smelling of soap and safety, and I breathed in the blessed scent and reveled in his nearness.

"Constable James Barnstable, at your service, miss. There you go." He set me back on my feet slowly so as to be sure

I wouldn't collapse, and leaned down to bestow a look of concern upon me. "It's all over now. Bob's gone. Tell me what happened and how you ended up in a place like this."

What was a proper lady to do?

There was only one option, and I did it without hesitation.

I burst into tears.

Chapter 17

Violet

July 24

"I had thought you would be excited."

I received no response to my observation, just as I'd received little or no response to the other comments I'd made throughout our journey that morning. Or for that matter, to little I'd said in the past twenty-four hours.

Though I hated to miss a moment of the scenery outside the carriage that had been sent to collect us from the Willingdale station—a view of the green, a glimpse of the Armstrong house, a hedgerow thick with hazel and hawthorn—I turned from the view, the better to give my sister a frown of displeasure.

"It's not every day we are asked to spend Friday to Monday with the likes of Lady B. I thought you would find pleasure in it, Sephora, otherwise I would never have accepted the invitation."

This, apparently, touched a chord, as Sephora deigned to grunt.

"You hardly care what I want," she grumbled. "You are here for your own purposes."

"Socializing with the fashionable set?" Honestly, I had to

laugh. The fact that I had packed but one trunk of clothing for our stay while Sephora had brought three spoke for itself. "You know I hardly care. You are the one concerned with what is all the rage in Paris, what Society is gossiping about, and how to look your best so as best to snag a husband. Lady B's guests will provide you the perfect opportunity to mix and mingle. Honestly, Sephora, I truly thought this would please you."

Certainly for the first time that morning, and possibly for the first time in the days since I'd been out of my bed and recuperated from my illness, Sephora turned her gaze on me. Her eyes were as blue as the sky. And as cold as ice. "I am not a complete idiot, Violet," she snarled. "Even though you like to think so."

"I never—"

"Never so much as called me a pudden-head to my face? Or never mentioned the fact that you have your own reasons for being here? You must. It's the only thing that explains why you would accept Lady B's invitation. Hunting parties? Dancing? Formal dinners and lively card games? Socializing is anathema to you. Therefore you must have another order of business, though for the life of me, I cannot imagine what it is. It certainly can't have anything to do with having fun. You don't know the meaning of the word."

The fact that this assertion might actually be true didn't keep me from bristling. "That's not what we're talking about. I accepted this invitation for you, Sephora, even though I'm just days out of my sickbed. You've had the mopes, and don't tell me it isn't true. I needed to get you out of London and get the cobwebs shaken from your head."

I did not mention that her barb had, in fact, hit a bit too close to the truth. Spending a few days as Lady B's guest would allow me the opportunity to continue my inquiries. If

I did not understand fun, Sephora certainly did not understand investigating, or my commitment to finding the truth, and justice for Ivy Armstrong.

"We might start setting things right," I told her, "with you explaining why a constable accompanied you home yesterday evening."

Her lips pressed together, she smoothed a hand over the skirt of her green-and-blue-plaid traveling dress. "I told you," she said, "I was out. Walking. I went a bit too far from home and got turned around. That kindly constable—"

"James Barnstable."

"Yes, he offered to show me the way. I told him I hardly needed the help." She tossed her head in a way that told me she had, indeed, needed all the help she could get. "But he insisted. Which was rather nice of him, don't you think?"

I thought back to meeting the young constable with his scrubbed face, his coppery hair, the air of concern he had when he handed Sephora over to me at our door. "He's a nice-looking and courteous young man," I observed.

"Nice-looking?" Sephora sighed. "I cannot think it's possible for a man of that class to truly be nice-looking. I mean, not in the way a gentleman is. I will allow he was polite and gallant. But then, we should expect no less from a public servant, should we?"

I refused to be drawn into a political conversation and instead, focused on the more relevant topic—at least for the moment.

"Perhaps the fact that you refuse to acknowledge the constable as pleasant to look upon has something to do with you comparing him to William Shakespeare."

The blank look she gave me only served to set my teeth on edge. I gritted them around a smile. "The man who sent you a message with his bouquet of flowers. I'm quite sure you remember him."

She did not rise to my bait. I did not expect her to. Whatever was bothering Sephora, she was very much keeping her own counsel about it, and that was uncommon. Sephora liked nothing better than drama. She loved to be the center of attention. The fact that she'd bottled up her feelings told me this was something serious, something that had hurt her deeply.

And that, of course, could only mean the flower sender.

Which did not explain the constable. Or the fact that Sephora's nose had been red and raw when she returned home on his arm.

When the carriage slowed, I set the thought aside and watched two fellows in woolen jackets and heavy trousers step forward and swing open an ironwork gate. They touched their hands to the brims of their caps when we drove through and on toward Bellington House, Lady B's estate. I leaned out the window for a look at a winding drive, a rose garden, a glass conservatory that flashed a greeting in the morning light.

"There is money to be made in newspapers, to be sure," I mumbled.

The way Sephora wrinkled her nose told me she did not follow my train of thought.

"Sir Leonard Thorn, Lady B's late husband. He made his fortune in newspapers and was knighted by the queen for using that platform to voice his support for her government."

"Tradespeople?" Looking as if she'd just smelled something particularly foul, Sephora sat back. "I had no idea."

I couldn't help but laugh. "It isn't as if he was out on the streets peddling the newspapers himself. He was a man of great importance. And really, Sephora, you'd turn up your nose at those in the trades? A tea plantation is as much a trade as a newspaper."

She ignored this pertinent fact and said, "When I was Lady B's guest, I saw how impressive the house is." As if to reassure herself it still was, she leaned toward the window for a look. "Yet I hoped on our visit we might meet a higher class of people than simply tradesmen. Some of the peerage, perhaps."

I ignored her snobbery to focus, once again, on the magnificent sights. The carriage rattled around a corner and the house came into view. It was an ornate Gothic revival with two sprawling wings that spread out from a central structure topped by a clock tower, all of it built of honey-colored stone. The house had turrets, oriel windows, and dozens of chimneys sprouting from a red-and-black-tiled roof, and its magnificence said something about Lady B's standing in the community, and probably about her guest list.

"You may yet meet a younger son or two," I told Sephora.

For the first time in days, she actually brightened. "Do you think so?"

"I think it is time for us to find out."

No sooner had we stepped out of the carriage than the massive oak door at the front of the house swung open and Lady B herself swooped outside and past the line of waiting servants who had been at the ready to greet us.

"Ah, the Manville women!" She folded me into a hug, then moved on to Sephora. "I'm so glad you're here. Come. Come inside and get settled. We have luncheon in just an hour, then croquet before tea. Dinner this evening. You have brought formal wear?" She asked the question of both of us, but I had no doubt it was intended solely for me. I wondered who'd told her of my dislike of formal wear. Adelia would have made my aversion to the latest styles sound like a compliment. Sephora, on the other hand, would tell the tale and make me sound an aberration.

I had no time to consider it, for a second later, Lady B whisked us inside and we found ourselves in a two-story gallery dominated by a stairway and watched over by what I assumed were generations of Thorn family ancestors, their faces—serious and important-looking—appraising us from the paintings on the walls.

Lady B instructed a footman to take our trunks to our rooms, pointed Sephora in the direction of the parlor where she could get a glass of lemonade, and grabbed hold of my arm to pilot me into the drawing room with its high, arched ceiling, velvet-upholstered furniture, and marble fireplace that dominated one wall.

She closed the door behind us. "Well?" She danced from foot to foot with excitement. "What have you found out?"

Were my inquiries so transparent?

This was something Lady B apparently did not hold against me. "I saw you in the village the day Sephora followed you, remember, and I hear you've been back since." She gave me a cagey look. "Don't tell me you keep coming around to try and retrieve your watch. Others may believe that, but I thought otherwise. I wrote to Adelia and she was circumspect but hinted you are up to something. You are here inquiring about Ivy. Of course you are. I should have known it from the start. You are half again as bright as dear Adelia and I would wager you are twice as inquisitive, though, really, it would take some doing, indeed, to be twice as inquisitive as Adelia."

Because I knew she meant this as a compliment, I laughed when Lady B did.

"I have not learned much," I admitted. "I did talk to the vicar."

"Yes, yes. Everyone knows all about that." She took my hand and led me to a circular settee near the fireplace and we sat side by side. "I assume you learned how he felt about Ivy. The poor man. I'm sure it still stings him to think Gerald stepped in and stole Ivy's affections."

"He had every reason to be jealous."

"I would think so," Lady B conceded. "But then, few men in these parts can hold a candle to Gerald. He is a handsome devil, accomplished, charming."

"Could he have killed Ivy?"

"Gerald?" She jiggled her shoulders to get rid of the very notion. "I would think you would be done looking for suspects after what happened between you and Dr. Islington on the bridge."

It was all the reminder I needed to step carefully through my investigation. Villages are hotbeds of gossip; my comings and goings were being noticed.

"The doctor claims not to have fought with Ivy when she returned from Oxford."

Lady B sat up. "Is that where she'd gone? She never said."

"But she told you she and the doctor had words?"

Lady B rose and went to the window that looked out over the gardens and, drawn by the sunshine that flickered outside, I followed. Before us was a sea of roses in every color of the rainbow, stone paths leading through them and to a fountain that sent up a spurt of water that sparkled every bit as brilliantly as the sun against the Ganges. Two golden-haired men strolled there. One wore a red cravat. The other, slightly shorter and rounder, had a lopsided gait.

"Cousins," Lady B explained. "Hackett is in coal, Dawes in shipping. Millions between them. And both unmarried."

I bit my lip and ignored the unspoken inference.

"It was Ivy we were talking about," I said. After all, I was there to discuss murder, not the possibilities of romance.

"Ah yes, Ivy. And the doctor." She spun and leaned against the window frame. "She told me only that she and the doctor had words, though she would not say about what." Lady B paused, and I couldn't help but think she was waiting for me to prove I had the information that would allow me to take the next steps in my investigation.

"Ivy had just returned from Oxford, where she met with Sally Gwinn."

Lady B sucked in a breath. "Ah."

"You knew her?"

"Not well, of course. As she was once Ivy's governess, it makes perfect sense Ivy and Sally would stay in touch."

"But not so much sense that after Ivy met with Sally, she was incensed enough to come back home and confront the doctor."

"You've spoken to Sally?"

"I've written her and haven't heard back."

Lady B pushed away from the window and took a turn around the room. It was a large room and she walked slowly. I do believe she did not return to my side until she'd made up her mind about what she wanted to say.

"Sally Gwinn was a servant, after all, a governess, so I had little interaction with her and therefore cannot tell you much. I sometimes saw Sally come and go with Ivy and we exchanged pleasant words. And then one day, Sally simply disappeared."

"Are you saying—"

"I don't know what I'm saying," Lady B admitted. "I am

simply reporting the facts. One day, Sally was living at the Armstrong house and taking care of Ivy. The next day, she had vanished."

"And when you saw her no longer?"

"It was very soon after Ivy's mother met her sad end, and such a terrible and confusing time." She shrugged. "I once mentioned Sally's absence to Ivy, but she was just a child and knew nothing. Ivy left for Miss Simpson's Academy soon after. I talked to her father about Sally's disappearance from the village, of course, and he . . ." Lady B frowned. "The poor man was so shaken by his wife's suicide, I think he hardly noticed Sally wasn't there. But later, someone . . ." Here, she paused, thinking. "I'm sorry, I don't remember who. It's been a very long time. But someone told me they'd seen Sally Gwinn at the railroad station late one night. Dr. Islington was seeing her off."

"To Oxford?"

"This is the first I've heard as to where she might have gone."

"Sally wrote to Ivy and her letter must have contained something tantalizing. That's why Ivy went to see her. And what she learned in Oxford upset her. As to exactly what that was, I suppose only the doctor would know."

"You'll have a chance to ask him." She patted my arm and smiled because, of course, she thought (quite wrongly) that I did not have the courage to do it. "Islington will be here this weekend. I hope you don't mind. He's a neighbor and I could hardly—"

"It's fine," I assured her. "I would like a word with him."

Her cheeks paled. "Not about . . ."

"You said it yourself, he is the only one who would know. Unless Ivy confided in Gerald."

"Well, he's still in mourning, of course, and he won't be here."

"Perhaps I should pay him a call."

"You really are too cheeky." The way Lady B smiled told me she did not hold this against me, but she had no opportunity to comment further. A servant knocked and told her Edith Cowles had arrived, and Lady B swept toward the door.

"One more thing," I said before she walked out. "A man named Reginald Talbot. He was a doctor. Have you heard of him?"

Thinking, she tipped her head. "Talbot? I don't believe so. He is certainly not from Willingdale."

With that, Lady B departed and I was left wondering why a visit with her governess had upset Ivy and caused trouble with Dr. Islington, and how a stranger named Talbot who had died in the far-off Indian Ocean figured into the story.

❧

By the time I arrived in the dining room for luncheon—cold joints of beef, fruit, bread, cheese, and biscuits—Sephora had already changed her clothing. As miserable as she had been in London, as ornery as she'd been on our journey to Essex, she was as sprightly there amongst Lady B's dozen guests as she was beautiful in a gown of shimmering pink silk. Just as I went to the buffet, her sweet, ladylike giggle filled the room.

Perhaps my strategy had worked after all, and I congratulated myself. Perhaps all that was needed to chase away Sephora's long face was a chance to display her formidable (if shallow) social skills.

I'd barely had a chance to sit down at the table to consider this when I caught Dr. Islington's eye from across the room.

The doctor, it should be noted, turned away, and sat as far from me as was possible.

At that very moment, a man wearing a red cravat slipped into the seat next to mine.

"Miss Manville." He tipped his golden head by way of greeting.

Hackett or Dawes? Coal or shipping?

Whichever cousin this was, he was a man of forty or so, with something of an overbite and one eye that strayed while the other stayed focused on me.

"I am Walter Hackett," he said, "and I wonder if I might have a moment of your time."

Since he had already set down his plate and settled himself, asking my permission seemed a moot point.

I stabbed a strawberry with the tip of my fork. Coal it was. "What can I do for you, Mr. Hackett?"

His gaze darted across the room to where my sister was speaking with his cousin.

Dawes. Shipping.

"It is your sister, Miss Manville." Hackett's voice called me back from my musings. His good eye strayed to watch my sister take a seat at the table. She wasn't carrying a plate. No doubt she had commandeered Dawes to fetch her food.

Hackett sighed.

"Ah, I take it you've met Sephora."

"Only briefly. And I wondered . . ." He cleared his throat. "I wondered if I might ask your permission to play croquet with Miss Sephora after luncheon. I realize she is young and it is only right I make sure you have no objection, as you are her older sister and from what I have heard, a spinster."

I wondered what my marital status—or lack of it—had to do with Sephora and croquet and why Mr. Hackett thought himself obliged to mention it, but rather than point this out, I set my fork on my plate. "Of course you may, Mr. Hackett. As long as Sephora is agreeable." I did not add that I wished him luck. Sephora would think him too old. Sephora would find that red cravat of his too bold. Sephora would never tolerate the wandering eye.

He as yet knew none of this, so he smiled with all the ingenuousness of a child gazing into the window of a toy shop. "She is quite beautiful."

"And frightfully—"

Shame on me, but I was going to say *boring* simply as a way of warning Hackett he best be prepared to discuss nothing more than the latest hairstyles, the newest fabrics, the most popular colors. I never had a chance. Lady B strolled into the room, a glass of champagne in one hand. Her other arm was held on to by a man with cocoa-colored hair that looked to have been blown by the summer breeze into a halo of curls around his head and, damn me for a fool, but suddenly, absurdly, I found it impossible to think clearly.

The man was tall and his eyes were as green as oak leaves in summer. He had a stubborn chin and a way of sauntering rather than walking. Too sure of himself. Too confident by far. I should have known better than to be intrigued. And yet I could not help myself.

Unlike the other men who'd gathered for the meal, he wasn't dressed in tweeds, but in a dark coat and trousers, and he wore a gray vest over a white shirt. There was a gold chain hanging from his watch pocket, polished ebony cuff links at his wrists. Expressionless, he scanned the room, deposited Lady B in a chair at the head of the table, nodded politely to my sister when their paths crossed, and went to fill a plate.

"Did you read it?"

I had been so busy staring at the man (it is a terrible thing to have to admit to, but the truth nonetheless), I had not noticed Lady B had a copy of *A Woman's Place* tucked under her arm. Now, she pulled it out and waved it around and instantly, all attention focused on her. "Not the latest from Miss Hermione, but the edition before that. One of her best letters, to be sure."

"The one to Bewildered Suitor?" Edith was wearing a mossy green dress that did little to complement her sallow complexion. She wrinkled her nose. "Imagine being bold enough to say something so impertinent to a gentleman. That he should look elsewhere for a mate! Outrageous!"

Lady B laughed. "That is the whole point, Edith. Her brass is the very reason I read Miss Hermione's words of wisdom."

"It is why we all do," another woman commented. "The woman is bold, that's for certain. But admit it, Edith, she often says what we only have the nerve to think."

When Edith pursed her lips, her face folded in on itself. "What she says is not always practical."

"Like the letter from the woman who is searching for her beau?" This came from Mr. Dawes, now seated next to my sister, and at the same time I congratulated myself for expanding my readership and drawing even men to Miss Hermione's column, I watched my sister tense and stare down at her plate of meat and cheese. I wondered at this change in her demeanor. Was it the topic that disturbed her? Or was it Mr. Dawes she didn't like?

"The way I remember it, Miss Hermione suggested the young woman go out and search for the fellow." This comment came from the man who'd walked in with Lady B. An American by the sound of him. With a voice as smooth as aged whisky and as smoky as peat.

I scolded myself for noticing. After all, I had my investigation to think about, and that was certainly far more important than this stranger who drew my attention like lodestone to iron.

His plate in his hands, he stepped from the buffet to the table. Even if he had not been talking, he would have commanded the company's attention. He had good bearing, an assured stance. He set his plate down to my left.

"In this case, I think Miss Hermione's advice was irresponsible," he said, slipping into the seat next to mine. "Sending any woman out on such a mission smacks of—"

"Sensibility?" I suggested.

"Irresponsibility," he grumbled, and turned my way. "What if the woman was to get hurt?"

"What if she was to learn to use the brains God gave her and the resources at her disposal to accomplish her mission?" I countered.

He lifted his chin. "Impossible."

"If we keep telling the women of the world it is."

"And dangerous."

"The world is a dangerous place."

"Which is why we . . ." He glanced around the table and naturally, the men gathered there nodded to show their support. "The men of the world must protect the women in it."

"Chivalrous," I snarled.

"The natural order of things," he countered.

"If we still lived in caves," I pointed out.

"Or have yet to learn that each of us—men and women—have their own place in the world and that those places do not overlap."

I'd lost my appetite, and I tossed my serviette on my plate. "Perhaps where you come from . . ."

"Ah, you noticed Mr. Marsh is a visitor in our country." Lady B popped out of her chair. It was just as well. I had little left to say to the insufferable Mr. Marsh. At least in public.

Lady B waved a hand toward our end of the table. "None of you has yet to meet our American guest. This is Eli Marsh. From Boston."

"New York City," he corrected her. Apparently, he had something to say about everything. "Pleased to make your acquaintances. And thank you, Lady B, for including me in your gathering. I'm eager to get to know you better." He slid me a look. "All of you."

I bit my tongue and pushed back my chair.

"Leaving so soon?" I wasn't fooled by Eli's smile, and his looks no longer moved me . . . much. He'd be just as relieved to see the last of me as I was to put a good deal of distance between us.

"I feel the need for air," I told no one in particular. "If you'll all excuse me."

It was, after all, what country visits were all about. Comings and goings and garden walks, the chance to breathe fresh air and get the kind of exercise difficult to come by in the city. No one batted an eye. I wasn't even at the door when those gathered fell back into easy conversation.

All except Eli Marsh. But then, he was too busy watching my every move.

I could have ignored the prickling feeling of his gaze boring between my shoulder blades. I should have. But oh, how I hate to back down from a challenge, even one so small as this.

At the door, I paused, turned, and gave him a most intimidating scowl.

Eli Marsh simply smiled.

Damn the man!

Chapter 18

Dinner would not be served until eight. Since I was not particularly enamored of croquet even on the best of days, that meant I had time aplenty to walk into Willingdale and continue my inquiries. I cannot say exactly what I hoped to accomplish in the village, but I knew a change of scenery was in order. I had barely arrived at Bellington House and already I needed to clear my head and, while I was at it, erase the memory of Eli Marsh's impudent yet dazzling smile.

It was a fine day and I retrieved my straw hat (newly purchased to replace the one lost in the millpond) from my room, set it upon my head, and told myself a brisk walk was just what I needed. Thus prepared, I let my mind wander.

Dr. Islington.
Edith Cowles.
Sally Gwinn.
Reginald Talbot.
Eli Marsh.

No!

About to step outside, I stopped and reminded myself I

had more important things to consider than the unsettling stranger who had piqued my curiosity, caused me to forfeit my usual aplomb, and boiled my blood while he was at it.

I would not allow it to happen again.

I drew in a breath.

Dr. Islington.
Edith Cowles.
Sally Gwinn.
Reginald Talbot.

The names twisted and turned through my head, and I was so absorbed in considering them, I nearly knocked into Mr. Dawes.

He was the same age as Hackett, though not nearly as tall. They had the same brassy hair, the same mannerisms, the same squat, rounded nose. At first glance, they might be taken for twins, but on closer inspection, I saw both of Mr. Dawes's eyes were in working order, and that he had an odd way of walking with a sort of two-step roll, as if he was at home aboard a ship. He smelled of peppermint humbugs.

"I do beg your pardon." He nodded by way of apology. "I am Conrad Dawes, of the Dawes family of Southampton. I wondered, Miss Manville, if I might speak to you." Either excited or nervous, he listed from one foot to the other. "It is about Miss Sephora."

"Her skill at croquet is quite appalling," I warned.

"But she is beautiful," he replied.

"Mr. Hackett will invite her to be his croquet partner before you do if you don't get back into the dining room," I told him, and when he scrambled inside, tilting this way and that, I took the opportunity to continue on my way.

It was a pleasant afternoon and I was in no hurry. When I came to the Armstrong house, I knocked at the front door, but there was no answer. Stymied but not discouraged, I walked on and though I did not consciously mean to end up there, I found myself at the bridge over the millpond.

As it turned out, I was not alone.

There was an overgrown buckthorn bush at the far end of the bridge and just as I arrived, a pair of brown tweed trousers emerged from it, back end first. There were boots at the ends of the trousers and legs inside them, of course, but even though I neared, I could not tell who they might belong to.

At least until the rest of the person backed out of the bush and onto the bridge. A jacket emerged and the individual belonging to all that clothing stood upright.

"Good afternoon, Mr. Armstrong," I called out.

Gerald held a long stick and as if it had suddenly caught fire, he dropped it. His shoulders shot back. His chin came up. His expression was stone.

"Miss Manville." His bow was perfunctory. "I didn't hear you arrive."

I was closer now, and I looked toward the greenery he'd been poking. "Have you lost something?"

"Oh. That." As if it might actually make the stick invisible, he kicked it aside and went to stand at the parapet, deflecting the conversation, or so he thought, as easily as he had the stick.

"I often come here," he said, his voice soft, the words nearly lost in the rush of the water. "It is where I asked Ivy to marry me."

I joined him and, like he did, looked down at the swirling water. "No doubt your visits are bittersweet."

He set his hands flat against the stone and leaned forward.

"She liked to stand here and watch the water. She told me it brought back happy memories. And now, I stop here, too, more often than I should perhaps. I cannot seem to stay away. There is a pull to the place, as if her voice . . ." His words broke behind a strangled sob. He turned his face away. "I know she is not here calling out to me and yet, there are times, especially after dark . . ."

He shook himself away from the thought. "I was here the other evening and lost a button." He glanced back to where he'd been rooting around. "I thought if I came in daylight, I might have better success in finding it."

"And did you?" I wondered.

He shrugged. "No luck. I will simply have my tailor find another to match. And you are here in Willingdale again . . . with Lady B's party?"

"Yes. She was kind enough to invite both my sister and myself."

"And is she . . . Has your sister come out with you this afternoon? I would like to meet her."

"Luncheon," I explained. "And a bevy of admirers who are hoping to catch Sephora's eye."

"Lady B is a fine hostess. I wish you and your sister a pleasant few days."

He moved to his left and would have gotten around me if I hadn't casually stepped into his path.

"I am sorry to intrude on your memories and your grief," I told him, "but as long as I have come upon you, I wonder if perhaps I might have a word. Have you perhaps found a pocket watch? I had it when I attended Ivy's funeral luncheon and—"

"Ah, the mysterious watch!" Was that surprise I saw flash across his face? Or relief? "Edith Cowles said something about it the other day when she came to call, but as I have been occupied with the buying of a piece of land, I'm afraid I paid little attention. Now that I know it is yours, I'll have it sent around to Lady B's."

"I am so grateful!" I pressed a hand to my heart, pretending relief, and lied because it seemed rather anticlimactic to admit I'd bought the watch at a bazaar in Hyderabad and it didn't keep accurate time far more often than it did. "Papa presented the watch to me on my sixteenth birthday. As we were traveling then, I will always remember the occasion. I understand you will be traveling soon, too. It was Canada, was it not?"

"Canada, yes, I have some business interests there, gold mines."

"I am sure you will find it an interesting place, beautiful and—"

He waved a hand back and forth, a dismissive motion. "Forgive me, I'm afraid I do not explain myself clearly. I did have a journey planned, but after what happened to Ivy, I could not possibly . . ." His expression folded in on itself and I was reminded of how he looked that first time I saw him in St. Christopher's churchyard, a man whose very being had been shattered by the loss of his wife.

"I am sorry to bring up painful memories," I said. "How disappointing it must be for you to have to stay here and not be able to set out on your own adventure, especially as you were acquainted with the Arctic explorer, Captain Jack Trembath."

Gerald's expression hardened, but when he turned to watch the water and a bare branch that floated by, his voice was as smooth as butter. "My goodness, Ivy did share our family affairs with you, didn't she? Even down to the smallest detail."

"It was no small matter to her. She was abashed to think her mentioning it caused you to be troubled."

"Troubled? By Ivy?" He threw back his head and laughed. "My dear wife could be curious, and she could even be mischievous, but trouble was one thing she never was."

I leaned against the sun-warmed stones of the parapet and pretended to have to search for the right words. "Not even when she rowed with Dr. Islington?"

"How did you know?" He shot a look over his shoulder at me. "She told you, didn't she? It seems you and Ivy exchanged a great deal of information. Well, if she told you she had a row with the doctor, she must surely also have told you what it was about."

"She told me she was indisposed for days after. So much so, she missed the summer fete."

He let go a long breath. "She was . . ." Gerald raised his hands, then dropped them to his sides. "Ivy was always a lively girl. Always bright. Always cheerful. It was one of the things I loved about her. Yet that day you speak of . . ." Though the sun shone down fully on us, Gerald shivered.

"When she arrived home that day, she was in a state of agitation the likes of which I'd never seen."

"And she told you why?"

He shook his head. "I could get nothing sensible from her. She ranted about the doctor. She raved about her mother. I had no choice but to bundle her off to bed and go to Dr. Islington to beg for his help. He did what he could. What he had to do. To calm her."

"He gave her laudanum." Try as I might, it was difficult

to keep the condemnation from my voice. Though tincture of opium was effective as a treatment for pain, I had, over the years, seen it abused. Husbands who thought their wives too boisterous. Parents who believed their children too disobedient. The stupor brought on by laudanum solved their problems at the same time it created living automatons, euphoric one minute, uneasy the next.

"Ivy was not seen in the village for some time after," I commented.

Gerald nodded. "It is difficult for a man to stand back and watch his beloved wife descend into such a state, so I allowed the doctor to do what he thought right. He dosed her every day. Sometimes more than once a day. Ivy retreated into herself, sleeping for hours at a time, quiet and withdrawn. Then but a while later, she would wander the house like a vengeful ghost. Tearing through things, uprooting old clothing from trunks and books from their shelves. Dr. Islington's only suggestion for controlling her was more laudanum. More and more laudanum."

"And while he was administering it, did he explain what brought on Ivy's fury in the first place?"

Gerald shook his head. "He said he feared . . ." He swallowed hard. "Her mother was mad, you know. And Dr. Islington thought . . ." He slapped a hand to the parapet. "I refused to believe it. I demanded that Islington stop the treatment."

"And after?"

"Even without the laudanum, Ivy was not herself, that is for certain. One morning I found her weeping uncontrollably in the garden. The very next day, she was out of the house before even the sun rose. On her way to London, she told me, though she would not say why or where she was going."

"Shopping, no doubt," I said, because it was what he expected to hear. Still, I could not help but think of Ivy's visit to see Marguerite Talbot. An idea tickled at my brain, but it was not something I could mention to Gerald. Not until I understood it better myself.

"And when she came back to Willingdale?" I asked him instead.

"She was moody, cheerless. She was either locked in her room or she roamed the village."

"And she met Dr. Islington here on the night she died."

Gerald's head came up. "Did she? Someone saw them?"

"Betty told me—"

"Ah, Betty."

"A reliable witness?"

He thought this over. "I should think so, though why she hasn't mentioned seeing Ivy and the doctor together to me, I cannot imagine. You don't think—" He slid me a look. "Miss Manville, you can't be suggesting—"

"Not at all," I assured him. "Though I am curious as to what Ivy and the doctor may have had to say to each other after the way she confronted him and how vigorously he treated her malady. Do you suppose it has anything to do with Ivy going to see Sally Gwinn?"

"Sally . . . ?"

His shrug spoke volumes.

"Ivy's former governess."

"Long before I came to Willingdale, of course. And this Sally, she told Ivy something that—"

"I have no idea what she told Ivy. I thought perhaps Ivy might have confided in you."

Gerald was wearing a sporting cap and he removed it from his head and pushed a hand through his hair. "I'm afraid there's little I can tell you regarding the matter. My only hope now is for peace for Ivy's soul."

"And that you find your button, of course."

For a moment, his expression was blank. That is, before it blossomed into a grin. Still smiling, Gerald sauntered away.

I, on the other hand, was not prepared to abandon the bridge so quickly. For a few minutes, I watched the water swirl below me, looking for all the world as if I had nothing better to do and little more important to think about.

At least until I made sure Gerald was long gone.

Then and only then did I dart to the buckthorn bush and slip inside. I was not looking for a button. Then again, I trusted Gerald wasn't, either.

After all, buckthorn shrubs have thorns—one of them jabbed the back of my neck and I felt a hot drop of blood trickle under my collar—and it is not worth dealing with thorns, not for the sake of a button. But for more valuable treasure . . .

A beam of sunlight snuck through the foliage and something nestled in the dirt where bridge met buckthorn sparkled and caught my eye. I bent to retrieve it, but did not need to brush off the dirt that coated it to know what it was. A brooch of diamonds and opals.

The piece of jewelry Ivy had worn on her wedding day, and according to Betty, something not borrowed but stolen.

Before I left the shelter of the buckthorn, I made sure there was no one around and, certain I was alone, I touched the brooch to my skirt to gently wipe the dirt away.

And that's when I saw it: a shred of green fabric caught up around the pin. Only one thing could possibly explain it.

The brooch hadn't been removed by its wearer, or simply come undone.

It had been ripped from Ivy's clothing.

❧

I saw no one on my way from the bridge to the village green, but when I arrived there, Betty and Gerald were standing near the Crimean War memorial, their heads together, their voices too soft for me to catch a word of what they said. Instead, flattened against the wall of the George and Dragon so I could see and not be seen, I simply watched.

Gerald inched closer to Betty.

Betty giggled.

Surely, they were not discussing housecleaning.

Gerald stepped back, tipped his cap, and went on his way.

Betty watched him go and when he was finally out of sight, she turned on her heels, as sprightly as a dancer, her face lit with a smile.

Putting aside Gerald's increasingly strange behavior for the moment, I stepped out of my hiding place just as she walked by. Not wanting her to know I'd seen . . . whatever I'd seen . . . between her and Gerald, I quickly pretended to adjust the laces at the front of my walking boots then stood in time to say, "Oh, Betty, hello! May I speak with you?"

She didn't bother to wipe the grin off her face. "Don't know what about. Oh." Just that quickly, her smile dissolved into acid. "Ivy. It's always Ivy you're talkin' about."

"You help at the Armstrong house."

Her top lip curled. "That don't mean nothin'."

"It means you were probably there when Ivy was treated by Dr. Islington recently. She was agitated. Mr. Armstrong told me she overturned trunks and books."

"And near destroyed his own dressing room." Betty made a noise from deep in her throat. "Imagine doin' a thing like that. Made an awful muckle, she did. I spent days cleaning up."

"Cleaning up what?" I asked.

Betty wrinkled her nose. "Cleaning up what she messed, of course," she said. "Clothing and personal things."

"Papers?" I asked.

"I suppose." She shrugged. "Can't see what difference it makes."

I, however, could. Perhaps Ivy hadn't merely been distraught. Perhaps she had been searching.

I thanked Betty and continued on toward Lady B's. I should have been proud of myself for finding another tiny piece of the puzzle and still, I could not shake the uneasiness from my shoulders.

After all, the mystery of Ivy's death had just taken an unexpected turn. And I?

I was more confused than ever.

Chapter 19

July 25

I was glad to run into Edith at the sideboard in the breakfast room the next morning. I had seen her the night before at dinner, but at dinner, there were too many people near us, too many ears. Now, I greeted her and invited her to join me at a small table near the latticed windows where the morning sunshine streamed in and sparkled against the silver.

She set her plate across from mine. It was heaped with potted fish, veal and ham pie, kippers, and cold game, and made my own plate (toast and a slice of cold ham) look rather anemic. Edith started in on her kippers as soon as she sat down. I sipped a cup of excellent coffee.

"I didn't have a chance last night," I said, "to thank you for talking to Gerald on my behalf."

Her full mouth did not allow her to comment. She didn't need to. Her blank stare said it all.

"About my watch," I reminded her. "He had it sent over yesterday evening. I'm so grateful."

She washed down her food with a large gulp of tea. "I told you he was a kind and considerate gentleman."

"And by talking to him about the watch on my behalf, you kept me from visiting to ask about the watch myself."

She took the comment at face value. At least until she thought further on it. Then Edith's eyes narrowed. She set down her fork. "Are you implying that the only reason I spoke to Gerald about your watch was to keep you away from him?"

"Was it?"

She huffed and sat back and I thought she might rise and go to another table, but instead she offered a smile every bit as sharp as sun against silver. "Why on earth would I want to prevent you from meeting with Gerald?"

"For the same reason you avoided him when he was with Ivy. You had your eye on Gerald before Ivy returned to Willingdale. You were jealous when they married. And now that he is a widower and will be on the marriage market again—"

"That is preposterous!" She glared across her veal and ham pie at me. "Even if I had stopped to consider that Gerald may want to marry again—and I can tell you, Miss Manville, the thought has never crossed my mind—but even if I had, do you think I might be so worried that I would want to keep the two of you apart? That I might think of you as some sort of . . . rival?" Her voice rose on the last word, her sarcasm as ripe as the apricots on the tree outside the window.

For my part, I kept my voice low and even. "You have no need to think of me as your competition," I assured her. "I have no interest in Gerald Armstrong."

"And yet you keep returning to Willingdale."

"And you think it's because . . . ?"

I nearly laughed, but something told me Edith would not appreciate the reaction and now, I needed her to talk, not to walk away in a fit of pique. "I came here after the funeral to collect my watch. And now I am here at the invitation of Lady B. Just as you are. Do you think Gerald could possibly have an eye on the ladies so soon after Ivy's death? For as you say, he's an honorable man, and he is in mourning."

"You're right. Of course you're right." Placated for now, she stabbed at a piece of fish. "We have hardly even talked since the funeral."

"Yet he has certainly talked to Betty."

Her lips pinched. "That is only natural. She cleans his house."

I remembered the two of them on the village green. Their closeness. The sound of Betty's giggle. "This was not talk of cleaning."

I pretended not to notice her glare. "I thought he might have mentioned it to you as I have heard you and Gerald were good friends." As if it were the most important thing I had to consider, I sliced my ham and took a bite. "There is talk in the village that you two might have married."

For a heartbeat, she froze. "That is hardly news."

"But it does explain why you might expect him to turn to you again. It also explains why you might have been jealous of Ivy. My question is, were you jealous enough to cause the accidents that befell her?"

Edith's knife and fork clattered against her dish. "Are you saying—"

"Where were you the night Ivy died?"

Her mouth opened and closed and I thought that the fish on her plate must have looked much the same when it was hooked and brought to shore. Her outrage smothered her words. "How dare you."

"I only dare because I am searching for the truth."

"And you think that I—" She could not make herself

speak the words. "I told you the first time we met, Miss Manville, Ivy was careless. She tripped and fell into the millpond."

"She thought she was in danger."

"You can't possibly know that."

"But I do. And you were one of the people she suspected wanted to do her harm."

Edith scraped back her seat and stood, her chin as stiff as her spine. "Did she? Then that proves just what I've said all along, doesn't it? Ivy was flighty. And addle-brained. If you've listened to town gossip, you know as much yourself, Miss Manville. If I wanted her dead, I would have just offered her tea. And scooped the sugar into it with my own hand."

ൠ

That afternoon, I had just stepped into the grand gallery of Bellington when I had cause to let a curse slip out under my breath. If I wasn't thinking of everything Edith said to me that morning, I would have been more careful. I would have looked around more closely before I started down the steps.

Perhaps then I would have seen Eli Marsh leaning against the wall at the perfect spot to waylay me before I went outside, and then I might have been prepared to face him. Or better, avoid him. What was it about the man that left me feeling light-headed and hot-cheeked?

He was handsome, surely, but I had only to think of Ash to remind myself I'd met handsome men before.

He was a foreigner, and there is always a hint of intrigue in that, yet I had spent my life living in other countries, dealing with other cultures and other people.

Still, there was something about the man, something I did

not yet understand, and it was that mystery, perhaps, that left me feeling edgy.

And far more interested than I wanted to be.

But I had more important things to think about. I could not allow my emotions to get the best of me again.

"You were not at dinner last night," I said quite casually when I walked past. "Are you so quickly bored with our company, Mr. Marsh?"

He pushed away from the wall so as to step into my path. "You noticed."

"Your place was to be the one next to mine. I found myself talking across an empty chair to Edith Cowles for most of the meal."

"Ah, Mrs. Cowles. Was I to be seated so close to her? I suppose I'm fortunate that business detained me from joining you." His eyes sparked with mischief. "I did not have to worry about Mrs. Cowles spooning sugar into my teacup."

I gasped. "You know the rumor!"

"Everyone knows the rumor. That doesn't mean it's true." Our eyes met, but only for a moment. It was long enough to make me feel short of breath.

He, though, had no such problem. He lowered his gaze to assess my clothing.

He was dressed in a plaid Norfolk jacket belted at the waist.

So was I.

He was wearing leather boots.

Just like the ones I was wearing.

His head was bare.

There, our attire finally differed: my straw hat was perched on my head.

He looked down, too, at my walking skirt, short enough to reveal the top of my knee-high boots.

"You are expecting to shoot today," he said.

"Lady B did say clay pigeons."

"Yes, but surely—"

"Really, Mr. Marsh, I hope you don't have the brass to say shooting is only for men." I could not keep the acid from my voice. "You really must learn to suppress your outdated attitudes. Yesterday, you said you believed a woman cannot take care of herself."

"Which I did not mean, of course. Not in the way you think. What I meant was—"

"You said the world is too dangerous a place for a woman to negotiate."

"Which it can be, but—"

"You claimed the only way a woman might make her way safely through life is with the assistance of a man."

"Not because she needs it so much as because he owes it to her. Women, after all, are the glue that holds the Empire together."

I wasn't sure I believed his sincerity.

But I wanted to.

A thread of warmth tangled around my heart, and rather than let on, I made sure to keep my voice level. "Perhaps it is different in America, but here in England, many women shoot. Especially at parties such as this."

He did another quick assessment of me and, like it or not, I found myself shifting slightly foot to foot, wondering what he thought. "Are you any good?"

"I am not given to false modesty."

"Which means you're good."

"Very."

A slow smile lifted his lips and revealed a dimple in his left cheek. "I suppose we'll see."

There is nothing I like better than a challenge. Especially one I know I can easily handle. I made to continue toward the door. That is, until Eli cleared his throat.

"Before we go outside, I wonder if I might have a word," he said.

I am not proud of it, but I will admit that right then and there, my heart clutched and my spirits plummeted. And here I thought the looks and the comments and the playful banter meant Eli Marsh was interested. In me.

Disappointment squirmed through me, and at the same time I told myself it was to be expected, I vowed not to let it show. It did. The moment the words fell from my lips along with the tiniest huff. "Ah, Sephora."

"Sephora? Your sister? That isn't exactly—"

"Oh, go right ahead, Mr. Marsh." Disgusted—at him for his taste in frivolous women, at myself for caring, at my sister even though it wasn't her fault she was pretty and so lively, men were drawn to her like bees to flowers—I waved a hand and spun toward the door. "Partner her at luncheon. Teach her to shoot. Sit next to her at dinner tonight. Run off to China with her for all I care."

"You're jealous."

His words froze me in my path. I did not turn to him when I said, "She is my sister. And an heiress. I do not have the luxury of being jealous. I know her lot in life is to—"

"Have crowds of admirers swarming around her."

"Yes." I composed myself and turned around because I wanted to read his expression when I pointed out, "Mr. Dawes and Mr. Hackett are certainly taken with her."

"And you think that considering their fortunes, I wouldn't stand a chance with your sister."

"I think she would bore you to death."

He laughed. "What makes you think so?"

I might have told him it was a guess, but I knew that would not satisfy Eli Marsh. Instead, I stepped back, my weight against one foot, and looked him over as carefully as he'd measured me so short a time before.

"You are not empty-headed. I can tell as much from the knot on your tie. It's tidy, a bit too, if you ask me. And I know you brought no valet with you, so you tied it yourself. You are a careful man. You pay attention to details. That is . . ." I glanced down further to his boots.

"The business that kept you from dinner last night involved you being outdoors," I said, and I do believe it was the first time he realized there was mud on his heels. "You were out late, certainly past sunset."

"I might have picked up the mud getting ready to shoot in the garden this morning," he suggested.

I shook my head. "If that was so, it wouldn't be dry. That means you tracked through mud sometime after dark when the ground was damp."

"And you think your sister would not approve of me because of my tie and the mud?"

"I think my sister would not approve of you because you are not nearly as wealthy as Mr. Dawes or Mr. Hackett."

"And you know that, how?"

I smiled up at him. "Because you don't have a valet."

He had the good grace to laugh. "What you're telling me is that your sister cares for little except fashion and entertainment and a man's status in life. And I can tell, Miss Manville, you care for those things not at all."

"I think there are more important things in life."

"Like the collections at the British Museum."

Surprised he knew this detail of my life and not sure I liked it, I took a step back.

"I'm no magician," Eli assured me. "Lady B told me. She says you have the heart and the head of a scholar."

"You spoke with her about me?"

"Aside from being a bit untidy about my shoes and a bit too careful about my tie, I am endlessly curious," he admitted. "Why did you assume I wanted to talk to you about courting your sister?" He stepped between me and the door to the garden. "I don't."

"That does not tally with the usual course of events when Sephora is present. For surely you have noticed Sephora."

"Barely. But then . . ." His smile flared again, as hot and as sultry as the tropics. "I have been too busy noticing you."

I wasn't sure if I should be flattered.

Or worried.

I decided to toe the delicate line between the two. "Why is that?"

"Because I wondered . . ." Like a mesmerist, he gazed into my eyes, and against my will and my common sense I found myself leaning nearer to him.

"What did you find at the bridge yesterday?"

I bolted upright. "You followed me?"

"I was out walking and—"

"And you followed me. Why?"

"As I said, Miss Manville, I couldn't help but notice you, and when I came upon the bridge and saw a certain portion of a woman sticking out from a rather formidable-looking shrub . . ." He took a look at my backside. "I recognized you instantly."

I lifted my chin. "That is a rather bold thing to say to a lady."

"Not at all. I'm simply reporting the facts. Just as you do. Unlike most other ladies, you do not conform to fashion, Miss Manville. You wear no bustle. So naturally—"

"You might have made your presence known," I said, because it seemed a safer topic than my backside.

"I intended to. Before I saw you poking around. What did you find?"

"What makes you think I found anything?"

"You pocketed it."

"Did I?" I smiled. "It was nothing more than a button."

"I know little about vegetation, but the thorns on that shrub looked lethal. That was quite a thing to do, all for a button."

Damn, how I hated that he thought exactly what I had when Gerald told me he was searching for a button.

Which is, of course, precisely why I smiled. "It was a very special button."

His eyebrows rose just enough to let me know he didn't believe me for a minute, but there was nothing he could say to dispute my story.

Satisfied, I whirled toward the door and out into the garden.

The other guests were already gathered there, the women at tea tables set near the flower beds where they could observe the shooting from a safe distance and the men further on, checking their shotguns, discussing the advantages of side-by-side barrels versus over-under for clay shooting.

I ignored my sister when she waved me over to sit with her, marched to the shooting line, and requested a gun from the gamekeeper.

"Oh, come now!" I did not turn when I heard Dr. Islington's voice down the line. He wasn't speaking to me, but to the assembly at large. "A shotgun has a hefty recoil. We all know hearty country girls who can handle a shotgun, but I fear Miss Manville, being from the city, is not capable. It cannot be safe for any of us to allow her to shoot!"

"Then run inside and hide," Lady B advised him. "Each of my guests is welcome to shoot. There are clay pigeons enough for all."

There were, and while I waited my turn, I watched them launch from the trap on the far side of the garden, studying the arc the clay platters made through the sky, watching to see how the breeze made them wobble, making note of each shooter, his range and his skills.

Islington, it turned out, was a fine shot. He missed but two of his targets.

Simon Plumley connected with only two of his.

Mr. Dawes paused before he shot, bowed toward my sister, and dedicated his efforts to her. Sephora, predictably, tittered and blushed.

Not to be outdone, Mr. Hackett made the same declaration. Alas, he was more courtly than he was skilled, and he blushed furiously when he shot poorly.

Eli Marsh shot next and I will admit that seeing the ease with which he handled the shotgun, the way he made each shot (every one of them a hit) look effortless, I felt a touch of envy.

When he was done, he stepped back and looked my way.

An unspoken challenge.

I could pretend a sudden headache. Or a tender muscle.

I could lie and say that the men were such fine shooters, I did not want to compete.

But what fun would that be?

Instead, I stepped up to the line.

It had been some time since I'd shot, so I reminded myself I could not afford to be distracted. Not by my jitteriness. Not by Eli's gaze. And he wasn't the only one watching: Simon waved a hand to encourage me. Mr. Dawes and Mr. Hackett, so alike and so different, their shotguns broken open and cradled in their arms, stood side by side to observe. I had no idea where Dr. Islington had got to, and I didn't care.

I had to prove myself.

Like so many things, shooting stance becomes second nature when it is practiced often, and I had enough experience to fall easily back into the routine. I set my left foot at twelve o'clock, my right at two, both feet together at first before I took half a pace forward and let my weight come onto my left foot.

Another few steps and my feet were shoulder-width apart. I bent my knees slightly and put nose over toes (as is said in shooting parlance). When the clay pigeon was released, I swung.

"Not the gun or your head or your shoulders. Those must remain locked," I heard Papa's advice in my ear. "Swing from your ankles, your legs, your waist, your core."

I squeezed the trigger, heard the satisfying crack of the shotgun, watched the pigeon shatter and clay rain down.

Behind me, there was a smattering of applause, led by Lady B, but I could not afford to bask in the glory.

Another pigeon rose. I shot and shattered it.

And so it went. I matched Eli shot for shot, kill for kill, refusing all the while to look to see if he was still watching, to wonder if he was impressed. With one more shot to go, I could ill afford to have my concentration broken. And Eli Marsh could surely do that.

I positioned myself for my last shot, drew in a breath, put my finger on the trigger.

I cannot say exactly what happened after that. I only know something sped past my ear. I did not hear it, but felt it. A rush of air and heat. Right before my hat flew from my head.

The next thing I knew, the shotgun flew from my hands and I was on the ground. Eli was on top of me.

"Don't move." His mouth was close to my ear. "Stay put."

"But I . . ." I squirmed beneath his weight, but he would have none of it.

My heart beat double time, matching the rhythm of his. My breaths came hard and fast. His were suspended. I cannot say how long we were down there on the lawn, I only know that after the surprised gasps of our audience died away, and Lady B called out, "What's happening? Is Violet not well?" he pushed himself away and sat down next to me.

"She's fine," he called over his shoulder and with that, the others came running. I hoisted myself up on my elbows in time to see their boots as they gathered around me. "She slipped."

I struggled to sit up. "I didn't—"

"Slipped." The metal in Eli's voice told me he would not tolerate an argument. "Lady B . . ." At the same time he lifted me to my feet, he gave me over to her care. "Get her into the parlor. Now. Stay with her. All of you. I need to . . ." Scanning the garden and the house beyond, he backed away. "I'll join you all shortly."

With that, he took off running, and I was left to be patted and clucked over by the assemblage.

"Oh, dear! Your poor hat." Sephora handed it to me, but I didn't bother to give it a look. Lady B had an arm around my shoulders, already leading me toward the house, promising brandy to settle my nerves, though had she asked, I would have told her my nerves were just fine, it was my brain that was spinning with confusion.

Once in the house, she poured brandy for all and insisted I sit and sip, and I set my hat down on the empty seat next to mine on a sofa upholstered with green velvet and trimmed with mahogany.

It was the first I noticed the hole in the brim of my hat. The first I realized exactly what had happened out there in the garden.

Someone had taken a shot at me.

❧

"You're leaving." I was just about to enter my bedroom to change for dinner when Eli appeared from down the long corridor that led from the rooms where the men were housed. "I sent a maid in to pack your things."

"You've? Sent?" Because I could not quite make sense of this, I looked toward my closed bedroom door and when that did not help, I opened the door and saw not one but two maids fussing with my clothing and my trunk.

I shut the door again. "I have no intention of leaving."

"It's not your decision." Just as I had, he popped the door open, then grabbed my chatelaine bag, which was on a bureau nearby, and shoved it at me.

"You're leaving," he said. "Now."

He hooked his arm around my waist and I would like to say he escorted me down the stairs, but honestly, it was more of a dragging. "You're taking the next train back to London. Your trunk will be sent on."

"But I can't . . ." At the bottom of the steps, short of breath and out of patience, I pulled from his grasp the better to face him when I announced, "I'm not going anywhere."

"You certainly are."

"There is no reason for me to leave."

He propped his fists on his hips and it was that stance more than anything that sent my temper soaring. There was no one else in the gallery, yet he kept his voice to a low growl. "Someone just tried to kill you."

"You noticed."

"Of course I noticed. Why do you think I knocked you down? I'm sorry about that, by the way. I know how you English are."

"It was . . ." It had been an eventful afternoon and I had finished not one, but two glasses of Lady B's excellent brandy. I had no choice but to tell the truth. "It was quite gallant of you. You might have saved my life."

"And I intend to continue doing exactly that." He took my arm. "There's a carriage waiting out front. And don't tell me you can't travel in your shooting clothes. Fashion be damned. We need to get you home to London where you can stay safely inside."

"I thought I was safe here," I confessed. "The shot—"

"Came from the house, I think." Disgusted, he grumbled under his breath.

"And the other members of our party? Where were they at the time?"

"All there in the garden. Except for that doctor fellow."

"Ah." I can't say I'd expected it, precisely, but I wasn't surprised. "You've talked to him?"

"He says he was feeling poorly and went to his room to rest."

"You believe him?"

"I believe . . ." His sigh betrayed his impatience. "I believe there is a train from the village in less than thirty minutes and you're going to be on it."

When he tugged me forward, I locked my knees and refused to move. "I can't leave. I need to find out what's going on."

"I will do that." For just an instant, his hold on me softened. "I promise."

"But what about Sephora? I cannot leave without—"

"She is already in the carriage."

I might have complimented him on his efficiency if he hadn't been so busy hurrying me to the door. There, he paused, looked all around, and put an arm around my shoulders to bustle me to the carriage. Once I was settled, he slipped into the seat beside me.

Which meant we both had a perfect view of Sephora's thunderous expression. Her arms crossed over her chest, her lips pressed into a thin line, she ignored Eli completely, all her wrath focused on me.

"This really is too much, Violet," Sephora spat. "Dinner tonight was to be the highlight of our days here."

"And Mr. Dawes and Mr. Hackett were anxious to partner you. I know. Perhaps we might invite them to London for tea sometime."

She huffed and looked away, and as long as she was going to pretend neither Eli nor I existed, I took the opportunity to turn in my seat, the better to see him.

"Are you going to explain how you knew—"

"No."

"Then perhaps you might clarify why you think—"

"No."

"Really, Mr. Marsh. You owe us that much. You see how upset Sephora is."

"And I'm sorry for it."

His apology did not raise my sister's spirits. She sat as cold and as still as a statue, her breaths coming in short gasps that betrayed her anger. That is, until another vehicle clattered by.

"Oh!" Sephora's breath caught just as Gerald Armstrong sped by in a sprightly phaeton. Had she been paying attention to anything other than her own misery, she might not have been so surprised to encounter another vehicle on the road.

The train was waiting when we arrived at the station. Eli bundled us into our first-class compartment and stepped back.

"You're not coming with us?" I asked him.

"I have inquiries to make here."

"As do I," I said, attempting to protest once again.

He was bareheaded yet touched a finger to his hair as if he were tipping his cap. "A cab will meet you at the station in London," he told me. "The cabman is named Jericho. Make sure he identifies himself before you go with him."

"Yes, but—"

"You have nothing to worry about now, Miss Manville. And if you did . . ." His eye traveled to the chatelaine bag in my hands. "I'm sure you'll take care of it with your pistol. Now go home." He closed the compartment door. "And stay there!"

Chapter 20

July 27

I did not stay home.

And really, Eli Marsh should have not expected me to.

Nor should he have had the crust to issue such an order.

After all, someone had tried to kill me, and even before the train left the station in Willingdale, I had every intention of finding out who the culprit was.

As Eli promised, we were safely delivered to St. John's Wood by Jericho, and as soon as I saw Sephora scurry up to her room (no doubt to bemoan the fact that her visit to Lady B's had been cut short, as had her opportunities to bask in the glow of her admirers), I retired to the library to make plans. The next day was Sunday and therefore inappropriate for what I had in mind, but the next day after that, I was on an early train to Oxford.

I was already walking down Beaumont Street when the sun came up and touched the Ashmolean Museum with golden light, and seeing it, a pang of regret curdled my insides. Ah, to be a scholar and ramble through the museum's vast collections!

I shook away the thought and continued on my way, arriving at Hollyhock House where the garden was chockablock with blowsy roses, drooping dahlias, and weeds nearly to my knees. I was just in time to see Sally Gwinn open her front door and set a cat upon the stoop.

I hurried forward. "I'm Violet Manville," I told her. "I wrote to you."

She was a stick-thin woman with a pale face, and her sparse gray hair hung around her shoulders. She scowled.

Right before she closed the door in my face.

Surprised, I froze, but only for a second. I had not come so far to be turned away.

I knocked, and when she did not answer, I called out to Sally through the closed door.

"I am a friend of Ivy Armstrong's," I told her. "I am sorry to tell you, Ivy is dead."

She had not gone far; the door popped open instantly and when it did, Sally looked a decade older than she had just moments before. Her face had gone as gray as her hair. Her eyes shone with unshed tears. "It cannot be," she said.

I inched closer to the door. "Perhaps it is something best discussed inside?"

She hesitated but finally pushed the door wide open and when she shuffled into the parlor, I followed through what I can only describe as a maze of untidiness.

There were books and papers on the tables and the floor, cut flowers flung here and there that had never been put into water. I stepped over the cat's dish in the middle of the hallway, food dried and caked to its sides, and joined Sally in the parlor. When she cast aside a wool blanket so that I might sit down on a chair covered with cat hair, dust flew all around us. She slumped into the chair across from mine.

"What happened?" she wanted to know. "To my Ivy girl?"

"That is exactly what I am trying to determine," I told her. "I am so sorry to be the bearer of such news, but I do believe Ivy's visit here might have had something to do with her untimely end."

I had known governesses all my life, and I admired them. They were hard-working and intelligent. Sally did not disappoint me. She read through my words and her eyes narrowed.

"I made her promise not to tell anyone what passed between us."

"And she did not betray your trust. At least to me. I found out she was here in a rather circuitous way." I glanced around the room, at the clock, unwound and silent upon the mantlepiece, at a teapot without a lid on a table between us, at the way Sally held her hands on her lap with her fingers twined so as to try to disguise the fact they shook uncontrollably. She was old, and she was ill.

"You were her governess," I said.

"Many years ago."

"You left Willingdale unexpectedly. Soon after Ivy's mother died."

She picked at the skirt of her brown gown.

"But recently, you sent Ivy a letter and whatever you told her in it, she was moved enough to come here to see you and learn the whole of the story."

"She did not reveal what happened on her visit here to you?"

"She died before she could, but it is my intention to learn the truth. I believe she would have wanted me to know it. But I cannot know the truth of what happened to Ivy, not until I have all the information."

"There are things best left unspoken."

"Yes. But when it comes to murder—"

Sally gasped and fell back against the chair. "You said dead. You didn't say . . ." She could not bring herself to speak the word.

It was harsher than the poor woman had any right to hear, but it needed to be said.

"Pushed into the millpond and drowned."

Her shoulders slumped. "You think what I told her the day she came to visit—"

"I cannot say. Not until I hear the entire story. I know after Ivy came here, she returned home and confronted Dr. Islington."

A sound burst from the old woman, half laugh, half cough. "Did she? Yes. I think she would have the courage. Did he confess? To what he'd done to Ivy's mother?"

I cannot say what I'd thought to hear from Sally, but it wasn't this. I sat up, tense and expectant. "Whatever you told Ivy, the doctor tried to keep her quiet about it. After a rather ghastly row, her husband asked for the doctor's help and Dr. Islington dosed Ivy with laudanum."

"He used to do the same to Clementine. Laudanum. More and more laudanum. All in an effort to keep her quiet. She had opinions, you see. She spoke her mind. And the world does not like spirited women." Her gaze shot to mine. "I suspect you already know this."

"I know someone is trying to silence me, too."

"Ah."

"That is why I've come to ask for your help."

Considering this, Sally's gaze clouded with memories. "The doctor . . ." She looked away from me, out a window coated with grime. "You see, he was convinced he was the one who could find a way through Clementine's troubled mind. As if she needed it! He would have done a better service to the family if he simply admitted that being an intelligent woman and having no outlet for that intelligence, no way to express herself other than running a household or helping with charity work . . . well, I don't need to tell you. After years of being dismissed, years of being ignored and belittled, Mrs. Clague grew dissatisfied with her lot in life. She spoke up more often, more vehemently. She acted out. Albert, that is, Mr. Clague, he was not happy about it. Like most men, he expected his wife to be docile and obedient and when she wasn't . . ."

"He thought her mad."

"He called in Dr. Islington," Sally said. "And the doctor, he tried laudanum, and when that didn't work . . . well, he said he'd met some foreign fellow who talked about strange plants from exotic countries. Herbs and things." Her sharp gaze touched mine for a second. "The doctor acquired some such plants, and he distilled them and gave the concoction to Mrs. Clague. And they . . ." She shivered and squeezed her eyes shut. "Oh, the terrible sounds that came from the attic where she was made to stay! Ranting and raving and carrying on. It was awful, and the sicker she got, the more Mr. Clague begged for help, and the more the doctor dosed her."

The sadness pressed against my heart. "Until she could stand it no longer."

Sally hung her head. "The misery of her mother's death weighed on poor Ivy. That is why . . ." Like a pianist at the keyboard, she plucked at the arms of her chair. "I am dying, Miss Manville. Do not say you're sorry and do not say I must have faith and hope." Though I had no intention of saying either, she stopped me from even thinking about it by holding up one trembling hand. "I could not let Ivy go on believing a lie. I wrote to her. After all these years. Ivy had a right to know. About all of it."

"You mean about her mother."

"I mean . . ." She gestured around the room. "You see, I knew what Dr. Islington was doing. And early on, I told Mr. Clague I thought the doctor's treatment, this new and supposedly miraculous medicine, was unwise. He would not listen. He was a desperate man. He believed Dr. Islington knew what was best. But I watched the doctor, and I knew. Oh yes, I knew. He would sometimes ask me to help subdue Mrs. Clague while he dosed her. So you see, I was there." Her eyes grew distant. Her voice, quiet. "I was there when he gave her the largest dose of that dread potion of his. When she thrashed and called out and screamed. When she died."

My blood ran cold. "Then she did not take her own life?"

She shook her head. "The doctor made it look as if she had. And he . . ." She bit her lower lip. "A governess does not have an easy lot in life. Perhaps you know this, Miss Manville, for you strike me as a woman who has had to make her own way. If a family is dissatisfied, a governess can be dismissed. If a child is unruly, the governess is made to take the blame and is dismissed. And if she has no references, no prospects . . ."

"But surely you did, the family respected you. Ivy loved you."

For an instant, a smile brightened her expression. "And oh, how I was fond of that child! But the doctor, he said if I told anyone what I knew, he would make sure I never found work again. He had Mr. Clague's ear, I was sure he would fashion some story and I would find myself without a position and with no prospects. And the doctor, he paid me . . ." She pulled in a stuttering breath. "He gave me the money to buy this cottage and to care for myself all these years. But only if I promised to never breathe a word about what had really happened."

"But now—"

"What the doctor could do to me does not matter now. I had to tell Ivy the truth before I die."

"And when you told her, she went home and confronted the doctor."

"And is he the one who killed Ivy, do you think?"

I did not expect Sally to have a mind as suspicious as mine. When I gasped, she laughed.

"What he did to Clementine Clague, experimenting on her so, was nothing short of murder," Sally said. "It isn't hard to imagine he might do it again to guarantee Ivy's silence. After all, he had to keep his secret."

The pieces of the puzzle fell into place. "And once she'd spoken to you, Ivy knew that secret. Dr. Islington arranged for her to have accidents, the incident with the horse cart, the slate that fell from the church. And when none of that worked—"

Sally closed her eyes, mumbled a prayer. "It is my fault."

"You couldn't have known," I said, with real pity. While I wanted to judge her for not coming forward with the truth of Clementine's demise sooner, I knew all too well how the right choice can be made to seem impossible, especially for a woman on her own.

"I should have suspected," Sally mumbled.

"You can still help remedy the situation." I glanced around for paper, pen, and ink. "I will write what you say and if you sign it . . ."

"Yes. Yes." Sally Gwinn let go a long breath, releasing the

years of guilt she'd carried. "I will tell you what happened. Exactly what happened."

ೞ

By the time I returned to London, the signed letter from Sally Gwinn safely tucked into my chatelaine, I was feeling more cheerful than I had since the day Ivy's letter had arrived along with the newspaper clippings that hinted at her killer.

Dr. Islington had a secret, one he was desperate to hide.

Ivy discovered that secret, and so had I.

All I need do was to convince the local Willingdale constabulary of the doctor's guilt, and thanks to Sally, that would not be difficult.

What it was, though, was a task for another day.

I was encouraged, yes, but also exhausted. I would return to Willingdale the next day armed with the truth. If Ivy had threatened to expose the doctor, he had a plausible motive for murder.

And yet . . .

I stepped from the hansom that delivered me from the railway station to St. John's Wood, the questions that had plagued me all of my journey niggling at me still.

What of the accidents that befell Ivy? Those happened before she spoke to Sally and knew about the doctor's treatment of Clementine.

What of the mysterious obituaries Ivy had secreted in her diary? Was Reginald Talbot the man who had introduced Dr. Islington to the supposedly medicinal herbs that ultimately killed Clementine? Had Ivy somehow ferreted out that information and is that why she'd searched for Talbot?

What else had Ivy known about Dr. Islington that I had yet to discover?

I shook the questions from my shoulders as problems for another day. For now, I would simply present my evidence—and it was powerful—to the authorities. They would, no doubt, take the matter in hand from there, and then perhaps Ivy and her poor mother would find peace.

My mind made up, I had just walked up to the house when the door flew open.

"Oh, Miss Violet!" Bunty pressed a damp handkerchief to her red and swollen eyes. "I was not sure where you'd gone off to or when you might be back. I didn't know what to do."

All thoughts of Ivy and the unfortunate Mrs. Clague flew from my head, and I rushed into the house and put an arm around Bunty's shoulders so that I might pilot her into the parlor.

"Tell me." I deposited her in the room's most comfortable chair and pulled another one in front of it so that I might sit and look her in the eye. "What's happened?"

"It's Miss Sephora." Bunty burst into tears. "She's gone!"

Sephora

It was just as well there was little light in the room where I found myself. I could not endure anyone seeing my face. I knew my nose was red for when I touched my sleeve to it, I felt the sting of raw skin. I knew my eyes were swollen for I had cried long and hard. I could not catch my breath.

And I did not know where I was.

"Think, Sephora. Think." I lectured myself again as I had in the time—was it minutes or hours?—since I had recovered from a sudden bout of dizziness and a blackness that had settled over me and robbed me of my senses. "Think about what happened."

But I could not.

Blackness again smothered me. Sleep overtook me again.

I dreamed of the bouquet of flowers that had arrived Monday morning and sat up, wide awake, the pain around my heart lightened.

Arborvitae for unchanging love.

Pink camellia. Longing for you.

Red tulips.

Yes, red tulips.

A declaration of love!

Even in my misery and fear, I felt my soul sing as it had when the flowers arrived at our door that day Violet left early and never said where she was off to. Supreme joyousness overwhelmed me.

Franklin was alive and well. He had not forgotten me. He had not forsaken me. In the note nestled between the arborvitae and the camellia, he asked me to meet him at the bench—our bench—in Hyde Park.

And I had. I remembered that much. I'd dressed in the green gown he'd always told me made me look like a fairy princess. I'd carefully pulled back my hair and perched my most beautiful hat upon my head. With Violet gone, I slipped from the house when Bunty was busy instructing the maid as to her day's work, and I arrived at the park a full thirty minutes before our appointed tryst. Though I was so filled with love and excitement I felt as if I might burst, I sat down and waited for my dear Franklin.

And then . . .

The memories did not overtake me so much as they did elude me, and my bottom lip trembled and my tears came again. For I could recall little else. Someone behind me? A cloth over my eyes? Yes, and something bitter poured down my throat.

And then I remembered nothing at all. Not until I woke, groggy and confused, and found myself in darkness.

"Oh, Franklin!" My voice was no more than a miserable whimper. My heart ached and my mind raced.

What would he think when he arrived in Hyde Park and did not find me there? He would surely worry, and I hated to cause him such distress.

Would he believe I'd rejected him? Abandoned him? I would sooner die—yes, die!—than let him think so.

Would he suspect that something terrible had happened? How could he? For even now, I could not reason my way through the events. I only knew I was . . . somewhere, and that outside the single window that barely allowed enough light into the room to let me see my hand in front of my face, it was dark.

London?

I could hear none of the city's clatter and when I dragged myself across the room, one careful step through the darkness at a time, I saw only treetops. Someone had spirited me away, from my home, from Franklin. And as I had no enemy in the world, I could only imagine it must be the reprehensible brutes who'd assaulted Franklin.

Who knew what they had in store for me!

My hands out to feel my way through the blackness, I did a turn around the room and discovered a small couch, and I dropped onto it and gave myself to my misery.

Perhaps my tears would wash away the terror that filled me. Perhaps somehow—somehow!—Franklin would hear my mournful cries and he would come to save me.

Dear Miss Hermione,

It is what you might call a tragedy. There I was, doing all the work at my master's house, and doing my best with it as well. And there he was, him what used to serve with the army in India, asking me to brew what he called . . . well, I can't say as I remember what he called it, I only know it was a tea of sorts with spices and such in it.

Was it my fault I got the cinnamon that should've been in that tea mixed up with the hot pepper powder we keep in the kitchen? They do look alike, after all.

Oh, the master's face when he took a drink! And how he did rant and rave about what a foozler I was.

Miss Hermione, I am now in search of a new position, and me being but a girl and on her own, am asking what I should do next.

Wishing and Praying.

Dear Wishing and Praying,

It is called masala chai and it is, indeed, quite a delicious drink when properly prepared. Alas, you cannot undo what you have already done to your poor master's taste buds and must simply forge ahead. You will surely find another position, just as you have surely learned an important lesson. Pay attention, and next time, don't mistake the pepper powder for cinnamon.

Miss Hermione

Chapter 21

Violet

July 28

"What are we going to do?"

Bunty wrung her hands one second and wiped a handkerchief across her eyes the next, as upset as she had been the day before when she relayed the news that Sephora had gone missing. At the time, because it was the sensible thing to do and I'd hoped it would give Bunty a chance to sleep and thus relieve her misery, I had insisted I would take the matter in hand and have an answer to our problem the very next day but now, the very next day had arrived and I was no closer to the solution than I had been all during the night when, sleepless, I did my best to allay my fears. Catching up on the latest of Miss Hermione's correspondence helped. Thinking of where Sephora might be and what might have happened to her did not.

"I must go to Willingdale and reveal what I learned about Dr. Islington to the police there," I told Bunty, then stopped her with a look when I knew she would call my actions heartless. "I am not insensible to the matter of Sephora. You know I am not. I am concerned about her, Bunty, as you are. I cannot help but wonder . . ." It was afternoon, and I was seated at the table in the dining room, a cup of cold tea nearby, a plate of seed cakes, untouched, next to it. I drummed my fingers against the tabletop. "Do you think our one problem has anything to do with the other?"

"You mean this doctor fellow and Miss Sephora?" Bunty considered this. "For the life of me, Miss Violet, I cannot say if I would rather learn she'd run off with that William Shakespeare fellow or if I worry she might have fallen into the clutches of this evil doctor. I will tell you this much." She brought her fist down on the table. "If either one of those men do anything to hurt our Sephora, I swear to you, I will myself take that man by the throat and—"

"I fully understand," I told her, because I did not need her to elaborate. In the darkest hours of the night when sleep refused to come and I found no answers to the questions plaguing me, I'd had the same vengeful thoughts. Still, as satisfying as they were, they brought us no closer to finding justice for Ivy and her mother and, more importantly, to discovering what had happened to my sister.

"The doctor knows I suspect him," I said, reminding Bunty of what I'd apprised her of briefly the evening before after I'd warmed milk for her and taken it to her bedroom. "And I do believe he thought I was closing in on his secret even before I visited Sally. Otherwise he would not have tried to silence me at Lady B's party."

She waved a hand in front of her face and sank down into the nearest chair. "I do wish you'd stop reminding me of that dreadful day. But if this doctor thinks you know the truth of what he did to the Clague woman, why involve Sephora?"

"I believe it must be because he wants to silence me. And yet . . ." I grumbled. "There has been no message from him, has there? Why take Sephora or convince her somehow to go with him if he had no intention of using her disappearance against me?"

Bunty hung her head and dabbed her eyes. "I don't know. Oh, I don't know. I know only that Miss Adelia will surely have both our heads on platters when she discovers what's happened."

"Then we must make sure we find Sephora and catch the man responsible for both Clementine Clague's and Ivy Armstrong's deaths before Adelia ever learns the truth." Confident of both the soundness and the righteousness of my statement, I stood and so, when the front bell rang, I left Bunty weeping in the chair and answered the door before she could.

Constable James Barnstable was on our doorstep.

I was not surprised. I had, after all, seen the way he looked at Sephora that day he returned her to our home. I had noticed how concerned he was, how attentive, how smitten. When I sent a message first thing that morning to inform him that she had not been seen in twenty-four hours, he was bound to be as worried as was I. In fact, I was counting on it.

"Ah, Constable. You are available to offer your assistance today?"

"Yes, ma'am, I am." He stood tall. "I am afraid I had to tell a lie to arrange it. I have a grandmother, you see, in Devon, and she's a dear old thing and I never would wish any harm on her, but I told my superiors she died and I had a funeral to attend."

Since I would have done exactly the same thing, I naturally approved.

I stepped back to allow James inside the house, and while he gaped at the orange-and-blue paper on the walls, at the elegant carpets beneath our feet, I had a chance to look him over more completely than I had upon our first meeting. In spite of what Sephora believed—that a man of Barnstable's meager prospects could not possibly be handsome—he was a fine-looking lad, if a little thin. He had a steady chin, a firm jaw. His blue eyes flashed with indignation and a color not unlike that of his flaming hair crept into his cheeks when I explained my predicament.

Constable James Barnstable did not disappoint. With Bunty in tow (for she refused to be left behind), we left immediately for Willingdale and when we arrived in the village, we made our way to the small but tidy police station not far from the village green. There, James identified himself, told the sergeant who sat behind the front desk why we were there, and when I handed it to him, he presented the letter signed by Sally Gwinn, the one in which she detailed Dr. Islington's perfidy.

"Well, ain't that just the butter upon the bacon!" Done reading, the sergeant laughed, and it is only to be expected that Bunty, James, and I were confused.

At least, that is, until the front door of the police station banged open and two constables entered. They had Islington in darbies between them. The doctor, usually so self-collected, thrashed and swore, and when he saw me, a string of profanities so vile fell from his lips, it made James blush to the roots of his carroty hair.

I was not fazed, except by my confusion. "What's this then?" I demanded of the sergeant. "You cannot have known we were on our way to present you with Sally Gwinn's evidence and yet—"

"As it turns out, that there letter you brought helps us leaps and bounds when it comes to Clementine Clague's death, but as for the death of Mrs. Armstrong . . ." The sergeant stood and glared at the doctor. "Someone has come forward. A witness. Told us about how she'd seen the doctor and Mrs. Armstrong upon the bridge that very night she died."

"Witness!" Islington spat the word and turned his fiery gaze on me. "Exactly the rubbish this nosey parker here told me. A witness claiming I was there on the bridge with Mrs. Armstrong. It's preposterous. The woman was mad, and I wouldn't have dared go near the bridge with her. I would have feared for my own life."

"And yet it is Ivy who should have feared for hers." I stepped up to the doctor. "And now we know why. Sally Gwinn has revealed what you did to Clementine Armstrong."

His face flooded with color. His mustache twitched. His mouth opened and closed in silent protestation.

"She has provided all the details the police need," I told the doctor, "so there is no use belaboring your innocence. At this point, you would do yourself the most good by telling us what you have done with my sister."

He gurgled. "I don't know what you're talking about!"

"Spoken like the coward you are, Doctor," I said. "Yet I do believe you will reveal the truth. It is no wonder you thought to convince me Ivy had killed herself. You wanted to tie her death to her mother's. But once the authorities see Sally's letter and once the witness gives further testimony that you were with Ivy on the night of her murder—"

Islington grunted, "Betty."

The sergeant was a middle-aged man with a large belly and sleepy eyes. "Oh, aye," he said. "She saw you all right, and our Betty, she swears after she walked away, what does she hear but a scuffle and then a splash. A large splash."

A telling detail Betty had never shared with me.

When he tried to break free of their grasp, the two constables held the doctor tighter. Islington raised his chin. "Betty's lying."

"Of course you'd say that," I commented.

"Because it is true," he shot back, then breathed as if to steady himself and said, through gritted teeth, "I'll admit my methods with Clementine were, perhaps, experimental, yet my intention was only to help. If you know so much, Miss Manville, ask yourself this. With your letter from Sally Gwinn in hand why would I now lie about meeting Ivy that night? Now ask yourself instead, why would *Betty* lie? And, since she is lying, who might have convinced her to do so? And why?"

I would have liked to know more, but the constables dragged Islington back to a cell and a second later, a bang reverberated through the station along with a string of curses from the doctor. One of the constables called for help, and the sergeant went running.

I turned to my companions just as James asked, "Do you know what he's talking about? Who is this Betty? Would she know where Sephora is? Or perhaps the person she lied for might? Or should I sit down for a proper interview with that Islington fellow; maybe it's him we can't trust . . ."

As James worked his way down the rabbit hole I myself had spent the past weeks lost in, I tried to focus on what Dr. Islington had said. Who could have convinced Betty to lie? I thought I knew the answer. And yet . . .

An idea blew through my mind with all the force of a cyclone. As in such a storm, the detritus was scattered so that as yet, it did not form a complete picture. I needed time to think.

But the worry that pounded through me told me Sephora must be my first priority.

I led the way out the door and found that word of the doctor's arrest had gone through the village chop-chop. Half of Willingdale was gathered outside the small station. They stood in clusters, pointing, talking. Lady B, Simon, and Edith Cowles had their heads together and just as I looked over, Eli Marsh sauntered by.

Before I could formulate a plan of evasion, he closed in on me. "You've returned to the village."

"Obviously at a very bad time." I moved to my right.

Eli blocked my way.

"You were talking to the police."

"Yes." I offered a smile.

"Do you need some assistance?"

It crossed my mind to tell him I did, but that was before I thought back to my earlier dealings with Eli. He was as maddening as he was mysterious, as attractive as he was confounding. I needed neither to be distracted from my search for Sephora nor questioned about it. Not until I knew if Eli was a friend, or if he had other motives I had yet to ferret out.

"I'm quite fine," I assured him.

He looked me over. "I can see that. But what I asked is—"

"No, no. No assistance necessary." I had already turned away, but whirled back around. I couldn't resist a chance at learning more of the truth. "Unless you have determined who took a shot at me at Lady B's."

He glanced toward the police station. "With this turn of events, I should think that was obvious. What you haven't explained is why."

"Haven't I?" Another smile, this one wider and far starchier than the last. It was time for the conversation to change course. "Why are you still here?"

It was his turn to smile. "Because I haven't left."

"But it is now Tuesday. Yet you remain."

"While you have returned to the village, even though I'm quite sure I told you to go home and stay there."

"There have been . . ." I considered how I might word it. "Developments."

"To do with the doctor's arrest?"

I tried to emulate my sister and laugh in the bright and merry way she always did, but the sound fell flat. "How would I know anything about the doctor's crimes?"

"You know enough that he took a shot at you."

"How fortunate I am that he is a better doctor than he is a marksman."

"And now that he is under arrest, you are safe again."

I hoped Eli was right. Dr. Islington's guilt explained why I'd been followed after I first came to Willingdale, the incident with the hay wagon back in town. Knowing I corresponded with Ivy, Dr. Islington was afraid I knew too much.

I could rest easy.

Unless . . .

Eli must have been reading my mind. His eyes searched mine. "Do you think he killed Ivy Armstrong?"

"Do you think he didn't?"

"I think . . ." Eli stepped closer, his voice like the low rumble of distant thunder. "I would not stay here in the village longer than necessary if I were you. There may still be danger."

And with that, he whirled and walked away.

Not for the first time, Eli left me feeling edgy and annoyed.

Still, thanks to the earthshaking idea that had presented

itself when Dr. Islington accused Betty of lying, I was afraid he might be right.

I waved James over. "Can you go to the doctor's surgery?" I asked. "Have a look around for Sephora. And James, take Bunty with you. Keep her close."

"And you?" he asked.

"I need answers," I told him. "And there are people here who may provide them."

I saw James and Bunty off, then approached the green where Lady B, Edith, and Simon stood and when I neared, I wasted no time.

"Edith . . ." I looked the way of Edith Cowles, bundled that evening in a dark-colored gown, a shawl over her shoulders. "I must ask you, and please, don't think me rude—"

She had not forgotten our encounter in Lady B's breakfast room. That would explain her chilly manner and the way she looked down her nose at me. "Well," she sniffed, "if you're warning me you might be rude, I must say I expect you to be."

"Yes, perhaps. But you'll be truthful?"

"Ask your question."

I had no time to cushion my inquiry so as not to offend her. "When Gerald Armstrong first came to the village, you and he were friends."

Edith sucked in her bottom lip.

"Yet when Ivy returned from caring for her aunt—"

"Yes, yes." When she twitched, her shawl shimmied down her shoulders, and she set it aright. "It seems all of Willingdale knows how pathetic I am."

"But what of this detail?" I asked. "Did Ivy have more of an income from her father than you did from your late husband?"

Edith puckered. "When you said rude, I did not imagine you could be this rude, Miss Manville. How dare you—"

"Oh, stop being so priggish." Lady B put a hand on Edith's arm. "Violet wouldn't be asking if she didn't have a good reason, and it's not as if it's a secret. Everyone knows Albert Clague had far more money than your Will did."

Just as I suspected.

I sucked in a breath.

"What is it, dear?" Lady B wanted to know. "Where has that lively brain of yours led you?"

"To the truth, I do believe, and it all has to do with cinnamon and pepper powder! Lady B, the next time you see them, you can thank Mr. Hackett and Mr. Dawes. Like those spices, they look alike but are quite different."

"Hackett and Dawes?" She looked at me in wonder. "But surely they know nothing of this matter."

"They don't need to. Looking from one to the other, I always felt as if I was viewing one man in a distortion mirror. Hackett and Dawes are cousins, and so alike, it might be impossible for someone who did not know them well to tell them apart. I mean, aside from Mr. Dawes's peppermints and Mr. Hackett's eye. They are like cinnamon and pepper powder."

"Well, yes," she conceded. "But Violet, what does that tell us?"

"It tells us exactly what I told Sephora days ago," I called out, already racing to find Bunty and James. "You cannot always believe what you hear. Or what you see, either! And you should never, ever trust a wily man!"

Chapter 22

Just a few minutes later, I found James and Bunty returning from the surgery.

"No sign of Miss Sephora," James told me, though in truth, I did not need him to relay the information. Bunty sobbed quietly at his side, and that told me all I needed to know. All I feared.

"I thought as much," I told them both, but when James began to question me, I simply marched across the green, so angry at myself for being so slow as to not see the truth when it was staring me in the face, and so worried for Sephora's safety, I could not waste time with another word.

By the time we arrived at the Armstrong house, the last of the evening light touched the horizon and streaks of brilliant pink and apricot sparkled in the windows.

It was not the only illumination in the house.

Light shone from the first-floor windows of Gerald's bedroom.

And there was a guttering candle in the attic.

Seeing it, having my suspicions confirmed, my heartbeat sped and my blood raced. There were already deep shadows in the garden, spaces where the night—and secrets—lurked, and keeping to them, I signaled to James and Bunty to hold their place near the wall that surrounded the property. "Our answers lie within," I whispered.

James stepped up to my side, eyeing me one moment and the house the next. "You do not intend to go inside, do you? If anyone enters, it should be me."

"I've been here before," I told James, touching a hand to his chest to stop him, sure he would have sallied forth then and there and pounded on the door. "I know my way around. I may need your assistance and when I do—"

"Here." He reached into his pocket, withdrew his police whistle, and pressed it into my hands. "I will keep an eye on the doors in case . . . well . . ." As if he'd just fully realized he was inside a mystery he'd joined too late to understand, he shrugged. "In case of what, I am not sure. But I will watch and wait. Miss Manville, you have exactly ten minutes to do whatever it is you intend. After that, I am coming inside."

It was a reasonable plan and instead of thinking of all the contingencies that would make it go awry, I sidled through roses and delphiniums, stepped carefully around a patch of daisies, and peered into the parlor.

It was dark and empty.

I lifted the handle on the French door and when it opened smoothly and noiselessly, I breathed a sigh of relief. Lest it somehow lock behind me and make it harder to leave, I left it ajar, then froze, listening.

Somewhere in the house, a clock chimed the hour. Another answered it.

There were other sounds as well. The creak of floorboards overhead. The faint chink of glass upon glass. The high-pitched sound of a woman's laughter.

At the same time I slipped from the parlor and moved

toward the stairs, I pulled my pistol from my chatelaine. With any luck, I wouldn't have to use it, but as Papa always reminded me, being prepared was half the victory. Thus armed, I made my way through the darkness to the first floor and from the landing, saw a streak of light escape from beneath Gerald's closed bedroom door.

"You pledged it to me, after all, your *mainsme,* and I done just what you asked." I recognized Betty's voice, and Gerald's, too, when he answered.

"Have you ever known me to break a promise? Eh, have you?"

She giggled and she did not so much speak again as she purred. "You said that there brooch would be mine. You said as how you were ready to give it to me and that's why Ivy . . ." Her voice soured. "That's why she was always a'wearing it, so I couldn't get my hands on it."

Ah, just as the doctor had hinted. The one thing Betty wanted.

The one thing she could be convinced to lie for.

As eager as I was to hear more, I knew I could not linger. I scurried up to the second floor and from there, raced down the hallway and to the attic steps.

Just as it had been the first time I was there, the door to the attic was locked, but the key hung outside it. I stowed my pistol and unlocked the door and a moment after that—taking but a heartbeat to see who had entered the shabby attic room—my sister threw herself into my arms, and the tight band of worry relaxed around my heart when I saw her, unhappy but unharmed.

"Violet! Oh, Violet!"

We did not have the luxury of an emotional reunion and certainly no time for melodrama.

I shushed Sephora and kept my own voice down. "Do you know where you are? Why you are here?"

Tears streamed down her face and her words strangled on a sob. "I know only that Franklin was waiting for me and when I did not arrive to meet him, he may have thought me untrue."

I spared her a lecture. We did not have the time. "It is far more important to get you out of here." I tugged her to the door and hurried her toward the stairs. "How often does he check on you?" I whispered.

"He? I've seen no man. There is a girl, a rather dull and common one with mousy hair."

Ah, Betty. I was not surprised she'd been convinced to be part of the plan. She was simple enough and if I was any judge of people, she was also in love.

A powerful combination, indeed.

"Come." I latched onto Sephora's hand. "You must keep quiet, Sephora. Stop your blubbering!"

That much taken care of, I led the way back downstairs. The light still shone from Gerald's room, the voices—his and hers—still rumbled a conversation and giggled and there were a couple of moans as well which, I sincerely hoped, meant Gerald and Betty were far too busy doing other things to take notice of any disturbance we might cause.

I allowed myself the smallest exhalation of relief.

That is until at the landing, Sephora tipped her head, locked her knees, and refused to move. "That voice . . ." She forgot herself and spoke too loudly, and I waved a hand to remind her it was not in our best interests, but Sephora took no notice. She lunged toward the bedroom.

"No!" If my harsh whisper was not enough to stop her,

the fact that I held on tight and refused to budge should have been. "We need to get out of here."

"But Violet . . ." She gave the closed door another look just as Betty's wavering moan crescendoed. "It cannot be," Sephora muttered. "The voice is familiar. As was the face I glimpsed from the carriage that day we left Lady B's so hurriedly. I told myself I had to be mistaken. But now—"

"And at this moment, it does not matter."

My grip was forceful enough to compel her to move and we were soon back in the parlor.

Though I swore I'd left it open, the French door was closed.

"Wait." I stopped Sephora before she could near the door. "Someone's been here." I pulled my pistol from my chatelaine and ignoring Sephora's whoop—was it one of fear or surprise at seeing the weapon?—I scanned the room.

It was a good thing I did or I would not have seen the cold glint of another gun barrel pointed in our direction.

❧

"I am not afraid to shoot," I challenged our aggressor. He might be unseen there in the shadows but I knew where to aim. "If you're wise, you'll allow us to leave without incident, and no one will get hurt."

"Damn it, if you would just mind your own business like I told you to, we wouldn't have to worry about anyone getting hurt."

Eli Marsh stepped from the shadows, his gun now at his side.

I was not so inclined to lower mine. "What are you doing here?" I demanded.

"I thought I might rescue your sister, but as you have already saved me the trouble, I've apparently wasted my time. And point that gun in another direction, will you?" He closed in on us. "I don't fancy getting shot by a—"

"A what?"

It was dark and he could barely see me, and yet, I think he knew there was fire in my eyes. Eli chuckled. "We'll discuss that later, why don't we? For now . . ."

From the hallway, the light of a torch flared and shone directly in our eyes, blinding us all. "Drop your guns, both of you," a man's voice instructed us, and as if we needed prodding, he moved the light just enough to reveal the shotgun slung over his arm.

Eli let his gun fall to the floor. I, more reluctant but just as aware of our danger as he was, followed suit.

"There, that is better." The figure behind the light moved toward the wall and turned up the gas jet and light sprang around us.

Classically handsome.
Dark hair.
Strong jaw.
Broad forehead.

My voice overlapped with Sephora's gasp.

"Ah," I said, "William Shakespeare, if I am not mistaken."

❧

It might have been a good deal easier to think straight if Sephora did not let out a crow of merriment.

"Franklin!" Ignoring the shotgun—or perhaps simply not understanding its significance, which, I fear, was far more likely—she rushed forward. She would have kept right on going if Gerald Armstrong had not raised his shotgun and if I had not grabbed hold of her to keep her in place.

Her eyes wide and her expression wreathed in confusion, Sephora looked from me to Gerald. "What are you doing here, Franklin, my darling? Unless . . ." Her discombobulation dissolved and she grinned and pressed a hand to her heart.

"Oh, Franklin! You are my hero! You came to save me! I knew you would. But you must know, these people . . ." She looked at me and she might have looked at Eli, too, but I do believe it was the first we both realized that, sometime between when Gerald made his presence known and when he turned up the gas, Eli had slipped away.

So much for heroes.

"This is my sister," Sephora told Gerald. "And she came to help me, too. You are both so wondrous! Both so brave. But we must leave here as quickly as we can, my darling, before that nasty girl gets back and brings whoever it is she's working for, the person who had me locked away. You did not wait in the park too long for me, did you, that day I was supposed to meet you? I am sorry to have inconvenienced you so."

It was hardly the time for me to roll my eyes, but I simply could not help it. "Sephora." I said her name quite loudly in an effort to gain her attention so that I could talk some sense into her. "This isn't Franklin. It's Gerald Armstrong, husband of the late Ivy Armstrong."

"No, no." Sephora was so sure of herself, she laughed. "He is Franklin Radcliffe."

"Oh yes, I daresay he is." I lifted my chin and looked Gerald in the eyes, the better to see his reaction when I announced,

"And he is also one Mr. Dunstable Corvey of Edinburgh who sadly died in Africa a few years back, and Captain Jack Trembath, the intrepid explorer who was lost in the Arctic, and Reginald Talbot, too, am I not right? Poor Reggie who died at sea and left his dear wife, the woman who he'd always called his *mainnsamee*—his princess—in terrible financial hardship. But then, I expect that is how all the widows found themselves. After their husbands, this man, disappeared with their life savings."

"No." Sephora shook her head so hard and so fast, I wondered she could see straight. Or perhaps that explains why she couldn't. "You are certainly talking nonsense, Violet. This is Franklin. My Franklin. We have known each other some months now and yet . . ." Thinking, she squeezed her eyes shut. "I saw you here in Willingdale. And I thought you must have some perfectly good explanation for being here, but I never had the chance to ask you."

"And that is how it works, isn't it?" I was less intimidated by the shotgun Gerald aimed at my chest than I was at the thought of Sephora never realizing the truth. "While you are married to one woman, you are already concocting a new identity and looking for your next victim. Let me guess . . . you saw Sephora's picture on the Society page of the newspaper when that silly Lord Hatton fell from his horse. You read she was an heiress and you decided that after Gerald Armstrong's unfortunate death in Canada, a place where he was supposedly going with all of Ivy's money, Sephora would be your next widow."

"Widow?" Sephora's voice racketed to the ceiling. "Violet, what on earth are you talking about?"

"The truth," I told her. "You see, this man creates identities for himself. Then he woos wealthy women. He marries them and takes their money on the pretense of investing it in foreign places. A few months later, the women receive word that their dear husbands are dead. The money, of course, is gone, too. And Gerald here . . ." I looked his way. "I know it's not your real name, but I cannot think what else to call you. Gerald goes on to change his name and his appearance. Sometimes, he crafts himself an Arctic explorer or has a full beard, as Reggie Talbot did, and calls his wife his *mainn-samee*. Only Betty, she got the word wrong. I heard her upstairs. Mainsme. It is not a common thing to say. Betty could have learned it nowhere else. Other times, Gerald transforms himself into your Franklin, Sephora. And what did Franklin look like?"

"Like this man." She swung out an arm to point at him. "But they surely cannot be one and the same. Franklin wears glasses and he has the most luxurious muttonchops."

"And the most vivid imagination." It might have been a compliment if I hadn't added a note of acid to my voice when I looked Gerald's way. "Ivy found Captain Trembath's death notice, and she was curious. She might not have thought any more of it if she hadn't discovered Corvey's and Talbot's and the other one as well when she was drugged and rooting through the house. And she started asking questions, didn't she? After she found Trembath's obituary you thought to get rid of her—you are, of course, the one who arranged her accidents. But once Ivy found the obituaries, you knew you had no choice. And how easy it must have been to know the doctor would be accused of the crime. All you need do was convince Betty to lie for you by promising her Ivy's brooch, a promise you never meant to keep."

"What's that you say?" Betty appeared from out of the darkness in the hallway, her hair disheveled, her anger aimed at Gerald. "You promised me again and again. You told me the brooch was mine."

"Which is why you considered it stolen by Ivy," I said to Betty before I turned again to Gerald. "You and Ivy had a scuffle on the bridge on the night of the strawberry moon, and before you threw Ivy into the water, you ripped the brooch from her dress. But then you couldn't find it. Even if you had, I don't think you would have ever given the bauble to Betty."

"What!" Betty slapped Gerald's arm. "You told me! You promised!"

"Shut up!" He swung out an arm and would have clapped her on the cheek if Betty didn't move faster.

It seemed her brain was just as nimble.

She saw the truth of the matter then, as surely as I had seen it there outside the Willingdale police station, and she froze.

"You had me lie for you." She spewed the words and all her frenzied anger. "You told me if I helped you, I would not only get that brooch, but then I would be your wife."

"No!" I am sure Sephora timed neither her banshee wail nor her spasmodic leap forward, but I took advantage of both. Lest she be injured, I stuck out a foot to trip up Sephora, and when she went down, sobbing and with arms flailing, I made my move.

I leapt forward and knocked the shotgun out of Gerald's hands and at the same time he turned and ran from the room, I located my pistol and snatched it up.

I caught up with him just as the front door burst open and Eli and James rushed inside. It was Eli who struck a punch that knocked Gerald to his knees, and it was also Eli, not James, who produced a pair of darbies, wrenched Gerald's arms behind his back, and clapped them on.

James helped Eli haul Gerald to his feet.

His face flushed with a color like blood. "You will pay for this," Gerald screamed at me.

"I think not." I faced him, my pistol where he was certain to see it. "But you will certainly be made to pay. For Ivy's death. For all the misery you caused the women you lied to and married and stole from. You are a blackguard and you broke my sister's heart." I did not even realize I'd raised my pistol and pointed it squarely at Gerald's chest until I was looking at him over the barrel. "You should be made to pay for that, too."

"And for arranging to have my purse stolen from me." The truth nearly strangled Sephora. "For you did that, too, didn't you? Because you couldn't risk Violet ever seeing that photograph I had of you." She hauled herself to her feet and stood at my side, her cheeks stained with tears, her eyes red, swollen, and suddenly and finally wide open. She proved it when she punched Gerald Armstrong square in the nose.

Chapter 23

August 7

It is not easy for a girl of Sephora's erratic temperament to recover from shock. Nor is it a simple thing for her to put the past behind her.

Not when that past includes the man she thought was her very heart and soul. Though Sephora and I often disagreed, I knew too well what she was feeling to add my judgment to her heartbreak.

Nevertheless, she somehow managed to make a go of it, and I knew there was hope for her yet a little less than two weeks after our business in Willingdale was concluded, when she walked out the door with Margaret Thuringer, the two of them dressed like duchesses and tittering at the prospect of being included at a dinner party hosted by Lady B, who was then visiting London. I had begged off on the invitation on the pretense of my health, and though I don't think Lady B believed me for a moment, she was kind enough not to press the point.

Bunty and I watched Sephora and Margaret climb into a hansom.

"Tea?" Bunty asked.

I had been in the library most of the day catching up on Miss Hermione's correspondences, and I stretched. "I think," I told her, "I would prefer something stronger."

"Miss Adelia has a cache of fine Scottish whisky in her dressing room. It's intended for special occasions, but with all we've been through these past weeks, I do believe this qualifies."

"I have some papers to take care of. You can bring mine into the library. And Bunty . . ." I called up the stairs to her as she climbed to fetch the whisky. "Bring a glass for yourself."

Even with Sephora gone, I felt the obligation to keep Adelia's library a safe and sacred place. I had barely closed the door behind me, though, when I knew something was out of kilter. It was not a sound, or a smell that alerted my senses and made me tingle. It was a feeling.

It did not take me long to determine the cause.

Eli Marsh was sitting on the settee, his long legs stretched out in front of him. "Does it really take women that long to say their goodbyes even when they're going to see each other in just a few hours?" As if that were some sort of malady, he shook his head. "I thought you'd never be done with that sister of yours, reminding her of this and that and how she must behave."

I had more important things to address. "How did you get in here?" I wanted to know, and while I was at it, "Where have you been? I haven't seen you since the night Gerald Armstrong was arrested."

"Alfie Brewster." He stood and sauntered nearer, dressed not in evening clothes but in tweeds meant for traveling. "That's his real name. Alfie from Liverpool. He's been lying to women for years now and cheating them out of their money. Man's a disgrace."

"And a murderer," I reminded him. "He'll be tried."

"And found guilty thanks to you."

I thought about the hidden death notices. "And to Ivy. She suspected something was wrong, something that had nothing to do with what Dr. Islington did to her mother. The poor girl." My heart ached for her. "She thought she was in love."

"She was in love. Trouble is, she was in love with the wrong man. And you know, I think she put the pieces together finally. Since the bulk of Ivy's estate went to Gerald, that will be confiscated by the Crown once he's tried and found guilty. But it turns out Ivy added an addendum to her will, a provision for each of the women Alfie had married."

It was enough to make me smile.

"And the infamous brooch . . ." There was a smile on Eli's face, too, when he continued. "I hear the honest citizen who found it delivered it to the police in Willingdale."

"And the police?"

"Betty was as much a victim as those other women."

I couldn't agree more. "It would only seem right if the brooch somehow came into her possession, don't you think? Poor, simple girl. Alfie had a way about him, didn't he? He beguiled them all."

I remembered the sparkle that was back in Sephora's eyes when she walked out the door and dashed away the bad memories. "Fortunately, Sephora was spared from any more misery. As for you, Mr. Marsh, you have yet to explain how you got into my library."

"You were upstairs fussing with Sephora." He said. "So naturally, Bunty just—"

"Bunty? She knows you're here?"

"Bunty knows everything. I thought you did, too."

Was that the ring of a challenge in his voice?

"I know you're leaving, but then, that is simple enough considering the way you're dressed," I told him. "And I know you were a brick when it came to arresting Gerald . . . er . . . Alfie. The fact that you had handcuffs with you at the time has been a thought that has quite occupied me since it all happened. Especially as they were Tower detective handcuffs."

"You know your handcuffs."

"It is to a lady's advantage to know as much about as many things as she possibly can. And after I saw them, I did a spot of research."

"Then you know—"

"They are not the most secure of darbies, but they are lightweight and easy to carry. They are used by the—"

A thought struck and I found myself staring at him, my mouth hanging open.

Which may explain why he smiled.

"The Pinkerton Agency," I stammered out. "Mr. Marsh, are you . . . ?"

"Eager to be on my way and catch my train? No, ma'am, I am not. In fact, I'd rather stay here and share a glass of that fine whisky Bunty's bringing down. Unfortunately, I have business on the Continent."

"Another felon to apprehend? Or . . ." It came to me in that one moment. "You're meeting with Adelia!"

"From what I have heard of her, your aunt is the kind of woman who expects a full report."

"She employed you. She knew what was happening because Bunty—"

"Is a faithful servant and like I said, she knows everything."

"And you—"

"Just happened to be in the country on other business. Just happened to talk to Lady B. Who just happened to remember me from another matter."

I was afraid my mouth was flapping and I snapped my jaw

shut, the better to growl from between my clenched teeth. "Adelia thought I couldn't take care of myself—*you* thought I couldn't take care of myself!"

"It wasn't me. And truth be told, I don't think it was your aunt, either. I just think she wanted an extra pair of eyes on you. And let me say, Miss Violet, keeping my eyes on you . . ." He clapped his hat on his head. "Well, that's the most pleasant thing I've done in as long as I can remember."

He'd already walked by me and to the door and I knew I should just let him go, yet I could not help myself. "Are you coming back?"

Eli grinned. "Would you like me to?"

I stepped closer to him. "That depends. Would it be for business? Or for pleasure?"

He let go a long breath and yes, I was pleased that it staggered just a little. I'd caught him off guard.

"Can't say," he admitted. "At least not until I try an experiment."

He never gave me the chance to ask what he had in mind. He scooped me into his arms and brought his mouth down on mine in the sort of slow, burning kiss that fills the pages of the silly romances Sephora reads. The kind of kiss that, until that very moment, I never knew actually existed outside the pages of fiction.

When we were done—it did not last nearly long enough—he stepped away and smiled. "I've brought you a gift," he said. "It's over there on the couch. I expect you to be wearing it next time I see you."

And just that quickly, Eli Marsh was out of the room and out the front door.

Damn the man!

My heart still beating double time, I walked to the settee

and found there a box from Lock & Co, the hatters. Inside, the loveliest straw boater I'd ever seen.

I perched it on my head and was still so adorned and smiling when Bunty arrived with our whiskeys.

August 10

Three days later, Sephora still had not tired of telling me every detail of her evening at Lady B's. I let her. It was good to hear her laugh again, and I was grateful she was recovered enough from the trauma of all that had happened to delight in the mundane issues of fashion and the foibles of Society once more.

Besides, with her chattering away, I had a chance to think. I had received a new packet of letters addressed to Miss Hermione that morning and though I'd given them only a brief glance, I knew there were a few that would be addressed in the *A Woman's Place* column.

For the present, though . . .

I was once again ensconced alone in the sanctuary of my library, organizing my thoughts, cleaning off my desk. Ivy's letters were there, and I scooped them up and went to the filing cabinets with them.

Unfaithful Husbands?

Not the best place to file the letters since Gerald . . . er, Alfie, was a bigamist and, legally and morally, not Ivy's husband at all.

Comportment, Disrespectful Children, and *Mothers-in-Law* did not fit the situation, either. Nor did *Manners, Morals,* or *Mourning*. Perhaps I would need a new category.

Thanks to the organizing I'd already done there in the

library, there was one file drawer that was empty, and I took a sheet of paper from the desk, scrawled a heading on it, and inserted it at the front of the drawer. Satisfied, I deposited Ivy's letters and her diary inside and closed the drawer, one marked *Murder*.

Acknowledgments

Writing is a solitary profession. Still, no book is written in a vacuum. There are so many people who contribute to a book's success!

Among them is my editor, Nettie Finn, whose careful suggestions took a decent first draft and made it into a better book. The rest of the team at St. Martin's Minotaur is just as impressive, and I appreciate all their hard work.

My agent, Gail Fortune, believed in Violet and Sephora from the moment she met them.

My brainstorming group helped, too, with ideas and advice. Thank you, Stephanie Cole, Serena Miller, and Emilie Richards, for your suggestions and your encouragement.

On the home front, special thanks to David and of course, to Eliot the Airedale who sits patiently in my office while I work.

Of Manners and Murder has given me the wonderful chance to set my imagination free in Victorian England. What a splendid time in history! And how lucky I am to get to let my characters explore London with its fog and hansom cabs, and Willingdale, the ideal country village that holds so many dark secrets.

No acknowledgment for a book set in this time period would be complete without thanking my dad. He's the one who originally introduced me to Sherlock Holmes stories and planted the seeds for the love of all that is mystery.